The Four Winds From The Silver Mountain

By

R. Kane

The Four Winds from the Silver Mountain

by R Kane

This book is dedicated to my fans who make me feel invincible.

Thank you, my friends.

Book One

'Death makes angels of us all and gives us wings where we had shoulders smooth as ravens' claws' – *Jim Morrison*

'Cold is the water

It freezes your already cold mind

Already cold, cold mind

And death is at your doorstep

And it will steal your innocence

But it will not steal your substance'

'Timshel' – Mumford and Sons

This page intentionally left blank

Prologue

Sometime in the past...

She stood in the doorway of her small Adobe hut watching the four children play outside, it looked to be a game of tag, although she wasn't sure which child was supposed to be 'It'. If you asked her, the children didn't know either what with all four running from each other and screaming like mad, because it seemed as if a single touch from anyone would make them 'It'. So again, exactly who was 'It' she asked herself with a smile?

It wasn't young Sara, the young girl with the long dark hair and ebony skin to match, who hails from a tropical island south across the large ocean with its long white beaches and deep blue water. It wasn't the boy who ran past her, dodging her attempt to touch his shoulder with a quick side step. His name is Ru, and he wears his hair cut short in the style of his ancestors, as he is a direct descendent of the people of the Steppes, nomadic horsemen with a reputation of being such ferocious fighters that whole cities surrendered at simply hearing of their approach. Though, this evening, only three other children feared him, and one was Marisol who gave a scream and quickly ran away from Ru. She was born into a small village by the sea named for the explorer Cortes, brought into this world as her mother left it. Her father had died in the mines he worked months earlier leaving the little one alone, just like Ru and Sara.

All three children were orphans, their parents taken by an unseen hand which twisted each one's fate ever so cruelly. All three were supposed to die at birth or shortly thereafter, a death arranged before each even had a chance to breathe a single ounce of the air of this world.

Then there was John, her precious white hair.

He was an orphan as well, only his mother and father were alive, and thankfully somewhere far, far away from here. John didn't know this of course, there was no benefit to be gained by knowing his path into this world began as one of betrayal. How could it help to know your mother and father were just moments from selling you off to the mysterious ones who had seen your birth in visions and meant to kill you before you could bring about their predicted destruction?

And yet it wasn't just John who was alone in this life. It was all four children who were marked to be murdered before birth by a cosmic force, a God you might call it. A prophecy foretold by seers and oracles from days when man recorded words in stone would haunt the children before any of the four had even been conceived. Were these young ones, her adoring children she had come to love with all her heart, truly the 'Four Winds' those seers and oracles had foreseen? How could they be, so small and vulnerable as they were? Yet, she knew more than anyone else, there were awesome forces no man or woman could control, bring to heel, and these four were part of those forces.

Such was the prophecy, and any who tried to stop it or ignore it were fools for doing so.

A day of reckoning was coming and all four must be ready for it. The children must be prepared to meet and challenge the ones who would hunt them down for a final fight. It was why she had come to this remote part of the new Americas, this land of the Red Sky and high bluffs. She had been drawn here, pulled by that very same cosmic force to raise and protect the four who would one day bring about the end to a God.

"They look like they're having fun Grandmother."

She knew the voice, it was Kota, the man from across the oceans who soon would teach her little ones an ancient martial art to defend themselves physically against the ones who sought out their deaths. This was his task in this world, the physical, while her teachings to the children would be of the endless worlds just beyond the veil of this one, the 'Other Worlds'. 'Grandmother', it was the name everyone called her because that's who she was, the matriarch who looked after all who came to her seeking guidance. She was a shaman to most, a simple messenger who walked between this world and the next.

Or so she let everyone to believe.

Although there were those though who knew her true powers, these people were few as Grandmother kept her secrets locked away from prying eyes. "Let them have their fun, tomorrow they must leave this carefree life behind and begin walking a new, more dangerous path." She whispered letting the smile fade from her face.

Kota stared at her for a moment, seeing a beauty there in a face which may have been around fifty. Her long black hair showed just a hint of grey at the temples and her face was touched with just a brush of age lines. No one was truly sure of Grandmother's age, or her past, as she said nothing of the first and spoke little of the second. He did know, just like her, that some force beyond the everyday normal directed him here to this place. Kota was no shaman like Grandmother, but neither was he ignorant of 'Fate'. He was a master of an ancient teaching, a life bound to an art of self-defense taught to him by his father, and who was taught the art by his father before him. Kota stood just short of six feet with a wiry frame which hid a fierce physical strength, even at an age of 60 years. His dark eyes peered with a hard stare holding back an even more dominant will and determination.

An unseen hand had led him from his small village in Japan, from the small dojo his grandfather had built, just before it was destroyed by fire. He conveniently, and rather mysteriously, found passage across the oceans on a decrepit wooden air ship when none were allowed to leave the small Island nation. That old air ship was rotten, and should have fallen from the sky, especially during the mighty storm which overtook them, and yet he still made it this strange new land. The way he dressed, in a traditional black and grey kimono with his long grey hair tied into a braid, drew contemptable stares and low grumbles at the air station, in a place called Long Beach. Kota worried little though, as to how he would get to this place he kept dreaming of barely bothered him. The strange force had seen him all the way here, and just like the old air ship which refused to fall apart during the maelstrom, there was suddenly, and conveniently, a man and woman who offered him a ride, right to this very spot. It was nowhere, in the middle of nothing really, and yet there were three simple sturdy huts among the hard plains of a new country. Then a small bit of movement caught the corner of his eye and Kota turned to see a person approaching the huts, someone leading a burro up the trail.

"Are you expecting visitors Grandmother" He asked, squinting against the brightness of the sun, even though it was starting to set for the day.

"It is just a man looking for help with his wife. I better stoke the fire and prepare myself." Grandmother answered while pulling the blue blanket tighter around her shoulders before walking outside to call to the children, who stopped at their play instantly. "Time to go inside little ones, I have work to do."

There was a single collective 'Awww," from the group before Sara looked up excitedly and asking a question with a single blur of words. "Can we watch you work from the windows Grandmother?"

Before she could answer, all of the children were begging and pleading as little ones do, beseeching with high pitched voices to watch her work. At first, she looked at them quietly, let them carry on for just a second or two. She then raised a swift eyebrow, with a quick stern expression, that instantly brought all four children under control. Every set of those youthful pleading eyes locked with hers as her own silent stare told them not another word would sway her. It might even bring a punishment, but then with a small smile she let her deception drop.

Teasing them was so very easy.

"Go inside and watch from the windows. Quietly mind you, with Mister Kota."

All four gasped at the wonderful news, then turned and bolted for the door of the large hut behind them. Grandmother chuckled and went to stoking the fire as the man and his wife approached up the trail. From the windows, the four children eagerly watched her with the quiet of a mouse, as the one who raised them greeted the visitors with a wave and a single word of a beautiful language, like the wind as it graced the hanging chimes.

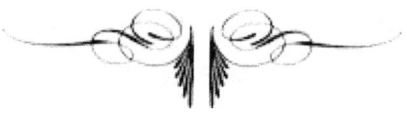

Sometime around 1900...

"What do you mean by 'it's all flooded'?"

The Captain's voice was pure gravel, grating and scraping with each and every syllable. He stood 6 feet 3 inches tall, and appeared just as wide at his chest it seemed. Every inch of him, east by west and north by south, was pure ill will if you crossed him. He glared at the sky pirate in front of him, the poor soul who had come back bearing the bad news of the now sunken treasure hidden here on Oak Island, which was a very large and very well-hidden trove of riches. It was part of the Templar hoard hidden here hundreds of years before, placed into several large vaults dug so deep in the ground it was said a man could fall for a quarter turn of the hourglass down the very shafts before hitting the bottom. The ones who created these vaults, special engineers and masons from a certain secret society, were brought in to ensure the treasure would never fall into anyone else's hands but the rightful owners. These engineers built booby traps, false shafts which led to phony rooms with empty chests, and special aqueducts which would flood everything if triggered. Which apparently, was exactly what happened to the ones who came looking for the hidden treasures before the pirates.

"Everything is underwater Captain, all the shafts and vaults including the main one, filled right to the very top. There's even a few holes old Billet never mentioned and those are filled up." The man stated minding each word carefully.

A loud grumble went through the crowd of pirates standing in the darkness of the woods with the moon high in the night sky, yet barely making any thing visible beyond a foot due to the thick canopy of leaves above them. There was no one left on the island since most of the workers from the company searching for the treasure were long gone, which meant the pirates had no worries of being seen. It seems treasure hunting be an expensive business, argh! And the company paying the bills must be all out of money to pay a wage, a lone figure in the crowd thought, and it took all her might not to giggle.

The Captain ground his teeth in anger and frustration as the others around him began to speak, tossing out bad ideas left and right like rats from a sinking air ship.

"What if we send a man down the main shaft? Someone who can swum good?" A pirate brought up and all at once it was soundly rejected with spittle, belligerent cries, and harsh words.

"Ain't no man here got the lungs to dive that deep you fool!"

"And if he did, why would he risk his neck to do such a thing? We ain't even sure what shaft leads to what room." Another spat among the chorus of rancor, but then everyone quickly shut their mouths when the Captain bellowed out a growl. It was low, but loud, and unless you were willing to challenge the man it came from, it meant to stop making any kind of noise.

The woods instantly dropped to an eerie quiet and the lone figure started to hope it meant they would be on their way soon. She hated being here on this island, which she heard was cursed, and her skin crawled when any piece of this place touched her bare flesh. The only thing she hated more was the idiot Billets, and the map he gave to the

Captain back in London. That cursed old sailor, who had actually sailed on ships that floated on the water and not the air, had a tale about buried treasure which the Captain couldn't resist hearing, and guess what my friends? Billets had a map too, damn his old wrinkled hide.

"It doesn't matter if we had a man who could breathe water like a fish, the same as we take in the air. We don't know which shaft is the right one, or didn't you hear Tripe here when he came back." A man to the right of the Captain snapped breaking the silence. Out of the whole crew, he was the only one who could have spoken up and not been shot between his very eyes. He was Jacks, 'and don't forget the 'S' at the end!' he would tell everyone, and he was the First Mate here on the Captain's crew. He was the trusted advisor, somewhat, for the leader of the pirates and sometimes the only sane voice in this rabble she thought as the Captain watched his First Mate handle the 'boys'.

"The company that's been looking for the treasure, they dug up a bunch of holes all over the island, all crazy like. Without orienting the map Billets gave us with the cross made from boulders, and the keystones there after, we're not even sure which hole is the right hole to swim in." Jacks carried on, shaking his head, helping the 'boys' along in the thinking process.

She looked around the group and took mental note of each and every one of them, realizing everyone had forgotten about an integral part of finding the treasure.

The map had to be aligned with the markers.

Yes, the map was a good reference for the shape of the island, but without orienting it to the boulders and the keystones, it was nothing but old parchment paper, not even worth the ink used to mark it. You could eyeball a spot and start digging, much like the treasure hunters who were here before, and come up with naught but an empty hole. The crew hadn't even started looking for the boulders, or keystones, during their haste to just run like a bunch of flighty geese, right for the center of the Island and the spot marked as 'Vault 1' on the map. Now, the daunting task of finding the treasure was starting to sink into everyone's thick head. They had to find the boulders, then the keystones, and then line everything up correctly before the first spade could touch the dirt they were standing on.

And all of that could take days to complete.

"You there, holding back the smile, what's your name lass?" The Captain's grinding voice brought her out of her thoughts with a snap.

She didn't realize she was smiling, at least till it was too late Still, with a solid backbone, she spoke up with a strong voice. "Fade Captain, my name is Fade."

"Fade eh? Well tell me, Fade, how the hell you came to be on my crew?"

It was a test, a trick question to see how she'd react. The Captain knew everyone on board his air ship. Every single pirate. One did not come and go but by his leave, and his leave alone, and he made it a point to know everyone's story. He had to know about everyone, because too many disloyal souls in a crew can lead to a mutiny.

She gave her head a shake, sending her long auburn hair so full of curls it looked like a bush spit out by a hurricane. "I fought my way on Captain, and I'm willing to fight to stay on."

The Captain's eyebrow raised just a little as he turned to Jacks, who spoke up for Fade with a nod and a smile. "She's a devil with a blade and an even better shot. Twitch found it out just after she came on board."

"Ah," the Captain smiled at the name while turning and staring at Fade, "so you're the one who took Twitch's arm at the elbow, eh? What, did he try to go where he wasn't asked to go?"

"I belong to no man and I don't like being touched. Twitch found both out, and if he had stuck around a little longer instead of running off like a dog, I'd have taken more than his arm." Fade answered back with every ounce of truth her being held. She was no man's plaything and never would be, not now at 16, nor a 100 more on in years. Yes, she was a handsome woman with all the right parts in all the right places, but Fade was more than a wench in some corset and breeches. She was going to be a captain herself one day and no pirate, or protectorate, or anyone would stand in her way.

The Captain stared at her for a long minute in silence before busting out in unexpected laughter which sent chills down everyone's spine, including Fade. She knew the Captain's reputation, and that scared her just a little as the large man turned to Jacks. "I like her, she can stay."

"Oh, I agree, but I'd really like to know what she' do right about now! Go dig in some random spot, or try and decipher this map?" The First Mate answered, then asked.

Damn, another test, Fade thought as she looked from the Captain to Jacks. "I'd get back on the air ship and leave this island in my memory." She snarled with a flat tone.

"You'd just leave all this treasure behind for someone else to take?" The Captain asked, the growl in his voice lowered, but still present. Maybe she had impressed him, she thought.

"We were never meant to find it Captain, and if we were, will then the whole crew would be bathing in gold coins right now. Billets said the legend was, the one who paid the heaviest price would be the only one who would find the treasure, and we haven't paid our dues yet from what I can see. It's why we're standing here in the dark looking like new born fools."

"What kind of price do you think old Billets meant?" A man in the back asked and Fade turned to answer him with a blazing glare. She always looked a man or woman in the eye when replying because it was the only way to make sure you got your words and your point through their thick skulls.

"I'm not sure, and I really don't give a damn to know." Fade said before turning back to the shadows of the Captain and Jacks. "The treasure is cursed, just like this damnable island, and anyone taking possession of it will have nothing but the spoils that come with curses for the rest of their days."

The woods fell silent again and Fade wished the light were better so she could see the Captain's face. She could read his expressions pretty well when she could see them, and she was curious if her words had damned her or brought her some form of prestige. She would never know because before either could answer, one of the lookouts from the beach ran up to the group, huffing and puffing out breath, but thankfully still able to convey a message.

"Captain, it's the Stray Dogs, they're here."

The Stray Dogs were the crew of one Trevor 'Butcher' Rollins. He fancied himself another Blackbeard, a chip off the old Edward Teach block, complete with a thrashed man-of-war he called 'The Queen Anne's

Revenge II'. The only problem was Butcher had no beard, his air ship could barely fly, and he lacked any of Teach's vile nature and evil ways for which to be dangerous with. Everyone around Fade began to pull out various sized sabers, knives, and guns of all types. The clicking of hammers being drawn back drowned out the scraping of metal on metal as swords were pulled from protective sheaths. Fade smiled a little as she thought old Butcher was about to meet his worst nightmare. A real sky pirate crew who could fight like all the devils in Hell itself.

"Where is he setting in?" Jacks asked quickly.

The panting pirate turned and pointed in the direction he had come from. "In the cove on the east side of the island. He hasn't seen us or the ship yet." The lookout offered just before the familiar gravel voice called out.

"Well then, come on boys, and miss! Let's go greet old Rollins with a handful of animosity and a mind full of warfare!" The Captain smiled evilly before turning heading toward the cove with his crew following. Fade started to follow when Jacks cut her off, his sweet looking body blocking her path.

"You truly ready to fight to stay here?"

She only smiled and drew her cutlass with one hand and her long pistol with the other. "You impress me tonight Jacks, and I might let you touch what cost Twitch his arm?"

Fade was by Jacks in two long steps, smiling with the knowledge she was about to go and get into a nice fight, and maybe a better one afterwards.

Sometime during 1921...

Pain ran rampant through his body, sharp and stabbing. It matched perfectly with the agony in his soul at the moment.

Wahkan looked down to his injured right arm and saw a lump just above the wrist, seeing the joint was also at an odd angle he knew the bone beneath the flesh was snapped in two. With his luck, probably a greenstick fracture. He held his injured appendage with his left hand, cradling his forearm to keep it from moving, but it seemed every thump of his heart sent a spike of agony right into his brain from his arm. He looked down to see his legs were still attached to his body, and with a grimace, he moved both an inch or two, just enough to confirm the limbs were still together and not a match to his broken arm. Wahkan gulped down a large gasp of air and then pushed with those intact legs to roll onto his back from his side, now looking up to the ceiling of the room where he was pretty sure he was going to die in.

He could hear them talking, the only two beings left standing in what was earlier today a road side diner, which it was before all hell broke loose. The remains of the booths around him blocked his sight of the rest of the place, but not the sound of the two who were fighting for his life, his very soul. Wahkan breathed deeply again, while holding his broken arm perfectly still, and fighting back the pain of his physical injuries as he listened intently.

"He is mine, John Greywolf. You have no claim to his soul as I do."

The voice should have been deeper, from a two pack a day habit and hard drinking. Wahkan knew this because the voice should have belonged to a man who went by the first name of Enoch, no last one known. He was the de facto leader of the murderous gang Wahkan had been tracking, running down for the last two years, and he was never this polite. The gang had killed a small group of Indigenous People just across the border which separated the Homeland from the States, a small town in what was once part of Kansas. The men of this gang had killed his family, his father and mother and sister, murdered all three without provocation or reason. They didn't even take a thing from the family home, just killed the trio of gentle souls and then left like the wind.

"I have never laid claim to any soul, but Wahkan refused you Dagon, you and your offer both. He can leave with me if he wishes, or he can walk away down the road, which ever fate he chooses it will be with his free will and not your influence, Nightshade."

Nightshade?

Dagon, that name sounded familiar. Wahkan fought the fog of pain in his brain, trying to focus, and pulled up the memory of the name Dagon. He had heard it somewhere before, along with Nightshade, but the memory was hazy, what with half the synapses in his head being used up by the shock he was feeling from being injured.

"He killed Devlin and Jamison with his own hand, Shaman. He never hesitated, or balked, when he shot them, even though I told him doing so would damn his soul. Wahkan is mine; now or later it does not matter." The voice of Dagon stated in the cold, but polite voice, which wasn't even a close to matching Enoch.

Wahkan rolled his head to the right looking back toward the back of the diner, back to where he saw the body of Devlin under a table and the feet of Jamison sticking out of the booth. Yeah, he shot them both, dead before they hit the ground. 'I had no choice' Wahkan thought. 'Both drew on me first and I was reciprocating, but that wasn't the full truth of it. I came here looking to kill these three men, these murderers, and I damn near did it till Enoch fought back and broke me like an old chair.' He sighed heavily from his thoughts while trying to ignore the pain. 'And now look at me, busted up on the inside with a broken arm on the outside, lying still here on the floor like Aunt Bessie's best rug.'

The voices snapped Wahkan out of his mental turmoil again.

"I know what Wahkan has done Dagon. I also know of your plan to take his soul and of your influence on Devlin and Jamison to ensure your plan worked. I know that is what brought him to this place at this specific time. Your vile intention and nefarious guidance. I know you had Devlin and Jamison kill Wahkan's family so you could force him to avenge his loved ones and fall into your trap. You have had this night planned for so long, and it was so close to being successful."

'What?!' Wahkan thought with disbelief. 'I was played this whole time? This ending here tonight, these long two years, it was all part of a plan?'

"What do you mean by 'close to being successful' Shaman?" The conniving tone of Dagon inquired.

There was a long pause; too damn long as Wahkan grunted and pushed his injured body to a sitting position with the aid of leaning against a bench. He could see the pair now, John Greywolf standing just a few feet away in what was the open entrance to the diner. He turned his head slightly and spotted Enoch, or Dagon now, standing between the booths and the stools by the long open counter. Damn, Enoch, or Dagon, or whoever, looked scary now with eyes that were jet black and skin as white as a man missing most of his blood.

"You can't tell can you, Nightshade?" John asked. His white hair was pulled back into a pony tail showing the smile on his face easily. That damn black hat with the wide brim and tall crown adding to the look of the shaman as some strange mystic.

"I cannot tell what?" Enoch/Dagon growled with a snarl as he retorted.

'Yeah, what am I and Enoch missing here John?' Wahkan asked no one in particular while sitting quietly thinking to himself.

The Shaman only continued to smile, looking out from under that black hat with the beaded band. "Has your plan truly worked, is the soul you've waited so long to possess really yours now Dagon? Maybe you should take a quick look and see?"

'Now what the hell did that mean?' Wahkan asked silently again as he swallowed hard. He watched as Enoch/Dagon looked incredulously at John for a minute before closing his eyes with a snap. Wahkan was happy for not having to look at those black pits for a second, but then both were open abruptly, back as Enoch/Dagon's eyes shot open with a jerk.

He suddenly looked quite upset Wahkan thought, for whatever he was. Dagon, who had tricked him to kill in order to possess his soul was very pissed at the moment.

"How is this possible? How can he deny ME?"

The Shaman shook his head and spoke calmly. "He invoked the Great Spirit before walking through the doors to the diner. He called upon the One to watch over him, and in doing so, ceased any claim you might have had to him, Dagon."

'I did', the large man thought with a smile forming on his face. 'I asked the Great Spirit to look over me and guide my hand.'

"No, no, that is not possible, it is not ALLOWED!" Enoch/Dagon screamed with a shrill, ear piercing voice.

"It is more than allowed Nightshade, it has been done, and now it is time for you to leave this world, Dagon. It is time to return to your realm Nightshade."

The last from John was like a slap to the face, and Wahkan was sure if Enoch would have drawn iron on the Shaman for saying such a thing, then this Dagon would most certainly take exception with those words. And as sure as the sun would rise, the being did, because he growled even deeper. "Try and send me back yourself, John Greywolf."

Even while sitting on the floor, Wahkan could easily see the large Bowie knife John pulled from the sheath he kept strapped sideways at the small of his back. He could see the Shaman spin the knife in his hand so the spine of the blade ran up against his forearm and the pommel was just an inch or two past the top of his fist.

"I sent your brother Silas back to your realm Dagon as well as Malfeus, you will be no different if you force my hand."

And there it was. The challenge accepted without hesitation.

'It was just like a few minutes ago, when I walked in here', Wahkan silently told himself. 'I locked eyes with Devlin and Jamison, knowing full well there was no backing down coming and no mercy expected, and then we were pulling our guns and slinging lead.'

He wondered how these two were going to fight, because neither was reaching for a gun, and Wahkan figured a weapon like a pistol wasn't the way this was going to go anyway. Wahkan breathed deep, waiting silently while watching intently both the Shaman and Enoch/Dagon. Someone's going to make the first move, they always do, and this thing is going to end in the blink of an eye.

Then Enoch/Dagon abruptly stepped back and smiled cruelly. "The Indian is your shaman. Know this though, one day I will repay you for interfering in my affairs. Mark my words, and mark them well, John Greywolf."

"And I will be waiting for that very day Dagon," was all John said in reply before the spot where Dagon was standing flashed with a white light so bright it blinded Wahkan.

His hand was busy cradling his broken arm, so Wahkan had no defense against the bright glow except his eye lids, which had little effect. He sat cringing in the simultaneous pain of his broken arm and the light, both flooding his brain with a sharp crescendo of agony. Then it was gone, the light and the pain from it, allowing Wahkan to open his eyes again and see the scene. As he did, he noted John was next to him now, squatting down while resting a hand on his shoulder, the same one which held the large knife from before, the blade now home in its sheath on his back.

"I can safely say you've seen better days my friend." John said with that knowing smile.

"Yeah, I think I did pretty good though. It took Enoch using everything not nailed down in the Diner here to beat me with before I'd go down to the floor." Wahkan smiled back. He remembered getting hit with a stool and a sizable part of the cash register before everything became a blur.

The shaman couldn't help but chuckle while reaching under Wahkan's arm, but before he could help the large man up, a question from Wahkan stopped him cold. "Why'd you come back for me John?"

"Would you have left me to a similar fate my friend?"

The counter response was a good one, and with anyone else he'd have said yes, because these days Wahkan had little use for friendship. The fact of the matter was, after the war, coming home had been a hard change. He had seen so much death in those trenches over in the war, and then to come home and find his family killed, well Wahkan had no friends because he didn't want any. There was just the impending confrontation with Devlin, Jamison, and Enoch. That was it. Nothing else mattered to him at all, nothing but seeing these three men into their damn graves with a one-way ticket to Hell.

But then he ran into John Greywolf.

"Probably, but I'm not a good man John, not these days." Wahkan replied begrudgingly, for having to admit the slightest chivalry he didn't even believe in himself.

The shaman nodded and continued to smile, "but every day gives way to another, a brand-new day with new paths and choices Wahkan."

The large man looked at John with a wide confused eye. He had been around the shaman for a couple of months now, and he was discovering his companion would say things like this. Little parables with hidden meanings, and all the damn time! When Wahkan remained quiet, and lost, the shaman titled his head and nodded. "Tomorrow is a new start Wahkan. You can begin to walk a new path, or wait until the next day when you are ready to do so. Just know, every man and woman can change, we are not bound to be one kind of person, or do one permanent thing with our lives."

'Oh, so that's what he meant', Wahkan thought as a laugh started to rise from his chest. 'And here I thought I was nothing more than a killer.'

The large man felt John suddenly begin to lift him up by his good arm, and the laughter stopped as he wasn't given much choice to get to his feet. "Damn, I guess I'm going home with you."

"Zheng said he wanted me to make sure you came back in one piece."

"Really, why's that?" Wahkan asked walking toward the exit with ginger steps. He was sore all over, from his eyelids to his big toes.

"He wanted the chance to say, 'I told you so', I think," John chuckled and Wahkan couldn't help but laugh again even though it hurt like hell.

"Nice. Now I'm going to have to take bunk from a ghost! My life's already changing."

Part One

The bed was warm. It was the kind of warm one would crawl into, ball up, and fight any and every attempt to take it away from you. Yet, when there was a knock on a door somewhere in the hazy fog which was the state of the mind of one Camille, she began to stir sensing an end to the warmth was coming. She felt the bed shift, the portion of the precious warmth was moving, moving away from her and leaving, which made Camille groan low. No, she thought sleepily, don't take it away just yet, not this magical...

"Coming," a voice answered the knock, and she felt the bed move again as someone stood up, and even through the fog of slumber Camille knew this was important.

She forced her eyes open just an inch while lying still on the bed, refusing to give up on the dissipating warmth, and caught a glimpse of Fade walking to the door to her personal cabin dressed in her night shirt. It started coming back to the Magi then, in small bits with brilliant flashes in her mind, of all that had happened the day before. The flight on the Protectorate Air Ship, the semi-successful attempt to retrieve the Joris Stones, and the fight to get the air ship to the Yards after Fade had dispatched it with her unmatched skill in the air.

"What news is there?" Fade asked the man at the door, his face just visible as the portal was cracked enough to allow the conversation to occur but not much else.

It had been a long day, and Camille had fallen straight to sleep after climbing into bed with Fade, even falling into slumber as the Captain spoke. They were talking about something important, or at least it felt-

"We're just outside the city Captain, tucked away high in the clouds as you ordered." The man answered, Fade's second in command Mr. Hayes.

Then Camille remembered then, the memory coming back with a snap, why she was here with Fade on board her air ship the Crescent Moon. They had been talking about John and Wallace, two men both cared for deeply, and even sharing her worry about the Engineer was not enough to hold back the need for rest and sleep. Camille watched as Fade nodded to Mr. Hayes while giving an order.

"Good, no one followed us during the night?"

"No Captain," the second replied with a shake of his head, "We weren't followed, paid close attention to keeping our course a mystery. We're hidden away now, but there's an awful number of lights floating everywhere round the city. The sky's filled with all kinds of Protectorate ships and haulers."

What city are we just outside of? Camille thought, wondering for the first time where she, and everyone else, had gone while she slept. Were they even around New York still?

"When you kick the hornet's nest Mr. Hayes you have to be ready for the bugs to protect their home." Fade replied with a nod before continuing on. "Have the crew ready my whip while you take the Moon low enough to let me fly into the city."

"Aye Captain,"

As soon as Fade closed the door after Mr. Hayes turned to leave Camille was up in the bed looking worried, her voice filled with the concern. "What's wrong with Wallace and John?"

The Sky Pirate Captain crossed the deck of her cabin with long steps grabbing her pants off the floor. "I don't know if there is anything wrong with them Camille, but I intend to find out."

"I'm going with you." The Magi stated with the emphasis on all four words. Camille slid to the end of the bed and began to get dressed as did Fade, and she quickly asked a question. "Where are we? Are we still flying around Manhattan?"

"No," Fade answered buckling her pants then picking up her corset, "we flew to Chicago through the night."

"Chicago?" Camille gasped with some shock as she slipped her pants on.

Fade waited a whole second before carrying on with the conversation. There was no time to waste if they had plans on catching John and Wallace. "Yes, I had Mr. Hayes take us here on a not-so-direct path so we'd arrive alone and in secret."

"Why are we in Chicago? Why are Wallace and John in Chicago?"

"John has a friend here in the city, and with the trouble he's stirred up, I'm sure the shaman will be going right to see her first thing."

That was right, Camille thought as she reached for her corset as well, there was an elderly woman on the West Side who everyone knew specialized in the 'old ways'. She hailed from Western Europe, and as such, she was wise in alternative medicines, remedies, and other arcane things. The immigrants who poured into Chicago inevitably ended up on the West Side, and all found their way to her small shop, searching for unique cures and ancient wisdom from the old country.

"He's going to see Twyla," Camille interjected lacing up her corset quickly with a practiced hand.

Fade nodded as she began to pull on her boots, "because she's one of the few he can confide in."

The last from the pirate slowly, and mercifully, vanished till the room was quiet. Camille could see the small twitch in her friend's cheeks and corner of her mouth, the only sign of pain she would ever show. Fade was as strong as any man, stronger that most the Magi had met, and yet she still felt the touch of loneliness.

"Maybe he goes to her because she is the only one who understands what he has...seen." Camille offered, trying to reach out and comfort her dear friend, and yet when the reply was quick and fiery she was not hurt. She expected it really.

"If the man would stop and talk to the ones who care for him then he would have more than just one old lady who understands him."

And with the end of the retort the room fell silent again. Camille knew to let her friend have some space, Fade was more than capable of asking for a hand, or a word of reassurance. In truth, she was just as stubborn as the shaman the Magi knew, so it was no wonder that the relationship found a quick end, or had it Camille was thinking as a knock at the door broke the quiet. We are in Chicago, chasing John she continued to think as Fade yelled out.

"Enter, we're dressed!"

The door swung open immediately and Mr. Hayes walked in a couple of steps speaking. "There's new trouble Captain."

"What is it?" Both Fade and Camille asked in unison, the voices intermingling so perfectly Mr. Hayes stalled, confused for a moment, before answering.

"The man on the Hertzian Wireless picked up a transmission between the Protectorate and the local Magi House, about Miss Camille here."

The pirate looked to her friend quick, with a concerned expression, as Camille inquired as to what was intercepted. "What was said?"

"Your to be detained the moment you step inside the Magi's House Madame, and then handed over to the constabulary forthwith, no questions asked."

The words were like thrown daggers, each one sinking deep into Camille's heart with soul wrenching pain. All she had known from a young life was the Magi, the elders and the Umbra, a family which had raised her and praised her and rewarded her work with magic. Now, the ones she had looked up to and sought the admiration of were hunting her down, like rogue Weavers who had defied the law of the land. She was nothing more than a criminal, one to be hunted, and by the very people she had wanted to please so much.

"This can't be Mr. Hayes; the man must have heard it wrong."

"No, my Captain, I was standing beside him the whole time the transmission was broadcasting. We both heard the same thing."

Fade spun to her friend, who looked about ready to expel her breakfast on the deck, if she had any food to throw up that is the pirate thought. "This isn't right, can't be right."

She was still reeling from what Mr. Hayes had said, to the point answering Fade was not possible for Camille. She was just trying to breath when Mr. Hayes threw just a little more weight on top of the pile already sitting on the chest of the Magi.

"The Magi were told to be on the lookout for the two Weavers as well. Both lasses get the same as Miss Camille, locked up till the Protectorate come for them all."

"The Weavers? They know the Weavers are here in Chicago?" Camille snapped, the shock of the moment instantly dispelling.

"It looks like I was right about where John was going to end up, and someone else figured it right as well." Fade spoke, looking from one face to the other in the room with no pride for being right. She only shook her head slightly as she continued. "If the Protectorate and the Magi are looking for the Weavers then they'll be after John and the others, as sure as I'm standing here."

"This means the Umbra will be out in force, and in number, blanketing the city. We have to find John and Wallace before they do or we will never see them again." Camille whispered, the words slipping out low on a long exhale.

The room was quiet again, for just a minute, before the pirate looked to her friend and spoke. "I think we're about to kick the same hornet's nest John did."

"Hornet's nest Captain?" Mr. Hayes asked looking confused with a raised eyebrow. The First Mate would never question his Captain, even if she were talkng about flying bugs, but it did seem a rather percuilar time to be asking about insects.

"I need to be dropped off near the Magi House in Chicago, not so close as to draw attention though." Camille suddenly ordered and the request brought a pause to the First Mate.

Mr. Hayes looked to his captain for a moment confused and then back to Miss Camille. "Beg you pardon Madame, but didn't you hear what I told you? The Magi and Protectorate are looking for you and it's not to ask where you spent the night."

"I know Mr. Hayes, and thank you for the concern." Camille smiled as she started to fix her hair.

"All right, I'll play this game, why do you want us to drop you off in the proverbial lions den?" Fade asked getting her belt off the floor.

The Umbra, or former leader of the elite hunters, shook her head signaling she would not be dissauded from her plan. "I have to warn Ezic to stay away or else he'll be sought by the Protectorate just as I am."

"Ezio?" Fade and Mr. Hayes quipped at the same moment.

"Yes, Ezio," Camille smiled holding her chuckle in at the sight of her dear friends while continuing on. "He was the one who suggested to me there is a secret conspiracy between the Magi and Protectorate. If the Umbra are hunting me they will certainly be after him."

"And you have a way to warn him, which just happens to be in the one place where you go you get put in shackles?" Fade inquired with a heavy dose of sarcasm as she clipped her sword on her hip.

"Just like John and his secrets, I have my own my friend. I know of a way to get a message to Ezio through a mutual friend. I have to do this my Fade, to leave my second without a warning would be kin to betrayal." Camille explained.

She had expected Fade to say something to stop her, to persuade her that this was a fools errand, but the Sky Pirate just looked to her friend and smiled. "We can drop you off anywhere you wish, on one condition?"

"And that is?"

"You be careful, or else I'll have my crew fight any and every Protectorate in this city to find you." Fade promised, and like any pledge, it touched Camille to her very soul.

Oh my dear sweet friend, the Magi's warm smile said silently, I will always be safe.

Across the dark morning sky, toward the North Side of the city, another pair was waking in the early morning. She had been sleeping so well, deep and restoring, that Boles never felt her love Wells get up. It was only when the dark-haired Weaver reached over with the intention of wrapping her arms around the smaller body of the green haired Weaver did she discover the missing form. Boles patted the empty space twice, and then with a snap, sat up looking for the one who should have been there. After her sleep filled eyes adjusted, she spotted Wells at the door, the portal cracked just enough to allow the Weaver to look out.

"What are you doing?" Boles asked with the befuddlement one might have when waking too quickly. She started to sit up as Wells whispered back.

"I think John is leaving the ship."

Boles slid on her robe and crossed their room with silent steps to huddle next to her love by the cracked door. "Why is he leaving?"

"I don't know," Wells sighed eyeing the hall beyond their room with worried eyes, "has the ship stopped? I can't tell, it doesn't rumble or shake like any of the other air ships I have been on."

The dark-haired Weaver shook her head, sending her long curly hair tussling. "I don't know either, all I feel is the strange tingling from the walls and floor where I touch. Wait, how do you know John is leaving?"

The question brought Wells attention away from the door and hall beyond and to her love Boles. The green haired Weaver's brown eyes were filled with the same concern as her voice as she whispered. "I had a dream about him."

"Oh my heart, it was just a dream and nothing more." Boles smiled, reaching up to stroke her companion's beautiful cheek.

Wells though, only shook her head and sighed, "no it was not Boles. It was like the dream I had the night before we were discovered by the horrible man who sold us to the equally horrible men in the brothel. It was the same feeling of dread as the one I had the night before Isaac was killed."

Boles breath caught in her throat, right below her larynx, stealing any words she would have proffered, if she could speak at all. The mention of both times when Wells prophetic dreams had come true was enough to throw the dark-haired Weaver off from consoling her love. Then voices could be heard, a door farther down the hall opened, and any chance or thought of soothing Wells was lost as both ladies turned to looking out the door. Out in the hall they could see nothing for a moment, just hear the recognizable voices of the three men who had come to their aid the day before.

"I'll drop off a list with the market so we can restock the kitchen and ship."

The voice was even, calming, with a slight Southern drawl, which was John both Weavers knew. The mysterious shaman who knew so much about them it was actually scary, and yet so safe in the same instance. There was no need for secrets because he knew the true person behind the mask, and more than that, what made you feel truly safe, was the fact he made no judgement about that person. You could be who you wanted to be, were meant to be, and never worry if you were accepted as a friend.

"We can pick it all up on the way back in, no problems."

That was Wahkan, his deep voice easily distinguishable. He was the protector, the one you would never have to ask to be by your side Boles thought and the image struck her funny. She had built a psychological wall and guard against men, and women, for all the years she had been with the Magi's. A deep distrust of everyone due to the treatment she was forced to endure, only with Isaac that wall had begun to crumble until she was taken again and locked away. Now, after looking into the large man's eyes and his hard-set jaw, Boles felt that guarding wall was wavering once again because, like with John, she felt she could trust this man with her life.

"Since Wahkan will be taking care of the ladies, I'll be looking to meet some old friends, that's if he doesn't mind of course?"

Now that voice was easy, the Scottish accent ringing like music to the Weavers ears. It was the engineer of the ship, the one called Wally, the technoist who built the box which kept things cold and the boiler which kept the rooms warm. They could see the large side burns on his face and the bowler hat on his head. Just like the others, he was a protective soul, a quiet man who preferred his tools and machines to human contact of the open world due to some tragedy in his past.

"Now that hurts me to the proverbial bone Wally. You don't want to spend the day with me?" Wahkan said with a mock hurt. The sound of it made both Weavers instantly smile and fight to hold back a giggle.

"Well, as sweet as you are you big dobber, I am afraid I'll have to decline the offer due to a more pressing engagement." Wally responded with his own mock pain.

Then the three were passing by the door and the light from the hall instantly disappeared sending the room into the dark for a moment. Then it lit up again as the group passed and they continued to talk.

"Yeah, and what's more important than John's request or me for that matter?" Wahkan shot back.

Wells stood at the door a moment longer waiting till the three were gone before opening the door quietly so she could look out. The group was down the hall now, just passing the kitchen, and still carrying on.

"I'm betting it's an old boiler, or broke down engine, something that hasn't run for a very long time and only Wally can fix." John smiled.

"Nah, my guess is it's some new tool that can do something neither of us understands but keeps Wally up at night all excited." Wahkan retorted quickly.

They were down by the stairs now, ascending the flight one step at a time, and Wells felt a sudden need to catch up, to keep the men in sight. She felt it so strong she bolted from the cover of her room, out into the hall, chasing them down with silent steps. She couldn't let anyone leave yet her mind and fear screamed, not yet before giving them a warning.

"Wells!" Boles hissed trying to stop her love but watching with horror as the green haired Weaver ran after the men. She barely had a chance to stay a step behind the girl as Wells ran quietly after John, the three still talking.

"You keep it up you two and there'll be no hot water to bathe with!" Wally remarked, which was quickly followed by a rather jeering comment from the ghost Zheng.

"That would not bother Wahkan. He does not bathe!"

The jest sent a hearty laugh through John and Wally while Wahkan only eyed the helmsmen of the Gāi Gōng De Tiānkōng while firing back with a grin. "Keep it up Hui and you'll find yourself back in the Waiting World."

Zheng Hui was going to reply to the large IP. He had a response ready to fly when a figure flew past Wally and Wahkan both, knocking into them as she passed. Wells gasped as she came to a stop by the one she had chased after so desperately. "John, wait!"

The shaman turned and smiled, looking down at the small Weaver as she reached out and grabbed his arm. He was wearing his usual white shirt under the custom hand-crafted leather vest, the one with the ends of the cords holding the material secure hanging down past the sides of his waist, and his goggles and his black hat with the beaded band. "Good morning Wells, I hope we didn't wake you with our good-natured fun."

"No, you didn't," she blurted quickly shaking her head, "but you can't leave your ship today."

The suddenness of the statement, as well as the apprehension, was not missed by the white-haired man whose eyebrows raised slightly from surprise. "And why is that my friend?" John asked calmly.

There was no response, no answer at first from Wells, but then another voice broke in speaking for the Weaver. Boles pushed her way past the stunned Wally and Wahkan while calling out. "Wells had a dream."

"A dream?" Wally whispered looking to the large IP, but Wahkan only shrugged his shoulders and watched.

"A dream, about me?" John asked lowering his eyebrow before smiling handsomely. It was nice, to know only a few short hours ago the Weavers were suspicious and closed to him and the others, but now open and even concerned. "What was this dream about Miss Wells?"

The Weaver swallowed hard while pulling her robe tighter around her shoulders to hold back the pre-dawn cold. Or maybe it was the fact she noticed all the eyes of everyone had settled directly on her and the attention was more than unsettling. Whatever it was, Wells mustered up her courage and spoke in her beautiful British accent.

"I saw you talking to a shimmering spirit, two bodies trying to be one but not able to." She began, stopping only long enough to take a breath, long enough for John to shake his head. The eagle feather tied to the cord which hung off the rear of the brim twirled as he spoke.

"I will be fine Wells, there isn't a need to worry."

"No, no, that wasn't the danger." She sighed shaking her head, the pair of long green bangs whipping from the motion. "The shimmering spirit was just talking to you, something else was coming for you, something from the dark of the shadows."

She was obviously upset, it was easy to see, and with a calm voice Wally tried to ease the Weaver and her concern. "John will be fine lass, he's a big boy you know."

"Yeah, he'll be fine Wells. It was just a dream." Wahkan added, his usually hard voice softer and his words kind.

Boles stepped up to Wells side and tried to make the three understand why her love was upset. "You don't understand. Wells, me, we both have dreams from time to time which come true. If Wells saw something in her dream about you John, then you need to listen to her!"

Just like the moment before, when the concern in Wells voice caused John to pause, the same happened now. Precognition, it was nothing new to the shaman, but to be the one seen in a dark vision was not a thing to take lightly, and John did not even though he acted as if he did. He looked to the dark-haired Weaver still smiling, there were things he must see to immediately leaving no time to calm the ladies. "I heard her Boles and I will be careful. Now, while I am away Wahkan will take you into the city and get clothes for you both."

It was the tone of his response, the calm, which only made Wells more concerned. It was like the shaman didn't believe her and that frustrated the Weaver like nothing else. "Snakes, something that is akin to snakes, it means to kill you John. You have to stay on the air ship, please!"

The impassioned plea should have sent at least a sense of urgency through John Boles thought, it did for her, and yet the shaman only smiled on unaffected and gently removed Wells hand from his arm. The move may not have been a dismissive one but it could easily be seen as such. "Thank you for the warning my friend. I will see you both this afternoon when I return."

"You don't believe her?" Boles whispered, partly in disbelief and the rest with a growing frustration, just like her Wells. To be ignored, set aside like this, it was too much for the dark-haired Weaver to take.

"You know, you two have a decision to make, a very important decision." John nodded before turning and walking quickly to the opening in the rail. There should be a gangplank or something Wells thought, a long board one could walk down to leave the air ship, only there was nothing by the rail as John readied himself to step out into the thin air. The green haired Weaver gasped again and yelled, a question she didn't even know she wanted to ask.

"What decision?"

The shaman stopped, paused a third time, looking over his shoulder to the Weavers. "Where will you go now that your free of course?"

Then he was gone, a ghost, as he stepped off and dropped out of sight. Boles gasped as Wells ran to the rail and looked over. She knew the shaman had fallen to his death, she just knew it, but as Wells looked over she watched as the air ship slowly pulled away from the roof of a building. And there, walking quickly, was John strolling across the top of the building toward a door set into a small dormer.

"He didn't believe you, just like everyone else." Boles sighed angrily from where she stood.

"Come on ladies, go lay back down for a bit. We have some time before we have to meet the Mouse." Wahkan said trying to sooth the more than apparent frustration.

Boles spun and walked by him shaking her head, "he dismissed us like we were fools."

"Oh lass, Brother John doesn't think such a thing." Wally chuckled trying to help just as Wahkan had.

Wells turned away from the rail just as the ship turned away from the roof and look dejected, so much so it made the two men ache. "I need some coffee."

Wahkan could only watch as the pair walked back into the air ship, one looking low and the other as angry as a bear. He wondered just how much this would affect their decision when Zheng spoke up from behind them. "They do not understand John or his way, but then neither did any of us when we first met him."

"Yeah, I just hope they don't make the same mistake I made is all." The large IP remarked before following the pair of Weavers into the ship. Wally trailed his friend, walking along in silence leaving Zheng alone on the main deck. As he watched them disappear the helmsman only smiled and whispered.

"No my friend, they won't make the same mistakes. I think the Weavers will surprise us all when the time comes."

The door wasn't locked. It was always unlocked when he came to Chicago. John wondered who was tasked with making sure it was accessible when he arrived, was it someone his friend, the Witch, knew personally or did she just leave word with a person and that someone walked up and opened the lock. Maybe he would ask once he arrived at the shop the shaman thought as he quickly travelled the stairs, ending up on the bottom floor in just a few minutes. The day was just starting, the sun still below the horizon, and yet the sounds of the working men and women in the tenement could be heard easily through the thin walls. Some child in one of the apartments was awake now, and crying loudly, while a man somewhere else screamed at his brother. It seemed money was the factor of the argument John noted as he walked briskly, exiting the building and out onto the street without looking back. Not a soul had seen his passing, no one person in the building could claim to witness seeing the man dressed in a leather vest and black hat as he walked through their living quarters.

Out on the street, the shaman turned right and began to walk just as fast toward the center of the town, East, as the goggles around his neck jingled from the leather strap. He had been dropped off from the Tiānkōng in what the locals called 'The West Side' of the great city of Chicago. It was called 'The Gateway' by most, if not all, of the immigrants and former slaves who came to the city looking for work, for a life and a new beginning. The term wasn't used with admiration or respect, least not by the ones who had to live in the 'accommodations' of this side of town. John passed by dwellings which had seen better days, walked on ignoring the smell of the common people as it surrounded him. The North Side wasn't like this he thought, the ones living there having the means financially to ensure it would never be like this on their doorsteps. The North Siders had the political power to keep the ones who had nothing more than dreams and hope to their side of the street one could say. A man stepped out of building ahead of John, and the shaman slowed just enough to stay behind him, and then quickly cross the street in long quiet strides. The man must have felt something, sensed the presence of another walking up, because he turned just in time to see nothing but the dark of the pre-dawn behind him.

The shaman went by the man on the other side of the street as he stood looking for whatever it was he felt. John moved along with a single purpose keeping his steps quiet and his thoughts contained, that was till he passed a small alleyway ahead. As he crossed the mouth of the narrow passage, the shaman barely noted the existence of the alley, but then he froze just two steps past it. John turned slowly back to the alley and spoke with a smile.

"May I ask why you are hiding in an alley here in Chicago my brother?"

A man, dressed similar to John, stepped out of the shadows and responded with a friendly air. "I wasn't hiding. I was talking with someone while waiting for you."

"Who could you be taking to in an alley this early in the morning Ru?" John asked the man, obviously his brother.

"I stumbled upon a very nice gentleman ghost from Ireland who just recently passed. He was telling me his story my brother and it was very intriguing."

"Ah, the ghost of the Irish, they always tell the best stories. Why is he staying in the alley?" John chuckled with a nod to his brother as Ru approached.

"He passed over only a few months ago, due to a tragic accident where he was employed, a place where cattle are butchered by the hundreds. He refuses to leave the alley because he can watch his daughter walk to and from school there. He can watch her grow and enjoy what little he can see of her."

The shaman from the Steppes of Mongolia stopped by his brother and grinned, the long flowing hair of his moustache and goatee framing his face perfectly. His facial hair, jet black at one time, was now peppered with grey as it draped down several inches from his chin. Ru was shorter than his brother, by a few inches, and dressed the same almost with tan pants tucked into calf high moccasins and a white long sleeve shirt under a waistcoat. Only where John's vest was brown tanned leather Ru's was a bright blue with flowing gold embroidery along the edges and around his waist was tied a large red sash. Ru's hat was different from John's as well, not the wide brimmed black type, but the fur of a fox, complete with a tail running down the back with beads and feathers tied to long appendage.

"Really, that is a very interesting story, but how did you find him?" John asked with a raised eyebrow.

"I saw him standing there in the alley, all alone, and curiosity got the better of me I guess." Ru chuckled before exhaling with fondness and leaning in to hug John. "You look good brother, especially after what happened in Brooklyn."

John hugged his brother back with a hard squeeze while speaking with the same fondness. "There was never a moment to worry my brother."

"Tell that to Sara and Marisol, both are unhappy with your choice to just walk into that place yesterday." Ru stated as he stepped back away from John, the fond smile changed to worried one.

"You've talked with our sisters as well,"

The shaman with the skull cap sighed again and shook his head, "you know those two. They talked and I listened, quietly."

"Ah, that bad eh?" John asked before turning to restart his walk toward Mother Twylah's. He waited till Ru was in step next to him as his brother answered.

"It was more like they talked and I could only agree with a nod between them. It has been decided, by our dear sisters, that you take too many risks, foolish risks at that."

"But those are the only risks worth taking brother. Well, I hope I fare better when we finally meet later. How is Sara?"

Ru gave a chuckle and a shake of his head, "you won't and you know this as well. I am relieved to see she is much better. The poison still weakens her a bit, but she is the strong one among us and her recovery is almost complete. She is helping Marisol, tending to one of the 'problems' that has come up from our actions yesterday. It seems, by intervening for the Weavers, we have set other actors in this story into rash motion."

John laughed with his brother as the pair walked on down the sidewalk, making their way to the shop of one witch, Mother Twylah. After a minute, John looked over and asked a sudden question which had come to his mind. "tell me, what are you doing on this side of town brother?"

"Mother Twylah sent me to unlock the door so you could come down from the roof." Ru answered with a look of surprise, as if John should have known the fact.

The shaman with the black hat gasped, winked, and clapped his brother on the shoulder before speaking. "So, you're the one who comes and unlocks the door to the roof?"

"No, I am not the one, but it does make me think, who does she have come and unlock the door for us?"

"I have no idea who it is, but just like that, the mystery remains," John laughed again.

The pair moved along the street in quiet for a moment before John could sense the happy mood was beginning to shift ever so subtly.

His brother was about to ask a serious question, a very important inquiry. And just as Ru turned to him John shifted his gaze to meet his brother w th an easy calm as the shaman from the Steppes spoke.

"The Nihods, they know we are here in Chicago. The one we seek, the shadow who attacked Sara, has followed us, all four, to this point and place just as we knew it would."

It wasn't the exact question John was expecting, just the preamble to set the ground on which the conversation would happen. "I know, I sensed the shadow's presence while coming down the steps from the roof. The Snake knows we are close to finding the one who crafted the poison which almost took Sara's life. It knows the alchemist is the path which will lead us to its realm, or so we hope it thinks this."

"Yes, I see this as well, which is why I wonder if this meeting with Laken Malus is such a good idea right now. The interaction with the Weavers only adds to the chance of our true plan being discovered while we are here in Chicago. Our ruse was thin at best and now, it is even thinner." Ru inquired with a raised eyebrow and an air of concern.

John grinned and nodded, "it may be hazardous Ru, but we all agreed we could not leave the Weavers to their fate, in that brothel at the hands of Triosi. It is why we bartered with Isaac."

"I know John, it is just, we have set people in motion counting on certain actions to occur at certain times, if something upsets what we have started moving?" Ru asked letting the last trail off, a sign John knew too well, deciding to press his brother just a bit more.

"What is it then that worries you my brother?"

The shaman from the Steppes shook his head and spoke from his heart as he always did with his brother and sisters. "I see a crossroad ahead of us brother, where the plans of others will cross our path, but I do not see what may come when we all meet in the center of the crossroad. This plan we have set our wills too, you acting as the 'bait' for the Nihods, to draw out the one who was hidden from us, this is not what Grandmother or Master Kota taught us to be. And now, these Weavers and the ones who come for them, it is all a storm rising to swallow us brother."

John only nodded, "I see the same, sense the same brother, but I don't worry for what will happen next, especially when everyone's hand, as they say, is finally played."

"And why is that?"

"Because," the shaman in the black hat responded, "I know we will not be alone when that time comes. Our fate has moved the four of us to this point in time brother, we cannot run from that or avoid it, but we will not face what comes alone. We will have friends to stand by our sides."

"Then you know the Sky Pirate Captain followed you here, to Chicago?" Ru grinned while passing on the chance to mention Fade's name. He knew he didn't have to, not with John.

His brother only laughed once again and nodded choosing not to answer. There were somethings words were just not needed for John thought as he walked with his brother toward the shop of the Witch.

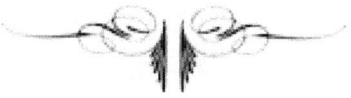

He watched from a safe distance, following the pair of shamans as both walked on toward the shop of the one called Mother Twylah. He had no name in this Middle World, just a body he could 'borrow' for the trips he needed to make. This body he took control of, it belonged to a man named Franks. He was not a very likable soul here in the Middle World because there was not much of anything admirable about him. Franks had no family to speak of and only a handful of friends to bond with, most who wouldn't lift a finger to help him if asked or begged. No, he was not a favored man by luck or the Gods, all save one. Franks was a particularly devout follower of Nidhogg, the one true God, a powerful and giant snake with one intent and purpose, to eat this Middle World and consume all in it. It was this piety, from such a disreputable man, which granted this entity the power to take over Franks, take control of his body and use like a puppet.

In truth, he was not a 'he' in the sense the humans who walk this world see each other. 'He' was nothing more than an entity of darkness, a shadow with no gender or tie to such a thing. Some might say 'he' was a demon, but that would not be correct either because 'he' had no power like a demon would have. 'He' was simply one of the dark followers Nidhogg, called on from the lightless world the God reigned from in the Other Worlds. A spy who carried out certain tasks, influencing outcomes in favor of Nidhogg, the one true God. The follower liked the pronoun 'he' though, it had become accustomed to the use due to all the times it had taken control of Franks.

So, Franks followed the two shamans close enough to keep a sharp eye, but with enough distance to maintain secrecy. He had been ordered to ensure the shamans did not find the one who created the poison to kill the West Wind. It must never be known he, the one called Franks, had been the one who had met and asked for the creation of the poison from the alchemist Gruder. Nidhogg, the one true God, demanded this and the entity masquerading as Franks would see to the deed himself.

Not a one of the Four Winds would ever know who had tried to kil them.

Part Two

On the outskirts of the great, and grand city of Chicago, just to the north, along the shore of the massive Lake Michigan, sits the newly built Glenview Protectorate Airfield. The facilities are the latest in modern design, from the three massive hangars which hold the many planes and steel air ships, to the main building and the barracks for the men and women of the Protectorate. There was little expense spared for the air field and it showed in the pristine image the complex displayed, and the task which it fulfilled every day. The protection of the city of Chicago, from the skies to the streets of the growing metropolis, fell to the men and women of the Protectorate and it was a job no one would fail at fulfilling. The air ships launched from the docks of the hangars and the planes flew from the newly paved runways to patrol and aid their colleagues who walked and patrolled the streets in the city.

This particular morning, as the sun was beginning to rise and light up the horizon on its long trek to cross the sky, the workers at the air field were busy getting the planes and air ships ready for flight. A special group of men and women worked with haste running around a pair of new and shiny bi-planes sitting just outside the doors of the hangar. These were no ordinary flying machines, no sir. These were the brand-new Curtiss P-6 Hawks, specially designed and steam-technology modified for the Protectorate alone and its newly formed Air Force. The planes were sleek with swept wings and bodies, the oversized engines and steam pipes glistened and shined even in the mechanically provided light of the field. And as the workers kept prepping the new planes for flight, two men walked up, pilots from their attire obviously, talking about the day that was beginning and what was their 'unique' orders.

"How in the hell do they expect us to fly and 'think' constantly about some air ship?" The pilot on the right remarked, more than asked, with disdain of his fellow air men on the left.

"I know it'll be a- "

"It'll be impossible, that's what it will be I tell you!"

The pilot of the left shook his head holding back the frustration he was feeling, for the orders his superiors gave him and the whiny wingman they saddled him with. "Yeah, it'll be tough, but that's why we get the big bucks and fly those new fancy planes."

"Yeah, I know, but why are we are looking for some goofy air ship when we should be trying to nail Capone for that massacre on the North side a few months back?"

It's like he's not even listening to me the pilot on the left thought. Yeah, there were bigger fish in the sea to catch, and after all the blood spilt on Saint Valentine's day the need to end Capone was more than needed, but orders were orders. "We can't go after Capone for that, remember, he wasn't in town when the hit went down. He was in Florida, doing whatever gangsters from Chicago do down there."

The pilot on the right started in again, on another tangent of the tirade, but frankly the pilot on the left was done. He tuned out his wingman and went right to his P-6 and started pre-flight checks. It was pure peace for 20 minutes, getting ready to fly overtaking the incessant whine of-

"Hey, is that Cruiser going up too?"

The pilot on the left looked up from his examination of the wing of his P-6 to see the large metallic air ship lifting free of its moorings and heading out of the hangar. He didn't answer his pain in the ass wingman, just watched as the Cruiser gained speed and altitude, slowly heading into the growing light of dawn.

"How may ships does that make in the air today?" The peevish pilot asked, captivated by the sight of the Cruiser breaking free of mother earth. It was nowhere near the size of a battleship, but with all the turbines whirring loudly lifting the gleaming air ship toward the sky, well it was still impressive.

"All of them, every air field is empty now." The pilot responded knowing full well the remark would only make his wingman ask another question, and another, and another.

"So, we're blanketing the city, for what?"

These were going to be his last words. The pilot had decided this before he spoke one syllable. "Whatever it is, it's above our paygrade so I'd keep my mouth shut, my eyes open, and my mind on some old Chinese Junk, got it?"

The peevish pilot only nodded taking the smarter choice of keeping his mouth shut. Whatever was going on, The Chain of Command had chosen not to give much, if any, information to go on and suddenly that was just perfect for him.

The man shuffled from the dark bedroom in just an A-shirt and his pants, both wrapped around a chubby belly, which were being held up by suspenders at the moment. The taller and well-muscled man who woke him stood stoically, just inside the stylish hotel room the smaller man owned, with its two large couches and two high-backed chairs. The taller man looked through the cracked door to the bedroom and noted the half-naked female body in the king-sized bed was one of the finer whores who worked for the brothel down the street. The smaller man made his way to the long bar made custom just for his room and motioned for the man behind it to pour him a Templeton Rye, the usual two fingers he always wanted in the same glass he always drank from. When your Al Capone, you get what you ask for the first time or you make sure everyone understands your displeasure at having to ask twice. The man behind the bar learned this not so long ago, its why he was missing his right ear.

The taller man leaned in ready to speak when Capone's pudgy left hand shot up ceasing any form of conversation instantly. With his right, he took the glass off the bar, drank the whiskey with a single gulp, and then put it back on the bar, and all the while his left hand never lowered, that was till Capone was ready to talk.

"You hear anything on the street about that thing Frankie?"

"No boss," the taller man stated quickly shaking his head, "no one's asking about the garage or anything."

"City Hall?"

"No boss, no one's asking for you."

"And those piglianculo's from this PBI, they looking into my business?" Capone asked while pointing to the glass once again, signaling to the man behind to bar to fill it again with two fingers of Templeton Rye.

Frankie shook his head for what seemed like the tenth time, which was a little frustrating, but when it came to the boss you did whatever he wanted. "No boss, it seems they have other business that needs their attention."

The boss of the South Side gang slowly lowered his left hand while raising the glass of Rye to his lips. As he took the drink down in a single gulp again Frankie took the meaning of the lowered appendage as a sign to carry on.

"I think those two Weavers from Troisi's- "

Poor Frankie didn't get far as his boss slammed the glass back down on the tabletop and bellowed loud enough to make the man behind the bar jerk then go completely still. Guess he hopes if he doesn't move Boss won't take his other ear Frankie thought for half-a-second as Capone pointed at him with his whole hand.

"Ah fanculo Frankie, you woke me for this merda?"

"No boss, no," the taller man started stepping up close and speaking quickly trying to head off Capone's infamous temper, "remember how I told you the Protectorate is busy doing their thing today?"

"Yeah, barely, I'm still half-asleep over here Frankie!"

"I know Boss, and I wouldn't have gotten you up if-n-this wasn't important." Frankie explained sensing he had gained a few minutes of a reprieve. "Those two Weavers, word is they're going to show up here in town, it's why the cops and the military are crawling all over the place."

"Really?" Capone asked back, the look in his eyes told Frank e his boss was awake now and wanted to hear every word he was going to say.

"Yeah Boss, there's so many air ships flying around the city you could walk back to Lincoln Park and never touch the ground."

"So it's true, the Protectorate raided Carlo's for these two broads?" Capone asked and the question sent Frankie into a quick succession of nods. It was enough for the smaller pudgy man as he slid the glass back to the man behind the bar and gave out an order. "We got too much heat on us right now Frankie, tell the boys to leave this be, no one goes near the two broads, got it?"

This time Frankie could only shake his head and the look the motion brought to Capone's face wasn't a nice one. "Boss, the Protectorate mignottas aren't the only ones who are looking for these Weavers from what I hear."

"That strunzo Moran, he's going to try and get them, huh?" Capone surmised, a low growl slipping past his lips as he finished. Moran, the leader of the rival gang to Capone and his Southsiders. The name alone incensed the smaller man like nothing ever had. Frankie only nodded and the growl went deeper as Capone walked past him heading for the bedroom again. He stopped just short of the portal though and turned back pointing a finger this time at Frankie and not his whole hand.

"Get the boys up, get the cars steamed up and gassed, and get the whips up flying, you understand Frankie?"

"Yeah boss, I got it." Frankie responded with a snap of his head.

"You make sure Moran and the Northsiders don't get those broads Frankie, use whoever you need to and do whatever you need to make sure this happens, capiche?"

"Yes Boss, it'll be done."

"Good, cause if Moran gets those two Weavers he'll hand them over to the Magi or Protectorate in exchange for something, I know that strunzo too well to see it different."

"Yes Boss,"

Then Capone was gone, back through the portal to the bedroom with the door slamming shut. Frankie turned to man behind the bar and sighed, "pour me two fingers there, will you Jimmy?"

The man nodded, got a second glass and reached for a bottle under the bar. Frankie stood there quietly waiting for the drink while his mind worked on what his next steps would be. He never expected to get this far with this whole thing so what was supposed to happen next Frankie had no idea.

Like Camille, the warmth of the covers wrapped Alice in a loving embrace, only unlike the Magi though it wasn't enough to send her back to a full and deep slumber. The only thing, the only one, who could do that had left the bedroom of the Whip just an hour before, stepping off the air ship in the dark on some side-street here in Chicago. She looked longingly to the spot in the bed where her Badu should be, where her Ezio had been all night next to her, where she wanted him right next to her once again. She needed him to be here, and not to fulfill some yearning. The need for sexual intimacy had been fulfilled quite nicely the night before. No, Alice felt something was incredibly wrong, out of sorts with the universe, and it may all be due to what Ezio was doing now, had gotten himself involved in with the Magi.

She exhaled with an anxious sigh trying to fight the want to tell the men at the helm of the Whip to turn this air ship around and head back to Chicago. Alice slapped the bed in frustration, fighting back the wave of neediness she felt. Ezio was a grown man who knew what he was doing, somewhat, in a roundabout way. He had found this Cabal, not stumbled on it, so he had to have a clue as to how dangerous these men in this secret plot at the Protectorate could be.

He had to know, right?

Alice reached up with the hand which wasn't holding the sheet to her naked body and covered her eyes while mumbling a rather nasty explanative in Italian. Why was she acting like this, like some school-

THWAP...THUMP

The distinctly loud, and abrupt sounds, coming from outside on the deck of the Whip made Alice sit up in bed with a jerk of her entire body. The hand clutching the sheets to her bosom could easily feel the sudden rush of her heartbeat, the muscle speeding up with the jolt of adrenaline that hit her nervous system like a hammer. Her breathing quickened, right after it started back up from being scared. Alice sat quietly listening intently for another sound, any noise really, and all she could sense was the eerie quiet that seemed to squeeze the fear which had wrapped around her lungs. There wasn't another thump, or whack, or anything for that matter and this unnerved her even more.

Well, she thought to herself, I probably shouldn't do what I'm about to do, but staying here in the bed naked is not going to help me calm down. Alice rose from the sheets and quickly slipped on a robe before quietly exiting the bedroom on her bare feet. The cabin of the Whip was a little cold this morning, probably from being aloft in the night sky, but she paid little attention to the fact or the cold. Alice crossed the room with the small bar, couches, and table with long strides keeping her approach to the hatch for the stern silent.

It was just the men Ezio hires to fly the Whip making the noise she told herself as she slid the door to the outside open. There's nothing to worry about at all Alice told herself quietly as she stepped out onto the deck in the growing dawn. A second later, still just a bit blind from going inside to outside, a rough hand clasped around her mouth squeezing hard. The same instant an arm reached around her, and with crushing strength, pinned her against a well-muscled body. Her feet were off the wooden deck in the same instant as her eyes caught sight of a man dressed completely in black from head to toe, his face painted as well to match his clothes. Yes, it's nothing to worry about all Alice thought as she tried to scream and only produced a whimper.

"We have the girl," a very rough voice whispered from behind Alice, actually the one holding her pinned to him. His accent was deep South, the 'R' drawing out longer than needed.

"Good, that's all the occupants then." The man in front of her stated, and with a nice British accent to boot.

"Signal the team, we're moving on with the plan." The man from behind ordered, to which the British man only nodded and pulled out a light from a pouch on his belt.

Alice watched, while fighting the hold she was in, which was useless because the man gripping her was as strong as a bear, as the second man flicked the light on twice, pausing before flicking the light on three more times, and then finally once. It was some sort of code because as soon as he was done a light off in the distance repeated the same sequence back. The man then flicked the light twice more before turning back and putting the light on his belt. "They're inbound, should be no more than two minutes."

"Roger, two minutes, no survivors."

The meaning of the last part of the statement by the rough voice wasn't missed by Alice, how could it be? No, she understood exactly what was happening, what was going to happen, to her. And that set off a panic in her mind as she began to scream into the hand and thrash against the arm holding her tight. When the other man only laughed cruelly as he pushed the lifeless body of one of the men Ezio hired to fly his Whip overboard, well, that only added fuel to the fear in her heart. Now Alice knew exactly what they had planned for her, only she wouldn't be dead when they tossed her over the side. Nope, she'd be very much alive, watching as the ground made a fast approach. So, she fought, and kicked, and tried to free herself from the man who was holding her, so much so Alice barely saw the other ship as it came out of the clouds approaching slowly alongside of Ezio's Whip.

"Calm down missy, you're not stopping this!" The rough voice demanded, adding a hard squeeze of his arm and hand for emphasis. The other man threw the last body of Ezio's crew overboard, then turned back to the pair, still smiling cruelly.

"No lass, you and your man should have left sleeping dogs lie. So now you both have to disappear, and not come back."

The other air ship slipped right up next to Ezio's Whip, only when the man holding Alice saw who was behind the helm he hissed low, right in her ear. "What the hell is this?"

The British man spun, looked at the person stirring the air ship, and was taken aback just a bit. There should have been another pair of men dressed just like he and his counterpart were, all in black with camouflaged faces. Only, well, the one standing at the wheel wasn't either of the men who were supposed to be there. Instead, it was a small woman, maybe 5'4, and she was dressed in a sweeping colorful poncho and a large brimmed black hat with a very recognizable trio of feathers pinned there by a colorful band that went all the way around the crown. She turned to the three on the deck of the other Whip and smiled, her dusky brown skin glowing it seemed.

"Hola, buenos días mis amigos, and what a beautiful morning it will be don't you think?"

The question was so out of left field, so unexpected, that all three on Ezio's air ship froze for a moment, even Alice stopped trying to break free from the man holding her to take in the little lady as she greeted them. So shocked were the three, the lady nodded and added to her introduction, "I am going to assume that at least two of you were expecting someone else, no?"

The long pause continued as the air ships sped along on the preset course, but then with a snap everyone began to move, beginning with the British man. He reached down with a lightning quick move of his hand, and from a holster on his hip that Alice didn't even realize was there, the man drew a strange looking pistol. It was black just as everything else he carried and dressed in, with a long square body which covered the barrel of the gun. The hand covering her mouth abruptly moved, releasing her to scream, or gasp as she did now, while she felt the man reach down and draw the same kind of gun. He pointed it at where the lady in the poncho should have been, and yet the space by the helm on the other Whip was empty now. The lady was gone in the blink of an eye, in the scant second it took the men to produce the guns she was gone into the air of the night.

"Where in the bloody hell did she go?" The British man growled, his eyes scanning the deck of the air ship just across the lightening dark from him.

Before the other man, who had now shifted his arm upwards to just under Alice's chin to hold her by the throat, could answer something came flying in from the bow of the Whip. She couldn't make it out as the object crashed into the side of the British man's head with a loud crack. It spun backwards, away from them, twirling in midair for a moment then falling to the deck. The man, whose head was now thoroughly smashed in, went stumbling from the blow, right into the transom and almost going over the side. The only thing stopping him was his own body, and the fact it was nothing more than a sack now, crumpling where it stopped against the rail.

"SHIT!" The man with the rough voice screamed as he spun in the direction where the object, Alice still didn't know what hit the man with the British accent, came from. She barely caught sight of someone ducking down low on the bow by the forward hatch, just as the man behind her did as well and yelled out.

"I'll kill her, I swear it!"

All right, I've had enough of this Alice thought, reaching up with both hands to grab the forearm of the man holding her. I've had just about enough of this jackass she thought with a hiss as she picked up her foot and then stomped down with all her strength on top of his foot with her heel. The appendage was covered with some thick leather, which bit into Alice's foot as she struck, but the pain mattered little to her. There was a loud crack as the bone broke, the man screamed, and Alice pulled with both hands freeing up an inch of two of space. She dropped down so fast she popped out of the man's grasp as he jerked away from her, but then Alice looked up just in time to see the business end of the large black gun he was holding. The barrel was dark and it looked as big as the opening for the Holland Tunnel back home in New York. This is going to hurt she thought, and it might have if not for the quick appearance of the lady with the poncho.

From the right, out of the air once again it seemed, she appeared dashing onto Ezio's Whip with a flash. The man with gun tried to turn back to engage her with his weapon, but the broken foot slowed him, and really, he never had a chance to stop her. She was too fast for him, even if he was in top form, and before the gun was even pointed at her the lady with the poncho met the attack with a counter. In stunned silence form the side, Alice watched as out from under the colorful cover she wore, the lady's hand appeared holding a cane, or what looked like a cane being it was a stick about two feet long. She was holding it her hand from the top, just an inch of two exposed above her fist, and with a vicious arc the lady brought the cane up with the bottom piece slamming into the man's hand holding the gun. There was another loud crack as another of the man's bones snapped. He bellowed with the pain, and the ominous looking gun went flying out over the side of the air ship never to be seen again.

"Ahhh," The man screamed, staggering back on a broken foot and clutching his broken hand for a brief moment. The counter attack was over, and even being injured, the man intended to fight back, using the pause he was in to pulled a long knife from his belt and growl at the lady in the poncho.

Make no mistake, there was no quarter in this fight, no mercy to be begged for between these combatants. The lady in the poncho met the challenge by spinning the stick in her right hand to hold it by the other end now while pulling a second from under her covering with the left. Yes, there was only one way this going to end, both fighters silently agreed to the terms with a single short stare, and then they charged at each other. The man swiped with his knife, a quick off balanced cut meant to draw first blood, only his blade cut nothing but air as the lady easily dodged the attack before slipping back in and countering with the stick in her right hand. The shaft hit him with a quick slap to the side of his head, and she followed the blow up with another from the left hand holding the other stick, another perfect strike to the other side of his head. Both blows knocked the man into a stupor as he began to stumble even more, losing his balance and perspective. How is he still standing Alice thought as the lady moved in and began to beat the man mercilessly with a flurry of blows with the sticks, from his knees up to his head and back down. The lady in the poncho moved so fast Alice could barely keep up, there was just a blur, and the continuous sound of blow after blow reigning down and cracking the man loudly. Then, after a minute, the lady stopped, stepping back away from the obviously half-unconscious man, who was only still upright because the side of the air ship was holding him up now that he was leaning on it.

"Is he dead?" Alice whispered staring at the bleeding man, who wasn't moving after being struck so many.

The lady in the poncho didn't answer, just stared at the man while still holding the sticks in her hands. Then the figure from the bow, by the forward hatch, came flying in, another woman, with a leap. Her feet barely touched the deck before she was spinning in a complete circle and kicking the man square in his chest. The strike sent the man right over the edge of the air ship without so much as grunt or a groan. In a blink, the man who had held her captive was no more, leaving the deck with a rolling backwards flip into nothing. The lady in the poncho lowered her sticks, and with a small turn, looked to Alice with a smile and nod.

"Si senora, I think he will be dead in a minute or two when he lands."

"Marisol, stop making fun of the dead. What will you say if meet the man one day in the Other World?" The other woman said with a small chuckle. The woman's accent was instantly captivating, as intoxicating as her physical beauty. She was tall, at least 5'10, with a long lean body and lovely dark skin. Alice noted she wore a hat like the lady in the poncho did, like the man in the strange flying ship who had rescued her yesterday from the fight at the brothel. Only her hat was one of the 'Stoker' variety, the kind a rich man might wear to a party while dressed in a tuxedo. The colored lady was dressed like the man in the black hat as well, with moccasins and tanned pants tucked into the boots. She wore a coat of dark blue, what looked like a Protectorate Officer's type, with the hem just below the waist and two tails flowing down the back. With the coat open, a white shirt unbuttoned at the top exposed her slim neck and the many necklaces she wore, but the hair spilling out from under the black steamer hat caught Alice's attention immediately. It was braided, sort of, in what she had been told was called a 'dreadlock', and scattered throughout the long cords was grey here and there telling Alice she was not a young woman.

"I think I will ask him why he killed two innocent men and threatened to throw this lovely senora over the side, or maybe I will just ask if he hit anything on the way down." The lady in the poncho winked causing the other to laugh more.

"Oh my sweet sister, how wicked you are at times."

"You two," Alice suddenly broke in looking from one to the other, "you're with the man in the black hat from yesterday. He wore a hat like the ones you wear."

"Ah, you have met our dear brother John I see. Tell me, was he injured in that foolish thing yesterday in Brooklyn?" The lady with the dreadlocks asked before suddenly leaning up against the wall of the air ship, drawing a quick response from the lady in the poncho.

"Ai, are you okay Sara?"

"I am fine Marisol. The poison weakened me more than I thought. In our younger days, I would have been up and moving with ease much earlier, but now it takes more time to recuperate it seems." The lady with the dreadlocks replied sweetly.

"Younger days?" Alice inquired still looking from the one shaman to the other.

"Si, my sister and brothers and I have all seen too many winters as our abuela would say. Though old, we may be, we are still formidable opponents." The lady in the poncho remarked moving the covering aside as she knelt down to grab the first man struck down.

She was dressed just like her cohort, moccasins and tan pants with a white shirt. She was thicker than the other woman Alice noted, not flabby or pudgy, just a curvy figure. The lady, Marisol wasn't it, easily lifted the man and with a heave tossed his body over the side to join the other in a free fall to mother earth.

"Being old is only a mindset, right my sister?" The one called Sara sighed while grinning still. She had walked over to grab something off the deck, the thing which struck the first man in the head, and Alice could see it was a fan made of solid iron. Yes, a fan, just like one a lady in the south would use to cool herself on a long hot summer's day. Only this fan was made completely of iron and probably weighed at least a good two or maybe five pounds.

"That it is my sister!" Marisol laughed walking over to the large wheel which turned the air ship.

Ok, this is so very surreal, too much maybe? Alice looked around the deck realizing that just a moment ago she was about to be tossed over the side, that was till the sisters here showed up and saved her. "Why are you here?"

"That is a very good question, one I am asked often actually, and I think it's because we are chosen from the cosmos to interact with this world so as- "Marisol began as she took control of the sir ship and began to turn it around.

"I think she means something else entirely sister. I am sure Alice here is asking how we came to be here tonight, on her lover's air ship." Sara broke in taking a seat on a small chair by the wheel.

"Oh, yes, that is what she is asking. Well, to be truthful, we were asked to come to your aid."

Asked to come to my aid, what was that supposed to mean. Then Alice truly 'heard' what the pair had said and her skin pimpled with a million goose bumps at one part. "How did you know my name?"

The light, and quite weird, mood darkened just a bit as Sara locked eyes with Alice and spoke with a calm that made the goose bumps on

Alice's arms grow just a little. "We will explain what is happening I promise, but we must first find Ezio and Camille. We need to ensure both are safe."

"Ezio, what trouble is he in?" Alice whispered as her stomach seemed to just drop, fell right through the deck she was standing on, from fear. I knew it, damn! I knew he was in trouble!

"The kind of trouble where the one you love may come to a very violent end, I am afraid senora." Marisol replied and the statement made Alice light headed. She had to lean on the side of the air ship as it all sank in, the dread of it, and she knew what the cause was. It was this evil Cabal Ezio has stumbled on, it had to be.

"Did you know the gang leader Al Capone stays at the Lexington Hotel? It is just a few minutes' walk from the Magi House?"

The question was innocent enough, meant to be nothing more than to point out a fact, and because the inquiry was wrapped in a sweet French accent it seemed even more pure hearted. The mood in the room, quiet and reflective, changed in an instant as a small Asian man walked over to look over the shoulder of the one who asked the question, a woman with long braided brown hair.

"No, a man with that type of a reputation living that close to the Magi's House here in Chicago?" The man asked with a small curious smile as he moved over to the side of the bed where the French Magi sat.

"It would seem so monsieur, it says here that he lives in that grand hotel just a block away from the House." The French Magi answered, holding up the paper where she had found the passage about Capone.

The Asian Magi took the paper, read the passage quickly, and then looked over to where a small table meant for two was positioned perfectly under a window looking out on the streel below. The Magi held the paper up with a large smile, "These Americans, every day I am here I am amazed it seems by their mannerisms, aren't you Adelaide."

"Oui," The French Magi replied with a nod and a sigh, "but I still miss Paris on a Spring morning."

"Well yes, nothing compares to Paris in spring, except for maybe Kyoto, or travelling the mountain trails of Iga."

"Then you will have to show me these beautiful mountain trails one-day monsieur." Adelaide smiled warmly at Tomo, almost with a hidden affection that she was unable to keep secret.

The Magi from the small island of Japan returned the smile with the same, if not more, warmth and nodded. "And you will have to show me Paris on a spring day, every site and sound."

At the table by the window sat the other two Magi of the group, both watching the exchange between the pair with rueful smiles. The man turned to the woman sitting on the other side and whispered as she took a sip of coffee from the cup she was holding. His accent instantly giving him away as a visitor to the Great US of A.   "Now I know for certain those two are together, in the bye-and-bye as they say."

"They don't say that actually," the woman replied smiling once again, this time at her companion.

"They don't? Then what do they call what they're doing?" The man asked with a wink, knowing full well the tease would be returned in his companions 'special' way.

"Sir, if I have to tell you what they call it after last night, then maybe we need to get your head checked."

"I did hit me noggin awful hard against the wall, didn't I my sweet." The man replied with a chuckle.

His accent was Australian, though where he hailed from on the continent none of the others in the room knew. Some in the Magi Society told stories he was from Perth while others whispered he was a wanted man from Brisbane and only the Elders from the highest ascension had saved him from a death sentence, bringing him to the US for his own safety. No one knew more, and all anyone was truly sure of was the man was very secretive and moved only when he felt sure of his footing, in every situation, which was the perfect match for the woman he sat across from. She was the same, secretive and introspective, only she was most certainly from these lands. Her past wasn't as shrouded in mystery as her companion's, but this only meant she was more guarded in her moves and relations with others. A fact which had almost assuredly kept the four from being in this lovely hotel room on the south side of Chicago on such an early morning.

"Do you think our benefactor will show Baird?" The woman asked looking at her companion, using his name to ensure he understood the playfulness of the conversation was at an end.

Baird, the Magi from 'The Land Down Under', knew well enough when his name was used that any kind of teasing banter was over, and as such his demeanor turned serious. "They won't show, not yet at least I feel Ellie, but we'll hear from whoever it is, this I can say for certain."

"Why is that?" Eleanor, her true name, asked before taking a sip of her coffee again.

"Whoever contacted us goes through all this trouble to just not show up? No, we'll hear from him or her soon enough, I just want to know why it has to be so damn early."

Eleanor swallowed her sip of coffee, silently acknowledging what her companion had said. After being contacted last night via a secret message delivered by courier, along with an envelope full of papers eluding to a conspiracy at the highest levels of both the Protectorate and Magical Society, the four Elder Magi had agreed, somewhat, to meet the one who had sent the message in the Hotel room provided. She and Baird had slept little through the night, between the coupling and going over the information in the packet there was no time for slumber, and really. she couldn't have found a way to sleep after reading what she had been shown. The coupling in the end had relieved the stress of discovering a nefarious plot in the House of the Magi, a place she revered and loved. The Philosophers Stone, a secret group was actually going to try and make one. The myth had morphed into reality, taken on life and energy when no one would have even considered it possible to create one. She had certainly not, until Baird confirmed what Isaac had been up to in the mansion in upstate New York.

"Why do you think this 'benefactor' chose us, we four?" Adelaide asked breaking Eleanor's train of thought.

"I think I know why," Tomo answered, smiling brightly as he always does when a chance to impart a bit of insight comes his way. and Baird only replied with a quick bit of wit.

"Is it because we were the only ones who were foolish enough to answer the knock at our doors last night?"

"Always," Eleanor and Adelaide both responded in perfect unison, both smiling while holding back a laugh.

"Well, there is that, which unfortunately is not a part of my theory, but maybe I will add it in later on." The Japanese Magi nodded, giving a small chuckle at the quip and the reaction. When no one offered any other words Tomo continued on with a raised hand. "First, we four have one thing in common, we were omitted from joining the 1st Ascension here in Chicago. We four will go no farther in the hierarchy of the Magi Society. We are, for all purpose and intent, no longer looked at by those above us which means we are the perfect ones to contact."

"Convenu," Adelaide said with a nod looking to Eleanor and Baird, "whoever brought us in knows we are not a part of this conspiracy due to being outsiders, so this person must assume we can be trusted."

"Hai," Tomo stated with a snap of his head causing Adelaide to return the nod as Baird moved the conversation forward.

"And what's the second part of your theory?"

"Simple, we all live here in Chicago, so whatever is occurring with this conspiracy, it will be at our doorstep here, very soon." Tomo answered, and the statement made, the room went silent for a moment as the other three pondered on the implication and meaning.

"I have to agree, whoever contacted us didn't have much time to put this plan of theirs' into motion. They chose the four of us here in Chicago because something is going to happen here and there was no time to find anyone else." Eleanor said putting her coffee cup down on the table.

Now the silence returned as the weight each Magi felt on their chests grew, built just a bit. The reality of what all this meant, all the subterfuge and conspiracy, it was just dawning on the four. No one had a word to say as the four considered with deep thought what the next move would be, if this benefactor would show that was. All four were still thinking as a knock at the door broke all concentration and even made Adelaide jump a little. Tomo looked to Baird for a split second, just a quick glance, and then he was walking to the door opening it just enough to glance outside. Eleanor sat in her chair tensed like a string being pulled tight, waiting for the one who had led them to this point with a secret message to appear, and when Tomo turned away from the door with no more than a second message she sighed. Damn, the Magi thought, another note from the shadows. Adelaide stood up from the spot on the edge of the bed where she sat and followed Tomo to the table where both stood waiting for him to read the note. The Magi cleared his throat and then spoke.

"Thank you for coming, I know what I showed you last night was not easy to believe or accept. I can only assure you it is the truth, a secret contingent of Magi and Protectorate officers will be making a Philosophers Stone, it is no longer a story passed along to children at bedtime. Isaac has already endowed a pair of Weavers with the ability to create that which was myth and a technoist is working to create the vessel which will become the stone."

Ok, Baird thought silently, taking in each word Tomo spoke with diligent care. We can believe the rumors as to why that old Galah Isaac was off by himself, locked away in that big house in the country. Yet, if someone like Isaac, who had no political ambition at all, was a part of this than anyone in the First Ascension in any city could be.

"I asked you four here for the purpose of revealing myself, to assure you this was genuine and not some hoax or something nefarious. I contacted you four, because out of all in the Society, you four are the most reasonable, the most open-minded, and the only ones capable of seeing the truth and thus stopping what would most certainly be the end of us all."

Now we're just being softened up Eleanor thought, being placated with niceties so we don't react too harshly when the other shoe drops, and it did, with a loud thud.

"Only my intent to meet with you has become impossible due to sudden circumstances. The Weavers Isaac bonded have been brought to Chicago, as unimaginable as that sounds, into the waiting hands of the Protectorate and the Magi Society. Right now, the skies are filled with Protectorate air ships and the streets team with Umbra and soldiers. The Weavers cannot be allowed to fall into the Cabal's hands or a nightmarish scenario will play out, one which this world may not survive I am afraid."

Everything just got a little more serious, Baird thought silently while his jaw set to grinding his teeth. This wasn't some game he understood, and after reading what they had last night, that fact was extremely evident. Now though, with the news Isaac's Weavers were in town, will that changed the landscape of this secret meeting drastically.

"And as if that were not enough my friends, the ones who conspire to make the Stone are moving to take the Weavers while tying up loose ends. They have ordered the arrest of the Umbra leader Camille and her second Ezio, both who only stumbled into this and now have their very lives threatened. I know I have asked so much of you four already, and to ask more would strain this weak association to breaking, but I am afraid that is what I must do. If you trust enough in what I have shown you then please, trust just a little more and go back to the Magi House. Go back and ensure both Miss Camil e and Ezio are kept safely away or I am afraid both will meet the same fate as Isaac."

With the last of the note read Tomo stopped speaking and looked up to his friends with a distant look. The words of the note hitting into his mind like a hard blow, the shock numbing but wearing away with each second the Magi contemplated the information in silence. The other three Magi acted the same, each going over what was written in the note, all except for Baird it seemed.

"There was no signature, really? Now, that seems rather rude don't it?"

Eleanor smiled with a cheeky grin at the obvious jab from her lover while Adelaide bit her bottom lip with a nibble, her thoughts coalescing for a moment before adding her perspective to this brewing storm of trouble. "I saw Miss Camille in New York once, long ago, during a visit I made there. She was very impressive, not only with her magic skill, but with her bearing as well. She seemed too capable to get involved in something like this, a sinister conspiracy like this."

"I do not think she is Adelaide, like the note states, she has accidentally found her way into this predicament. The question is, do we trust our mysterious agent and what he has told us?" Tomo pointed out with a small and quick nod to his companion. When he looked back to Baird and Eleanor he was greeted with an even quicker reply from the female Magi.

"There's no question there Tomo, in for a penny in for a pound they say."

The remark might have surprised Tomo and Adelaide, which in actuality, it did not as both never faltered in their expressions, and it certainly did not shock Baird. He had been around the Elder Eleanor far too long to be surprised by her actions, especially when it came to doing what was considered the right thing to do.

"All right, we're all in agreement then, when we leave this room we are in fully with this benefactor. We're going to see this to the end, well, because we won't have a choice not too, not once we walk out the door. We all agreed then?" Baird asked while also reminding the others of the stakes and the situation.

Tomo only nodded while Adelaide sighed and smiled, "as our Eleanor has stated so nicely, in for a penny and all."

Baird smiled, stood up, and then held his hand out for Eleanor to take as a gentleman does. There were no more words exchanged between the four as they headed for the door and left the room behind.

He watched the four leave the room from the safety and cover of the shadows at the end of the hall. When he saw them leave quickly by the stairs the young apprentice sighed heavily with relief. Cooper had worried the four Magi Elders would take the chance to leave this whole plan by the wayside and just stay put in the room. That would have been devastating to his needs to say the least, an outright killer.

No, Cooper thought, stepping out of his hiding spot and into the dull lights of the hall. He had to extricate himself from this hellish existence his father had put him in. For a long time, he had considered himself an ambitious young man, not so much so as to be ruthless, but enough to see himself as an Elder in the 1st Ascension. Then Samuels and Hamelin had shown him just what a ruthless ambition is, how powerful and dangerous it can be. Now, he had to put himself above everyone, and anyone Cooper had decided, including the four Elders who had just left. He had to be cold now, as cold as the Generals, to be free of this mess and the four who he contacted and had now procured, well they were unknowingly going to help him do just that. It didn't matter to Cooper anymore if any or all of the four were hurt or worse while following his orders, just so long as they followed what he asked them to do. He needed a distraction, and he knew Samuels would know he contacted the four Magi, and that meant he had the perfect distraction for what he had planned.

"All right Generals, it's time to see how ruthless I can become."

Part Three

Good evening, my name is John, as you already know. And you also already know I am a shaman, a man of a mysterious and mystical nature you might say, but not one of magic. I am no Magi who controls the energy gifted to me by a Weaver. What I am, what I do, is more complicated than what my friends who wield the very energy of this world do. Firstly, I was not born a shaman as say Miss Camille who was born able to control energy. I was called to this path, to walk it, as were my sisters and my brother. Though, like Miss Camille, I had no choice but to accept my lot in life as a shaman as she did as a Magi. I was never given a choice at that early age if I wanted to be a shaman. My sisters and my brother were never given the choice either, so like me, all three walk this path of mysticism. My power lies in the ways of the Other Worlds, of the old ones and Nature who created this world, and of the 'magic' both grant me. My path in this world is one of being alone for long periods of time, as is my sisters and my brother. Every shaman has to ready themselves to walk his or her path alone at some time, for the way of the medicine man is ever inward and never outward, always inward to the center of the soul. The answers to the mysteries of life are uncovered during the 'Journey' a shaman undertakes, and those answers come from the experiences of the medicine man's walk in this physical world and the one beyond.

Though I could talk to you for hours my friends, about my life's path and of my Shamanism, I will not go further with that discussion tonight. It would entail too much sharing of personal information that I am afraid is not part of what Wahkan started. His intention from the start I think was to stick with telling you of this adventure you have been listening to and I have to agree with his choice. Do not worry though, there will be more than enough time to share with you the tales of our other exploits and adventures.

So, at the moment, I find myself at what my brother Ru so perfectly called a crossroad in this plan of ours. I knew freeing the Weavers might cause a slight change to this course the four of us, my family, had decided on when Sara was poisoned. What I was not prepared for, what the souls I spoke with on the Field of Waiting had not foreseen, was the quickness of the response to the pair being taken would be from the ones who sought their return. In less than twenty-four hours the Protectorate, and the Magi who had killed poor Isaac after he successfully bound Boles and Wells as asked, were now flooding Chicago with personnel and equipment. Even the souls who have passed over cannot see every consequence a choice will bring. A single decision can lay bare so many possibilities, so many doors opening by simply saying yea or nay to a question.

As we arrived at the building Mother Twylah used as her shop, Ru gave me a silent nod then headed around to the back of the store to use the portal there to gain entrance. He would hide and keep an eye out as I met with Laken Malus. We both knew the 'Procurer' would not come alone, this we knew without the aid of seeing the future. Laken never went anywhere without their valet, Henrietta.

I have seen many seasons in my time, many people coming into and out of my life, and none more mysterious than one Laken Malus, that is if you don't count Fade. I wonder still what might have been had our circumstances been different, me and Fade. Would we have been able to be as close as lovers or just friends if our lives had not been taken in directions we could not avoid? Ah my friends, but those are thoughts and feelings for another time, so back to Laken Malus who some say is evil, a person you hastily avoid while making the hand gesture for the evil eye, for protection. I don't believe in evil necessarily, it's just a word created by others who have the need to explain the terrible things that happen to them and others. To me, Laken is nothing more than a mere human, like so many others of this World who follow the baser needs of the spirit. A being who put their personal pleasures above the spirit's and at the end of the day, is more than willing to live as such.

Once you understand this, then the word evil means nothing, is nothing, and simply vanishes from one's lexicon.

And so, I entered Mother Twylah's shop ready to meet with Laken and begin the inevitable negotiation any conversation with the 'Procurer' turned to. Swirling smoke, from a mix of white sage and lavender, lazily danced across the air from several burners in the store, twirling and floating through the ether like a dancing ballet of ghosts. The room was the usual rectangle shape and open, several small tables occupying the center, and all the furniture sitting neatly arranged on the hardwood floor. The walls to the east west were just long rows of shelves from the ceiling down to the floor, and lining the shelves were glass jars of various dimensions, each containing some object with its own special use. I noted some were filled with herbs and plants, some with crystals or feathers, and some with things better left unsaid. I looked north then and sitting behind the counter, which stretched the length of the width of the store, was the old witch herself looking as beautiful as ever. Behind her more shelves, more glass jars, and a small portal going to the rear of the store. If you have ever entered an emporium for ones who use spells and such, then this place was like a home away from home to you.

I have seen pictures of Mother Twylah when she was younger, hand drawn works of artistry depicting a woman whose eyes were pathways to a soul deep and wise. Her long brown hair was silver now and it framed a face which could still take a man's breath with its elegance and grace. She stood just at five feet, just the right height to stand at the counter and look up to her patrons, which is what she was doing at this very moment as I walked over.

"Good morning John, you look as handsome as ever."

As I walked up I could smell the peppermint tea, the aroma already energizing my mind and my spirit for the day ahead. It was a custom to have a cup while I talked with Mother Twylah, and as I should have known, she was prepared this morning for my arrival. "Good morning Mother Twylah, and thank you, though I think I am a distant second to your beauty."

My words had barely left my mouth before a scream erupted from the back, behind a set of swinging doors which bar people from the rear of the store, and more importantly, the stairs which lead up to the apartments for Mother and her family. The owner of the squeal came running out from the back, easily passing under the swinging doors without a care of striking the wooden shutters. I smiled as the little girl ran under the eave on the counter and right up to me with such an excited look I couldn't help but smile even more, a stuffed doll representing a bunny tucked under her right arm.

"Mr. John, it's really you!"

"Yes, little Taima, it is me!" I laughed shaking my head at the Mother Twylah's grand-daughter.

She was a perfect twin for Mother and those paintings I had been so fortunate to see. Little Taima is a bundle of limitless energy, and endless curiosity. She has no fear I know of, with the exception of her mother, who came out from the back shaking her head trying not to smile at her young daughter's preciousness.

"Taima, how many times have I told you not to greet Mr. John like a whirling tornado?" Tala admonished her daughter, or tried to. I could easily see the smile the middle-aged mother tried to hide but failed to do so. Even little Taima could tell her mother's anger was nothing more than frustration, and she only giggled running to Tala to be picked up and hugged.

All three were dressed in the same type of robes, a mix of deep purples and blues, with Mother wearing a black shawl across her shoulders. Twylah was the matriarch of this little family, the owner of the store, and just like all the women of the family before her she was a witch. Taima's mother Tala was a witch and one day she would have the store, and then one day it would be passed onto Taima. Magic was everywhere in little Taima's life and she had met many practitioners of the art, some very powerful, but for some reason I had become her favorite of them all.

Maybe it's because of my hat?

"Are you journeying tonight John?" Tala asked with a wide pretty smile. Her long brown hair was full of curls, like the infinite number of waves which spill onto a beach.

"No Tala," I answered still smiling at little Taima as she smiled back with an adorable grin, "I'm meeting someone here."

"Who are you meeting John?" Tala asked me, and before I could answer, the bell at the front door rang meaning someone was entering the shop. I didn't need a look to know it wasn't Laken but the other person I had been expecting. I turned and peered over my shoulder

Fade has never been one to visit Mother Twylah's shop unless it was for a very good reason or at gun point, I was hoping for the latter as she walked in. She wore her usual pants tucked into knee high boots, a black corset over her white shirt, but atop her fiery hair this morning was a wide brim black Cavalier hat with a set of large black and blue plume feathers pinned to the Ivory colored band. It was the hat she always wore when not striding the decks of her air ship the Crescent Moon as it traveled among the clouds, and it drew every eye like steel to a magnet. Fade's nose instantly wrinkled at the smell of the strong incense, and the move was just as sweet as Little Taima's grin I thought as we locked eyes, and then she was instantly moving toward me. In a blink, ignoring the three others standing around us, Fade confronted me with her usual directness.

"We need to talk, now."

"I know, and we will." I replied as from the corner of my eye I spotted a sly smile forming at the corners Mother Twylah's mouth.

"Ah, the thing in Brooklyn. Yes, John, a long is just what is needed I think, a long talk indeed."

Fade only nodded at Mother, and I could only grin as I answered both, "and we will I promise, as soon as I meet with the one who I came to Chicago to see."

"You mean she's not the one you came to see John?" Tala asked and just like before I had no chance to answer her.

The bell on the door rang out again, and I knew this time, it marked the arrival of Laken. There are many responses one has to seeing Laken, from the fear little Taima felt to the foreboding ill Tala sensed is what most people experience. Then there are those like Fade who greeted the 'Procurer' with a slight growl and eyes closed to slits, or whispers of old words meant to ward off bad omens as Mother Twylah was doing. I turned and looked at the door again spotting them standing there looking just as they always looked, dressed in an expensive Victorian dark grey suit complete with tails, a dark grey shirt, and cream-colored ascot to top it off.

Yes, before I confuse you further, I used 'they' instead of 'him' or 'her' when referring to Laken. You see, Laken may have been born a woman to this world, but that association never held true for them and as such means nothing to the one. Laken is not a 'her' or a 'him'. Laken is like I said, 'them' or 'they'. Now that I think of it, enigmatic is a word I would use for the 'Procurer', not evil.

"The mysterious John Greywolf as I live and see." They called out to me, walking into the store followed closely by a large bodyguard. One could never miss the entrance of Henrietta, a large man wearing a tightfitting waist coat and shirt with woman's makeup and painted nails.

"Good morning Laken, and to you Henrietta."

The bodyguard didn't respond to my greeting, just to the slight movement Fade made when she slid her hand toward the grip her long gun. Henrietta clenched his fist and locked eyes with her. The intention of the bodyguard was more than obvious, he meant to tear the Sky Pirate Captain apart if she made a threatening move. Thankfully Laken took the step to ensure a confrontation would never happen.

"It's fine Henri, sweets, nothing is going to happen to us in here. Not while our dearest friend John is around, right John?" They said with an easy discernible East Texas accent, the last word dripping from their lips almost.

"I always take the side of calm over a tempest Laken."

The Procurer snickered a little, and then looked left spotting Fade with wide eyes. "Good morning Captain, I don't think we've had the pleasure? I just love the hat by the way."

"No, we haven't, and I would know because I would have remembered someone like you." Fade stated with a cold edge meant to tell Laken to keep a safe distance. I thought for a moment that I would have to step in, and yet again Laken showed no interest in fighting or in confronting the Sky Pirate. Henrietta on the other hand, he may have worn pretty makeup, but the large muscled man was a brawler and he was ready to fight, growling an ominous threat right back.

"I think its best we conclude our business Laken and be on our separate ways." I said trying to hurry the meeting along.

"I'm not afraid of her or you, shaman." Henrietta snarled with a voice as deep as the growl.

"You want to put that courage of yours to the test? I bet I can make you blink?" Fade snarled in return, as I knew she would. The Sky Pirate had never backed away from a fight, not with any man or Protectorate Air Ship.

The tension was thick, like that bar of steel I mentioned earlier, in the store and I watched thankfully as Tala took Taima and headed behind the counter for cover. I sighed drawing some of the attention of Fade and Henrietta to me and away from the need to turn this into a physical contest. I never looked away from Laken and our eyes were still locked to each other as I spoke. "Do you have the information I came for Laken?"

"That I do John," they responded with a small grin and nod before continuing on, "but the price for what you want to know has changed I am afraid."

"Changed?" I asked with a raised eyebrow and suspicious tone to my voice. I half expected them to change the deal, but what this new cost Laken was now asking for had me concerned just a touch.

"Oh, its nothing you cannot handle my friend, the wise and arcane Shaman Greywolf."

"I won't walk into a trap Laken, no matter how much you hide the snare. I won't help one of your 'clients' either, no matter what you offer." I replied quickly, and assertively, letting them know there was only so far that I was willing to go for what I wanted.

I know at this point Fade and Mother Twylah must have been wondering just what I was doing. Here I was ready to walk away from this meeting, a meeting I had brokered mind you, with an individual as dark as Laken Malus with nothing. They probably thought it was for the best to leave, owing nothing to a dark figure like Malus was the prudent choice, but then that would mean this whole thing this morning had been for nothing, a farce. I know Laken though, and for them to suddenly change the price on an already struck bargain is tantamount to giving a refund, it was something Laken never did. They had a reputation for conducting business a certain way and with a certain arrangement, which means a deal is a deal no matter the way it was struck, and breaking a bargain was never good in anyone's interest. What it would take for Laken to threaten both of those aspects must be very, very lucrative...for them.

"This doesn't concern one of my regular clients John, though I will say you are in a way helping someone who bought something from me."

"Don't do it John, this doesn't feel right, at all." Fade whispered in my ear, her hand still hovering over the grip of her gun.

No, it didn't feel right, just like Fade had said, but it still wasn't enough to sway me from my path with Laken. It only made me wonder more what kind of an offer they were setting in front of me now. Laken Malus was a shadow in the city, a whispered name that drew the evil eye from old ladies and a shiver for the young ones as I've told you. Laken was everywhere and nowhere, no address for one to look up, but there was a phone number to call if you asked the right people residing in the wrong places for it. Laken Malus was the one you went to when no one else could or would help you, if you were willing to pay the price for their service. Laken was the go between for those unfortunate souls who needed to work with the devil to rise above Hell and they could find anything you needed or desired for a price. Malus dealt in the blackest of Magic and Spirits, so for one of their client's to be in enough trouble to force them to break a bargain made my mind whirl and churn.

"What kind of help?" I asked noting the angry look the question brought from Mother and Fade, both at the same time.

"Oh, only the kind you can provide Shaman Greywolf."

Now there was an answer with so many meanings and twists it could take a man a minute or two to think on it, which I was doing in quiet contemplation. I stood eyeing Laken, trying to decide what new game this was we were playing, when they leaned in and spoke with a malicious smile.

"I forgot to mention John, there's a young innocent life involved here, so time is of the essence."

And there it was, the trap I had tried so hard to keep from falling into springing up and around me. My grin turned to a hard line as my mind turned over what Laken had told me, how I was now entangled in this nefarious plan of theirs.

"You put a young one's life in danger?" Mother Twylah hissed at Malus like a snake.

"It wasn't me Mother. I only provided the name of an alchemist to create a potion for a certain ceremony you might say. What happens after I provided the name is of no concern to me." Laken stated with that malicious smile still eyeing me.

"It's the same alchemist, isn't it?" I asked already knowing the answer.

"What you want, the name of the alchemist who made the poison potion for Sara, is with the very one who needs your help. Miss Abagail Grouse is more than willing to supply you with the name, as well as a nice sum of money, for your help." Laken said while pushing a folded piece of parchment toward me on the counter.

I looked down at the paper as they withdrew their hand. It was neatly folded and for some reason looked as if it might bite my hand if I tried to pick it up. As I stood there, I heard Tala from behind the counter speak up quickly. "You can't expect John to do this, forced into your bidding like this?"

Yet that's exactly what Laken expected was going to happen, what they had planned on. Malus knew I would risk my very life to help anyone who asked, only the kind of people that Laken 'took on' as customers were the kind I wouldn't help unless the situation were dire, or an innocent were involved. The kind of 'clients' who found themselves in need of help after opening the wrong door at the wrong time, risking everything for some misguided reason or reward. Laken knew this about me. They would know that to get me involved it would have to be something utterly life threatening.

"I have a feeling Laken here doesn't expect much, her task was probably done the minute she walked through the door to this shop." Fade answered Tala, her eyes locking onto Henrietta.

For Laken, name calling and such was a waste of time. They had progressed beyond feeling anything from that kind of abuse, and yet the use of a pronoun would send Malus into a rage. I looked up from the folded paper just in time to see them snap their head toward Fade, a look of pure hate spilling from their eyes. If Laken had a weapon at that moment then they might have used it to shoot or strike the Sky Pirate, but then with that same quickness, the face on Malus changed and the evil smile was back.

"Very observant you are Captain. Yes, my services have been paid for by just meeting with John and passing on the name of the person and where he can meet them." Laken said with such a cold air I could feel the bitter burn of it as they turned back to me and continued to speak. "If you decide to meet with Miss Grouse, or not, I am free of any obligation from this moment on. Though, we all know, John here will meet with her and help in any way he can."

With that final statement, the meeting was done, and as such Laken and Henrietta wasted no more time on words with me. They both turned and headed for the door, stopping just at the portal for a moment, enough time to ask one last question. "Ah John, do you still have that marvelous pair of Weavers you took from old Carlo?"

"They are not 'mine' Laken, but yes, both are still with me."

"Hmmm, I could probably arrange a nice price for them for you if you wish. It seems those two are being sought after something fierce." Malus laughed with the offer. I didn't answer, and after a minute, Laken left with their bodyguard leaving the shop and the air instantly felt cleaner, lighter.

"I don't like her momma, not at all." I heard little Taima whisper just as the door to the shop closed.

"No one likes her little one, not even her own mother I'd guess." Fade answered and the last piece made me wonder. Laken's mother, what would the woman think of her dear daughter now, not what 'they' had become but what 'they' did to live. I was thinking on this more when I felt a hand touch my arm and I turned to look into the worried eyes of the fiercest Sky Pirate Captain flying today. "You're not going to do this John? This smells like a trap, a deep and dark one at that."

I shook my head and smiled trying to soothe Fade's concern, "the choice has been taken out of my hands."

I could see the flash of anger in her eyes. The frustration she felt at my decision, or the lack there of, must have been overwhelming for someone of Fade's demeanor. She lived her life free and her way, by her own rules and laws. She was free of all ties, or so she thought, but now I could see one tie there in her eyes staring back at me and I felt pain from it. A decision is coming for you my dearest one, and it will not be easy.

"If you are going John then let me add my aid." Mother Twylah said and I turned slowly, just in time to see her shake a bag.

The bag was the blessed receptacle for her beloved Runes. Mother Twylah was a powerful believer in the arcane, and in-place of 'The Bones' of the diviners of her past she used the Runes. To anyone else they looked just like ordinary flat rocks, stones of differing colors and types, each etched with a single strange marking. To Mother though, the Runes were the guides to discovering the answers to questions one had yet to ask. If you consult the Runes you might learn of a wondrous thing that might happen in the future or be shown a warning of probable disaster awaiting, you.

It was all in the handling of the Runes, of the reading, just like a deck of Tarot cards.

I watched as Mother stopped the shake after three exact movements, and then with a slow hand reach into the bag. She produced a single Rune in her fingers, the marking hidden from my sight, laying the stone down on a green felt cloth on the counter with a careful touch. Mother did this two more times, the same exact movements, pulling two more Runes out. She put the bag down, uttered a prayer in the old tongue of her country, and then began to turn each stone over with the same delicate touch.

Behind me Fade watched with eager and curious eyes, as did little Taima and Tala. It seems my fate was something to be interested in at the moment and when Twyla looked up with a concerned eye while Tala gasped with dread I never flinched.

Me, I already knew how this day was going to end for myself, no need to consult the Runes.

"We have added another change to our plans, I see."

My brother's sudden appearance, and his voice, caused Mother Twylah and her family to jump while Fade, well she just went for her pistol before cursing loudly. "Where the hell did you come from?"

"That we have brother, a small but very necessary one it turns out." I replied with a smile, as I looked to him.

"Everything has been small but necessary these days." Ru responded while walking over, leaning down, and smiling as he recognized the Rune on the counter. "Ah, you will have an adventure today I see. I hope it is a good one."

"This is John's brother, correct?" Fade whispered to Mother Twylah, who only nodded back watching the shamans intently.

"As do I my brother, and a quick one at that."

"Well, if it turns out to be a long affair we will just have to make another change, want we?"

I gave a laugh and a nod to my brother's humor, though it just brought on a look on incredulity from the ladies.

Part Four

The desk sat dead center in the large state room, not an inch off from perfect midpoint from all four corners of the quarters. It wasn't an ostentatious desk. It wasn't the desk of some narcissistic personality who wanted everyone who sat on the other side of the furnishing to know just who was in charge here. No, it was the desk of someone who cared little for such things. There was no name plate, no leather blotter, and not one piece of ornamental accessory to be found on the top of the middle-sized counter. The desktop was spartan, austere with everything where it should be, was supposed to be. A plain pen sat next to a plain and simple pad of paper. The handwritten notes on the paper were even in perfect straight lines, each line and sentence equidistant from the next. The stateroom was a perfect match for the desk, nothing out of the ordinary to catch one's eye, and yet it felt like everything was where it should be. Then the door to the state room swung open and a man dressed in the sharply pressed uniform of the Protectorate stepped in. The gold boards on his shoulders gleamed, even in the dull light of the electric lamps, and the medals on his chest seemed glued in place as not a one moved when he did.

General Samuels was a military man, born and bred to be a soldier and nothing else. He took off his hat and sat it down in its usual place, just at the right corner of the desk, the polished bill hanging just off the edge.

He took a quick seat in the chair and was just sliding into place at the helm of the desk when the door to the room opened after a single knock. Right on schedule, the young Lieutenant entered and silently walked over to the desk and handed over a large folder filled with papers. Samuels took it while his staff member waited, placing the folder on the desktop and opening it without looking up. He read the first three pages before speaking, again without looking up.

"Is everything in place Lieutenant?"

"Yes General, precisely as you and General Hamelin ordered." The young man answered quickly, obediently.

"The air ships are in place?"

"Yes sir,"

"And the air support, the new P-6's"

"Up and in the air sir, as ordered."

"And the pilots have been instructed on the 'special' needs of this operation?"

"Yes sir, they have been told of the special needs."

The room, a converted hotel room to an office now, was quiet as Samuels read more of the papers before initializing the bottom. He didn't speak to the young Lieutenant or even acknowledge him again. There was no need as the officer hadn't been dismissed, and as such, would remain in place by the General's desk until sent away. The door to the room opened again, no knock this time, and a woman wearing the long purple coat of one associated with the Magi entered. She wore a white ascot tucked into the folds of a white shirt and black pants similarly tucked inside knee high boots.

"Good morning Addison." The General stated coldly without looking up from his papers.

"Good morning Silas," the Magi stated taking a spot just beside the Lieutenant. He only nodded to the older woman and she only smiled back as the General was quiet again for a moment before speaking.

"Are the Umbra in place?"

"Yes Silas, positioned all over the city as we discussed. If one of the Weavers uses her powers, we'll know and we can descend on them in short time. Has there been any word on Miss Camille?" Addison answered and asked with a nod.

For the first-time Samuels looked up from his task and right to the both people. "Good, we can't afford a mistake like yesterday in Brooklyn. And no, there's been no word on Camille or her second Ezio."

"Her second, we're picking up Mr. Ezio as well?" Addison said with a small bit of surprise.

Samuels went back to signing the papers as he replied, "yes we are. I ordered it this morning after thinking on it last night. There is too much at stake here, for both the Protectorate and the Magi, to let these two Weavers slip away again."

"Yes sir," the Lieutenant snapped off quickly.

"We understand Silas," was all Addison offered checking and then tugging at the cuffs of her coat. She seemed to care little that another Magi was going to be taken in.

"Good, your excused Lieutenant." Samuels remarked sending the young officer into a salute before exiting the room.

Addison grinned as the man left, wondering if the young officer was this obedient to the General out of some respect and admiration, or if it was some delusional idea he may make rank faster if he acted like an obedient puppy around Silas. This whole operation was beyond Top Secret, no written record of it would ever see the light of day, so how could it be used to prove the requirements for promotion? Or maybe the Protectorate officer knew this. and as such, he had some thought of using it to force a new promotion out of Samuels? Well, that was highly unlikely due to the fact Silas was not one to be blackmailed, ever, which was proven just a minute later.

The door to the room swung open and this time the ramrod figure of Thales Hamelin entered. He was the equal to Samuels for the British Royal Army, a General in the Intelligence division. He was the human epitome of a British Bulldog. Hamelin's face was a chunk of pure granite, chiseled into the stern look he gave any and every one, except for Samuels. Which was the part of this treacherous relationship Addison found herself in which was so damn off-putting. The Magi could accept the lack of trust between all three, the fact they were committing a form of treason did not seem to bother either General, and she had no such concern. No, it was the fact these two unbelievably stubborn, hardnosed men had formed some kind of 'Members of the Brotherhood' bond, and that made Addison vey weary. She was not a member and she never would be The Magi knew this and that was the direct reason her paranoia was at such a high level when around the pair.

"Good morning Silas, I have some news we need to address first thing." Hamelin remarked while holding out a folded note to the Samuels.

For the first time since entering and taking a seat, the Protectorate officer looked up eagerly to other in his office. He took the note and asked a quick question. "What is it Thales?"

"Our mouse has finally decided to try and escape the trap." The British General remarked with a sour face, his usual look Addison noted as she asked a question.

"Would the mouse your referring to be a young Magi by the name of Cooper?"

"One in the same!" Samuels snapped looking at the note then back to turning through the papers the Lieutenant brought him.

"What is he trying to do?" Addison asked quickly, her voice tinged with confusion.

Samuels stopped on a page to read it while Hamelin took over the conversation. "Mr. Cooper has contacted four other Magi; with what we can only assume is the intention of leaving our enterprise."

Before Addison could ask a third question she was cut off by Samuels, who asked a question while this time looking up with a stern eye directed right at her. "Who are Adelaide, Eleanor, Baird, and Tomo? What rank are they in the Magi?"

The questions caught Addison slightly off guard, the emotion in the room went straight from cold to colder, like being in a very intense interrogation, which prompted a cautious approach to speaking from the Magi. Addison felt her paranoia jump a notch or two as she spoke with care. "The four are exceptional Magi, but unfortunately their skill was not enough to take them to the First Ascension. They were omitted at the last call, and as such, will remain where they are, at the Second Ascension."

"Do the four harbor a bitterness at being 'omitted' for Ascension, as you say?" Hamelin asked, his hard eyes joining with Samuels, upping the intensity of the questions.

That brotherhood, the one Addison had been thinking of just a minute or so ago, was now on full display as both men seemingly came at her with questions, each loaded with all kinds of a bad outcome.

"No," Addison spoke looking to Hamelin first and then to Samuels to finish, "they would not harbor such feelings. We Magi are students, bound to learn what we can of the energy we wield. We are no seekers of fame or politics, just curious of the gift we have been given."

The room was quiet again, both Generals staring at the Magi coldly for a minute before, with a sudden about face, Hamelin turned to Samuels and spoke. "I believe her, which means Mr. Cooper has now officially become a bother."

"And he's going to waste four innocent souls in his escape attempt." Samuels huffed before standing and holding out the paper he had been reading to Addison. As she took it Hamelin to her side began to speak again, almost narrating the words she was reading.

"Mr. Cooper rented a room last night at a hotel just down the street from the Magi House. The fool used an alias, which was smart, but then he showed up in person to pay for the room, which was very foolish."

Addison kept reading as the narrative being explained in the room kept moving with Samuels taking over. "The boy has neither the making of, nor the inclination, at being a half-decent spy. He had four individuals go to the room, each identified as one of the Magi I asked you about."

What she was being told, each and every fact, came from the report the Magi held in her hands. Addison read the words, and yet she couldn't make the connection to what all this meant, and as she looked up the bewilderment was apparent on her face.

"Why would he ask these four to a room at a hotel?"

"Well, if you are asking me, and I think you are, then I say our Mr. Cooper told these four all about our plan to create a Philosophers Stone." The British General stated emotionless.

"But why would he do that?" She asked turning from Hame in back to Samuels. Her hand holding the report unconsciously giving the paper back to the General.

"My first thought, is I have no clue. He's not telling them our plans in hopes the four will go to the First Magi of the First Ascension here in Chicago telling him what we're doing." Samuels answered in his own special way, as direct as possible.

"The First Magi knows what we are doing, Corrine is meeting with him this morning as I meet with you. We have his blessing and aid. It is the same with the Grand Magi of the World Council above him." Addison added with a shake of her head, her mind running at top speed with the onset of all this new information.

"Exactly, so what does our little mouse have planned Addison. This we need to discover as fast as possible." Hamelin snorted as the Magi nodded silently.

What are you up to Cooper? The question had no answer, not yet, as Addison kept the inquiry spinning in her mind. If he's not setting a strategy of exposing them all, and how could he with the four he had chosen, then what was the young man up to? It was not the obvious Addison whispered in her mind, so then it must be something with these Magi he brought together. She had to look deeper into their pasts. Whatever was happening, or about to happen, it had to do with the two men and two women he reached out to Addison decided.

The four were key to what Cooper was going to do.

"All right, we 'll put those four on our list of people to follow. If need be, we can have them picked up anytime." Samuels ordered stiffly, his eyes watching Addison very closely.

The Magi House of Chicago, it could, and has been, mistaken for one of the finer hotels on the South West Side of Chicago. The twelve-story building was built to be grand with a white granite facade shining in the morning sun. The home of the Magi was easily as spectacular as the Lexington, where it's rumored the notorious Al Capone stays, occupying the entire 5th floor of suites. Only, the ones who were granted access inside and allowed above the first floor could see the true lifestyle of the Magi. While the first floor was decorated in warm colors with plenty of chairs and couches and areas to greet visitors, the floors above were simple with very few lavish amenities. The floors above the first were just like any other hotel with rooms for Magi to stay in for a night or live, other rooms were open intended for groups to sit and meet. It was quite the normal living space, except for the rule of Ascension, which meant the higher floors were barred from being accessed by the lower Magi. The top floor, the penthouse, was reserved for the First Magi and his staff. You only went there when invited, and only then.

Ezio walked on toward the House, the building easily noticeable just ahead as he moved forward. He knew the Magi House here in Chicago was the same as the one in Manhattan, as it was the same as the one in Atlanta and even as far away as Los Angeles. Across the globe as well, in London and Madrid and even Kyoto, all the Magi Houses were the same, all twelve stories high and setup inside the same. With a sigh Ezio realized this was to foster a union, a sense of society and family where all were part of the same purpose and design. No one member was more important or better than the other, and as such every Magi was a cog in a wheel moving the society toward the same goal, the betterment of Magic. Yet, that beautiful ideal, was coming to a close, an end, due to the inescapable politic of Global Isolation. Countries, after the war, began to wall themselves off and cut off ties to others. This shouldn't have affected us he thought, we are Magi. We have no allegiance, or need for that matter, with politics, and yet here where are being corralled and separated.

The thought disgusted Ezio, all the ideas and knowledge that was going to be lost to this Isolationist politic was tragic. He shook his head to clear his mind and began to reach into his vest pocket for his watch when a hand took his in a hard grip and a harsh whisper cut in with a hiss.

"You shouldn't be out on the street! Come with me now!"

Before Ezio could react to the voice, which sounded very familiar, the hand gripping his with an overly firm grasp forcibly pulled him off the street and down an alley out of sight. Once off the street, and his wits gathered, Ezio pulled back on his hand as he set his feet to not taking another step. "What are you doing - Camille, is that you?"

"Yes, it is me," the Magi stated with the same harsh whisper she used on the street while dragging the taller man away. "You can't be out on the street Ezio and you certainly can't go the Magi House."

The look of utter confusion the taller man returned from her statement frustrated Camille just a little more as she sighed. "Where have you been this morning? I've been waiting in this alley for over an hour at least."

"I was having breakfast with someone, but why are you acting like this Camille, so secretive? And why are you in Chicago?"

The questions made Camille stop for a second, to gather her words for an answer, and the pause was enough for her to reign in her frustration as well. "I came to Chicago with Fade, following John and Wallace to hopefully catch up with them. And I'm acting this way because we, both of us, are to be arrested the moment we step foot into the Magi House or on sight if spotted on the street."

That look of confusion switched suddenly at her words, the explanation knocking the wind out of Ezio for a moment before whispering. He stiffened as his eyes squinted with surprise, "arrested, the two of us?"

"Yes, the Protectorate has ordered us to be detained by the guards at the House until they arrive to take us away. It's a miracle you weren't arrested just walking over here." Camille answered with another sigh, steadying her emotions even more.

"The Cabal, they had to be the ones who ordered us imprisoned, but how did they discover we even knew they existed?" Ezio asked back quickly, and for a strange moment Camille could see the pair playing their game again, back on the Air Ship from yesterday. There, standing by the rail, tossing questions at each other, waiting to hear if the answer bolstered a theory or contradicted everything. It was that very image that brought about the sudden realization to Camille of how the cabal knew of her and Ezio.

"Cooper," she whispered and the single name hit her tall friend like a thrown stone right to the stomach.

Ezio gasped at the same realization Camille came to, the betrayal now taking over both of their minds. The one person who had probably overheard what they were talking about yesterday, the very one who more than likely saw Camille running off to join the Sky Pirate Captain Fade. Then, with the iron grip of his will, Ezio calmed his mind and spoke, just as if the game they played while standing on the deck of the air ship yesterday was still going on.

"Cooper is working with them, the Cabal, but, why would he side with them? What does he have to gain from this act?"

"I don't know. I had very little interaction with him due to the fact he was just assigned to us." Camille answered with a shake of her head.

"Wait, I think I might know, but you won't like how I came about what I know my friend." Ezio replied and the words caused Camille to squint as a feeling of paranoia began to rise in her stomach.

"What is it Ezio?"

The tall man sighed and started to speak as he placed his hands behind his back in a pose meant to show his friend he was safe. "When Cooper arrived, I asked someone I knew to elaborate on his background, who he was and what information there was on his past."

"You checked into him?"

"Yes Camille, yes, I did, and I would like to say my natural tendency not to trust anyone was a waste of my time when it came to our young Mr. Cooper, but unfortunately, it wasn't I'm afraid."

The Magi eyed her colleague hard, her mind wondering just how much did Ezio know about Cooper, and the others in their Umbra group. She wondered for a moment just how much did he know about her and her past, the parts she had kept hidden from the light of day due to a cringing fear of anyone finding out. Then Camille did just as Ezio had done a moment before, she used her strong will to keep her wits about her.

"What did you find out?"

"Our Mr. Cooper is fine young man and Magi, only the same can't be said about his father. The man worked with one of the companies which develops and sells Steam Tech to the Protectorate, specifically turbines and weapons. Cooper's father, by all accounts, was a dedicated engineer, until the day his secret was discovered. Cooper's father had a very nasty second career."

"He was a spy?" Camille whispered

"Yes, from what I was told, the man sold both industrial and military secrets, including plans and schematics, to the highest bidder."

Camille took a moment to think about what Ezio had told her, run the information through her mental filters, and everything pointed to a single end. What she had learned from Ezio, what she knew of Cooper, it all came to one conclusion. "He's being blackmailed to turn on us."

"It is the only possible answer I agree. The man being an unwilling spy must be the only conclusion, and there is the fact Cooper doesn't seem to have the demeanor of one who willingly betrays another Magi for personal gain. The evidence against him is overwhelming, yet I think the possibility is very high he might have been forced into the position of being a spy." Ezio stated biting his bottom lip just a little as he did. It was the 'tell' he would let slip occasionally while in deep thought.

"And as such we cannot trust him any longer. If we see him, we must walk the other way."

"Again, agreed, but that does not alleviate our current predicament." Ezio commented looking over his shoulder and back toward the Magi House.

Instantly Camille knew what he was thinking, a nice consequence of being friends and colleagues for long. She knew her fellow Umbra so well she had come to anticipate Ezio's thoughts, and what she was reading was not good at all. "You can't go to the Magi House Ezio. The Protectorate guard the building and they will almost certainly catch you."

"I know Camille," he said turning back and looking at her deeply, "but I have an appointment I can't miss at the House."

"What possibly do you have to see to at the House?" She asked with wide eyes.

Ezio sighed and tried to explain. "Last night, as I lay in bed, I came to a sudden realization. I know the Cabal were the ones who had Isaac bind the Weavers, but why did they have him do this? What end would it bring for them to have two Weavers bound soul to very soul? Then I put two to two and came to four, as my grandfather was fond of saying. I finally understood what this was all about. The Cabal is going to make a weapon of pure energy, a bomb of monstrous proportions. The Weavers can and will likely be used to charge a specially constructed stone for them, I am sure."

The answer, well, it was a little hard for Camille to swallow at first. "A weapon, from a constructed stone?"

"Yes," Ezio nodded only once before quickly moving in just a little closer to Camille, "we both know, in theory, two Weavers bound will draw in more energy than one, why even a pair who have not been bound can pull together more. Now, what if Isaac was very specific and very precise in the pair he chose to bind? What if he ensured just how much energy these Weavers could draw by being very selective in his choice of Weavers? What if he sought two very powerful Weavers and bound them? Think for a second, with that much energy, the Cabal could make a bomb powerful enough to raze a city to the ground."

It was all starting to make sense to her now, Camille's eyes narrowing as the horrid truth began to fill her mind. "A weapon which can be carried right past an enemy's defenses. You could even send it via a pouch by a secret courier."

"Exactly, but then I began to get a grasp on what this plan entails. The Cabal has two very large obstacles to overcome. One, bringing forth the amount energy to create and charge the stone, which Isaac solved with the Weavers he bound. The second, and the more perplexing of the two issues, was where to find a stone to hold all that fabulous energy these Weavers were to draw in."

"There isn't such a stone!" Camille whispered, the certainty of understanding evident in her voice. Not once since learning of the insidious plan just a moment ago to create this weapon did she think about the most important part of it all, the very stone to hold the charging energy.

"Yes, the Cabal has too manufacture the vessel which holds the energy, a fake stone you might say, because there is not an organic one readily available in the real world."

"They can't use any normal stone or crystal, can they?"

"No, they can't. The stone must be made of a certain distinct organic and crystal makeup to hold all the energy that will be directed into it by the Weavers. I remembered something then and thankfully I had my personal notes on my whip."

"What?"

"I had a conversation with an alchemist once, three years ago, during an investigation. He told me of some news passing among his kind, that there was one among them in the Underground who had proffered a way to create a crystal strong enough to hold an infinite amount of energy, a Philosopher's stone if you will."

"That's just a fable, isn't it?" Camille asked quickly cutting Ezio off, her mind already treading down the path Ezio was taking her.

"Yes, of course it's just a fable, but without any known crystal to base any experimenting on, there is only hypothesis and theories about what will work and what will not. We should assume If the Cabal already had Isaac bind the Weavers then we also should assume they know of a way to make a stone to hold the energy. It was probably this unknown alchemist who gave them the knowledge and insight on how to make the vessel and I am sure they know of someone who can make it for them." Ezio explained as best, and as quick as he could.

Camille nodded, then grinned a little, as once more she connected the flurry of dots of information racing through her mind. "And your meeting someone who knows who this alchemist is?"

"Yes and no, I mean if it were that simple a question than I'd have a simple answer. The same alchemist I interviewed told me if the rumors floating around the Underground were true, and there was a good chance the rumors were, then he knew of only two people who could possibly make the stone real. The first is the one he knew for certain with the right laboratory and setting could make it most definitely, a woman by the name of Karina who lives here in the US somewhere. She's the best choice, the very one the Cabal needs to solve the second problem of creating their weapon."

"But these people in the Cabal, they have to know this too like you said, and by now they have this woman Karina helping them, or locked away." Camille retorted the obvious she thought.

"The woman went missing two years ago, just around the same time Isaac began working with the Weavers, so I can safely assume the Cabal already have her as you said." Ezio countered while looking around once again. The move was making Camille just a little nervous, what, with all the stress she was under at this very moment, it was understandable to get a little unnerved.

"If the Cabal has the woman already then why do you need to go to the Magi House?"

"Because," Ezio began while finally sliding his hands back round to the front of his body and using both to help explain, "there is a Magi here in Chicago by the name of Eleanor who is Karina's Aunt. I'm going to look at her personal record in the administrator's office. He might have some information, some obscure piece of insight written down, which could help me either track Karina down or lead me to her work notes. I need something more substantial than a rumor."

She sighed again seeing it was going to be futile to try and talk her friend out of going through with this crazy idea. The fact Ezio was taking all this on his shoulders was exactly why the man was a treasured friend she knew. He would never stop looking for answers and he would never let anything happen to the ones he loved. He saw this as a danger to those he cared for and as such he would try everything in his power to stop it.

Still, she had to make sure he wasn't going to just try to up and walk through the front door.

"Well, do you have a plan at least to get inside the House without getting caught?"

"Of course, I do. I hadn't planned on using it, but I guess there's no choice now." Ezio replied before going quiet which drew an immediate reaction from Camille. Her eyes went wide, her head bobbed a bit, and Ezio knew instantly what the move meant. She wanted, not expected, an answer and she wanted it now.

"Oh, yes, I know a man who can sneak me in via an underground tunnel. The entrance is around back of the House. It was put in to give egress of the First Magi if needed."

The answer wasn't the best Camille had ever heard, but it was the only one she was going to get. She backed down with a sigh and nodded, sending her long hair streaked with purple highlights shimmering just a little. "Then be careful Ezio, the Protectorate and the Magi both intend fully to catch us today. I have to go and find Wallace, make sure he is okay."

She finished and turned to walk away when her second's hand grabbed her arm lightly but forcefully, enough to stop Camille. She looked back just as he spoke.

"There is something you need to know, something that could be very disturbing."

The tone of the remark, the pure foreboding in it made Camille's heart almost stop. "What is wrong Ezio?"

The tall Magi let go of his friend's arm and bit his lower lip just a bit before speaking. "The other name the alchemist I spoke with about creating the stone, the only other technoist and engineer who could complete the task, it was Wallace McAndrew."

The ground suddenly dropped out from under Camille's feet and she almost fell with it. She reached up and grabbed Ezio's arm to steady herself for just the briefest of moments before speaking.

"The Cabal, do you think they would go after him?"

"I don't know," he answered truthfully while watching his friend gather and steel herself, getting back to the Camille he knew and trusted. "I think it would be better if you found your Wallace before anyone else does."

"Yes," Camille nodded quickly and firmly, "but how do I find one man in the city the size of Chicago?"

Ezio smiled, almost chuckling, before speaking. "There is a large Scottish neighborhood on the Near Northside. I'd bet all my money that's where you'll find him."

"How do you know that?" Camille asked with a small grin.

"Simple, there's a tailor there in the neighborhood called The Mouse. He's the best in town, maybe the whole Northeast of the US. Go to his shop and ask him about Wallace, he might give you a lead."

When Camille stared at him the Tall Magi shook his head, "I had him make me a coat once. I still have it and the stitching is extraordinary. His store in right in the center of the community."

The colored Magi only chuckled and shook her head. "Only you my friend, but please, be safe."

"I will my friend, you do the same. Keep your head down, find Wallace, and then get the hell out of town."

Camille only nodded before turning to leave the alley. She stole one last look back, one last time to capture an image of her friend. Ezio smiled and nodded quietly back before she turned and left. The Cabal had found him, and her, he thought while waiting silently. He wanted to give her time to slip away before approaching the Magi House. They discovered me he kept thinking. He knew they would, discovery was inevitable, but Ezio had never expected to get this far with his investigation undetected. It sure took this Cabal a long time to find out he was nosing around, I wonder why he thought? Then he just pushed the question away and turned to leave the alley.

It was time to see this through he told himself.

"The Generals, they are sure the Weavers Isaac prepared for us are here in Chicago?"

The question from the First Magi was direct, and with the weight of his sharp steel grey eyes added to inquiry, Corrine should have felt just a small twinge of intimidation. Truth be told, the female Magi wasn't fazed one bit by the First Magi's stare or his reputation.

Absalom rose to his present position as head of the Magi House in Chicago because he had never been swayed or distracted from his path to be the highest ascended Magi in the city. He was the youngest First Magi in the US, at a spry fifty-five years of age, and a man of color who was born to former slaves in the state of Illinois. Absalom left his parents at age six, entering the ranks of the Magi, and he never once looked back. He never went home to visit them, not once, not even when both passed away. No, to Absalom there was nothing but the Magi and his rise through the Ascensions. To the man there was only this world of Magi, magic, and nothing else. His quarters at the top of the Magi house was a perfect example of this philosophy of living a dedicated existence. Nothing gaudy or showy, just what a man deep into the studies of magic would need to live and grow intellectually each day. Shelves lined the walls where tome after tome was stored, and in the open spaces of the room, were tables with the tops occupied by apparatuses and instruments meant to probe the power of the energy he weilded. His clothes were modest Corrine noted, a simple dark blue coat over a white shirt and matching dark blue vest, the cuffs of the shirt showing just a touch past the wrist of each hand. The only thing which stood out was the large ring fitted for two fingers and the large purple stone affixed to it on his right hand.

"Yes sir," Corrine answered sitting in a chair across the desk dressed in a brand new deep colored purple skirt and jacket with button up boots. She had no problem dressing in the latest fashions, Corrine rather enjoyed being a little flamboyant. Which was strange since she rarely cared for company or attracting attention. "Eloy is certain the Shaman Greywolf will bring the Weavers to Chicago."

"And why does Mr. Eloy think this?"

"He thinks the shaman took the Weavers for a specific purpose and once that requirement is met he will turn them loose."

The First Magi nodded then asked another question. "And the shaman came to Chicago seeking sanctuary I presume?"

The man was very sharp, just as the hushed words passed round the Magi House said, Corrine thought as she spoke. "The shaman has several contacts here in the city. As you said, Eloy is sure Greywolf came here seeking help and safety."

"And we don't know the names of these contacts?"

The female Magi shook her head, the long blond braid of her hair never once slipping off her shoulders. "No, I am afraid, for if anything the Shaman Greywolf is a mysterious and secretive man. We know very little about him beyond what we have heard in stories."

"Now that is a shame," Absalom stated locking eyes with Corrine while speaking coldly, "but it is something we will remedy here quickly. Go to the Generals, have them ascertain all the information they can on the Shaman Greywolf, and then add what we know."

"What are we looking for sir?" Corrine asked with a slightly raised eyebrow. She was sure what the Protectorate knew would be just about the same as what the Magi knew about the reclusive shaman.

"A more complete picture Miss Corrine. One must truly 'see' one's obstacles before one can conquer them, overcome them."

"Yes sir, I'll make it my top priority."

"Also, check with Addison, make sure she and Eloy are prepared for their next steps." Absalom added with a quick snip.

"We still plan on taking possession of the stone from the Generals once it's been created, sir?"

The First Magi nodded as he responded, "yes Miss Corrine, immediate possession. To leave such a remarkable object in their hands would be an abomination. The Philosopher's Stone should, and will, belong to the Magi. It has been decided and thus ordered at the highest levels of the Ascension."

Well, Corrine thought silently with a nod, the man is a determined and driven man. She would hate to be in his way when he decided to move.

Part Five

"I look like a boy, a short ugly boy."

The complaint had to be the tenth one from Wells, or what might have been the tenth one Wahkan thought. Frankly, he had lost count of how many times she had complained. The normally calm, and compliant, one of the pair of Weavers had suddenly taken to stating her displeasure of the present situation. The group had left the Tiānkōng earlier, in an atmosphere that Wahkan considered more leaden than filled with excitement. Wahkan was sure there wasn't a lady on the planet who couldn't, or wouldn't, become excited at the chance of getting a new set of clothes.

And yet here were the Weavers, standing on a busy Chicago street, proving him wrong with each passing minute.

"You don't look that bad lass. I think my old coveralls never looked more at home then draped across your body."

"Stop it, we look stupid. These clothes don't fit at all." Boles added with a huff, the 'harrumph' at the end punctuating the sour mood both Weavers were in, and it was spreading it seemed.

"You don't look stupid, and even if you do look a little odd, Mouse will take care of you." Wahkan replied as he walked by a small shop with a fruit stand. Taking the chance to step away from the Weavers, and they're foul dispositions, he stopped by the stand and picked up a pair of nice looking red apples. As he paid, while Boles and Wells stood waiting and scowling, Wally whispered with a sigh.

"I don't envy you one bit my friend, keep your arse down and hopefully you don't get shot by one of them."

Wahkan paid for the fruit and turned with a raised eyebrow, "So you're just going to leave me alone with them?"

The Scotsman just smiled and nodded, "I am afraid so, my friends are waiting."

The large IP simply shook his head while smiling, "go ahead and run-away you coward."

"Remember lad, keep your arse down!"

"Uh-huh," Wahkan shot back as Wally disappeared into the crowd of the street. It was early morning, the day truly beginning, and yet everyone was out and about here in the city, moving with robotic precision to jobs and assigned duties. It was the same in the south, on the west coast, and even the North Wahkan thought, looking back to the Weavers. As he rubbed one of the apples on his vest, the dejected looks on the two young woman's faces made him feel a little low himself.

"All right ladies, let's get over Mouse's and get you some new clothes so Wally can get those coveralls back."

The remark wasn't meant to be anything but that, a simple remark, and yet the ladies took it a little personal. Wells threw up her arms and let out a cry. "See, you think we look ugly!"

"Now wait a minute-"Wahkan began as Boles jumped in with both feet, both hands, and every bit of her ill temper.

"You just let us walk around looking stupid and said nothing! I thought we could trust you!" She snarled.

"Stop it both of you " Wahkan snapped back, what little patience he possessed used up. The Weavers quieted down in a blink, the large man in front of them turning rather scary suddenly. He was sorry for frightening them, but Wahkan knew better then to back down at the moment. "Now listen, if I thought for a second you two would get hurt wearing what you have on I'd have done something, anything, else. The thing is, you're not being hurt and there was no other choice. I mean, you could have worn those frilly underthings we found you were wearing at Carlo's to walk around in, you rather do that?"

The spat was drawing way too much attention Wahkan noticed, people were starting to stare and some even stop to gawk. They had to keep moving, but first he had to establish some kind of respect and trust with the ladies. He was no hero type. He wasn't some white knight, but he was also not one to abandon someone in need, no matter how bad they angered him, and the sooner both of the Weavers understood this the better. After a minute of staring, from him to the ladies and they back, Wells nodded.

"Yes, we won't say anything about the coveralls again."

"Yes," Boles even added though her body language still screamed defiance, "we won't say anything else bad about what we're wearing."

"Good, now the store we need to go and visit is just up the block." Wahkan sighed before turning and heading that way. He didn't look back to see if the Weavers were following. He already knew both were just a step behind. Where else were Wells and Boles going to be? Neither Weaver was stupid and both knew right now sticking with him was their best chance for staying free.

Along a busy street on the Near North Side of Chicago, just where the those better off than most others gathered and live, is the small but well-known shop of a remarkable tailor and his sweet little wife, literally. The captivating garments created by the gifted hands of the 'Mouse' are sought after by the rich, and everyone else for that matter, but the rich mostly because they're mostly the ones who can afford his clothes. The Mouse was born in a small town, or village some might say, near Hannover Germany in 1879. His mother was as proud as a mother could be when he came into the world, even if he was smaller than all the other babies. His father, he was as proud as a father could be, at first. His son was named after his grandfather as custom in the family dictated, Otto Adalbert Buchwald, and great things were expected of the toddler, only the boy never grew to quite meet those expectations because, in the end, the boy never grew physically.

Otto was what people around him called 'a little person', at least the polite and nice ones. He stood just at four feet and three inches tall, not at all what his austere father had wanted for a son. It was the reason Otto followed his mother every day to the dress shop where she worked when he was not in school, the love she gave him that his father would not drew him to her like a starving man to a bowl of smoked ham and potatoes. Otto's mother made the best Tuffel un Plum. She was also a seamstress, a very good one, and as little Otto watched her work he learned. He watched her every move, every stitch she laid down, and before anyone knew it Otto was sewing and then he was working right beside his mother. The owner of the shop never looked at Otto with more concern or care than it took to look at the corner chair where customers sat waiting to be measured, but when those customers began asking for the little gentlemen with the exceptional skills, well he sure took notice then.

Life for little Otto, who was now in his late teens, was no longer a simple one. He was sought out instead of being shunned. He had customers waiting in lines, and sometimes days, to have garments made by his two hands. And yet he still only had his mother's love and his father's disdain. Otto was no fool. He knew those clamoring for his work had no care for him except his ability to sew. He was sure he would always be alone, with the exception of his pet mouse Hilda, which he kept in a small cage at his small apartment of course. Then one morning, as he was looking over the shop's appointment book, which was already filled with the names of those waiting to see him, a young woman entered the shop and Otto was immediately and forever smitten with her.

Inga Felgenhauer was just 19 in those late days of 1899 when she met the best tailor in Hannover and maybe all of the Weimark. She had long beautiful blond hair and a comely face, but because she was only four feet four inches tall, the suitors were rare, if any. Inga needed her newest dress taken in and a bone replaced in her corset, which is why she had come to the dress maker's shop this morning. Her friend had told her of Otto and his skill with a needle and thread, but she had failed to mention the tailor's handsome face, or the fact he had the most incredible eyes. When Otto came around the corner of the tall counter, when she noticed he stood just at her eye level, Inga Felgenhauer knew instantly she had found the man she was going to be with for the rest of her life and beyond.

And enter in the sanctity of marriage they did, in the spring of 1900, just after the snows in Hannover had melted. The pair were inseparable, in love, and were never happier...till 1918. Otto and Inga left their home, their country, that year fleeing a great pain and the rising revolt of the German people around them. They knew not where they would end up, but in America they had been told, all things were possible, and in the early days of 1919 Otto and Inga opened a new tailor shop in Chicago. A year later a strange man with long white hair and a black hat with a colorful band and large Eagle father walked into the shop, and Otto's life, once again, was no longer all that simple.

"Ah, Segne mich! It is Wahkan! Papa, come, our handsome Wahkan has arrived!"

Boles and Wells stood back in perfectly stunned amazement as they watched the tall IP kneel and accept the hug of the little lady, who seemed beside herself at seeing him. She wore the latest Victorian fashion they noticed, a dark blue dress with lace up boots and an exquisite black leather corset, all of it setting off the long grey hair which almost reached the floor. Even her grey eyes sparkled against her dress, or maybe it was just the fact she was so excited to see Wahkan the Weavers thought, both smiling just slightly at the sight. She threw both arms around his neck and kissed his cheek, and all the while saying something in German. Then, from behind a tall counter, a man, the same size as the lady, came walking up in a fast trot. He was also dressed in the latest fashion, a dark blue vest with a cream-colored wingtip shirt complete with a pocket watch in a small pocket on his small waistcoat.

"Oh my, they're the same size." Wells whispered watching as the man grabbed Wahkan's large hand with both of his in an exuberant shake.

"Like two little dolls," Boles whispered in slight amazement.

"Wir sind, was Mama? " The man asked in German with a smile while turning to see the two young Weavers standing in the rear entrance of the shop.

"Excuse us, we're sorry. We didn't mean anything by what we said." Wells quickly apologized, though the remark seemed not to bother either of the little people.

"Oh Wahkan, are these the ones John told us about?" The lady asked breaking away from the large man finally.

Standing up, Wahkan nodded and spoke. "Yes ma'am, this is the pair. Boles and Wells, this is Inga and Otto, 'The Mouse'."

"Ah, what pretty names, to match such pretty women!" Inga smiled taking one hand from both in each of hers. "Oh, but why did they dress you in Wallace's old things?"

"It's all we had Inga, the other clothes were...inappropriate for a pair of ladies to walk around in." Wahkan answered and the response drew a quick look from both of the Weavers. Strange, Boles thought as Wells smiled, it was nice to be called a lady and not something akin to a possession one strapped to their belt.

"Well, well, these clothes will not do for such beautiful Frauleins, will they Mama? I know just the dresses- "The Mouse began before his wife stopped him cold, turning around while still holding both Wells and Boles by the hand.

"Ja, ja, we will try on the ones we finished just this morning. Those skirts, with new corsets and shirts, will look beautiful on them!" Inga declared leading the Weavers from the back room to the front of the shop.

The Mouse only laughed and followed while Wahkan closed the backdoor and made sure it was locked, both locks. Then he went up front to keep watch, and enjoy watching Inga and her husband dressing up the Weavers.

Part Six

"Why do we have to be alone Grandmother?" Sara asked in a young voice that strangely suited her age and gangly body.

Our matron and teacher turned to us with her eyes warm and her smile small, just a hint of a contrast against the tan features of her face which age was beginning to mark. She stopped making the small corn cakes we loved to eat as her grin broke the brown sandstone look of her cheeks, a small slit of white teeth appearing as she spoke. "We are not alone little Sara. We have, all around us, the spirits which gather and speak to us. Our spirit guides, who show us our path, keep us company as we live each day. We have friends like Mr. Kota who come to us when asked and others who seek us out when they have need of our help. I do not think we are alone at all."

I thought for a moment on the answer my teacher replied with, as did my sisters and brother, and even though it was just a moment of hesitation she had already read our minds and was talking again. She did that quite often, almost knowing when to continue without asking. "But I think you are asking about a different type of companion?"

"Will we ever fall in love Grandmother?" Marisol asked quickly, an urgency in her voice I had never heard before.

Grandmother sighed, shook her head slowly, and we all instantly knew the answer would not be one we would like. "No, my little Marisol, there can be no closeness with another, no love like you wish for. You can give no more of your heart than that which friendship needs because there will be no one who will look at you with their sacred heart once the true path of your life is known."

"But why grandmother?" Sara asked with a quick exhale, her voice full of disappointment. I looked from her over to my brother Ru and saw his face was expressionless. I knew he had the same thoughts as Marisol and Sara, that we might end up being alone in this life, and yet he barely seemed bothered by what was being said.

"We shamans experience this life in ways no one else can imagine Sara, and in ways no one else can understand. We can ask some, with open minds, to accept this life we live and hope they will accept our hearts. But you my children, my precious ones, you are more than just shamans, more than even I am. Remember, you are special my little ones, meant to do a great deed saving many souls, and because of this you have been marked by the sigil of the Great Serpent, to be destroyed by its followers. Anyone you let into your life will be in the same danger you are. That is not fair to you and even more unfair to the one you love. Alone you must walk this path my children because you cannot let an innocent be hurt by your fate."

"But we will stay together Grandmother, all of us as a family?" Ru asked suddenly, and it was then I understood his fear. While Sara and Marisol worried they may never find love, Ru simply wanted to keep what he had now, his beloved family close. And yet, once more Grandmother answered with words no one wanted to hear.

"No Ru, a day will come when you and your bother and sisters will have to part and live away from each other, only visiting in Journeys. The chance that the Great Serpent would strike and end all of you with a single stroke of its reach is too dangerous to allow. I know my children these words hurt, but take to heart that the day for leaving is very far off from this one, and you all have a lot of work to do before you may leave."

Then she went back to making the flat corn cakes we would eat for dinner with our roasted meat, and I sat quietly watching her every move. I knew how she would answer, knew before she spoke the words we hated to hear. My teacher may have been wise beyond her long life, but I had learned to 'see' more with my eyes in my short life than my brother and sisters. She was only partly right, our Grandmother, only hiding one fact from us. The Great Serpent may send its followers to kill us, but it was only because the snake knew we four could destroy it. The Great Serpent was scared and it was rightfully so, which was something we could use against it one day when the final fight would happen.

I made myself a promise that very night, one day we four brothers and sisters would destroy the Great Serpent before it could kill us, and we would use its very fear of us to do it.

"What are you thinking about John?"

We had stopped by an old condemned building, one of the many in this part of the city, the part the occupants called the 'Southside'. The street was empty as no one ever visited here to this part of the city, why with it dying and all? That was the sad story actually of this place called Chicago, a city filled with so many souls of such different backgrounds and yet never able to harness that uniqueness of life to better this city, to make it grow and soar. Fade's question, her sweet voice, broke me from my trance as I stood on the street. The memories from that night were powerful, but nothing has ever had sway over me as much as her voice. I looked away from the surroundings to her, smiling as I gathered myself, putting my mind to the here and now. "Nothing but what must be done my...friend."

The last came out wrong, and with a pain in my heart I could not let show. Grandmother's words could never be truer as I watched Fade's face harden just slightly, for just a brief second, before turning back to her usual expression. Behind me I could easily picture Ru, could see his expression in my mind, and I knew he was quietly waiting to see if the truth would, could, come.

"Can you tell me at least what must be done? Will you tell me that small bit at least?"

Her questions were valid if not stinging, both deserving nothing more than the full truth, and yet after living forty-two years in this world by a certain set of rules dictating secrecy, I found it hard to speak the truth to her, my heart's desire.

"Typical John, why should I expect anything else from you." I heard her whisper in frustration, stinging me even more.

Yes, that is my way, was my way at the time. As Grandmother, who had taught us for so many years before she passed, I kept my secrets locked away and I kept them locked away tight. But now, with what I and my brother and sisters were about to do, what I needed from Fade, the way of my former life was no longer acceptable I decided with a new and fresh courage. A new path was needed now, for us both.

"The truth Fade, is in five days I will be dead, killed by an ancient but still powerful God from the Other World, called Nidhogg."

My answer struck her like a hammer to the heart, with her abrupt gasp, it was more than easy to tell. She let go of the handle of the sword on her hip and tried to speak but couldn't, the wind knocked from her lungs I knew. "My life has been a secret and reclusive one because Nidhogg has marked me, and my brother and sisters, to be hunted and killed. I have lived this way because I could not dare endanger an innocent soul with my fate, and never such a beautiful one as yours. I would never dare endanger someone I care for, someone I love so much."

The last must have slipped past her observant senses because Fade never once reacted to what I finished my remarks with. She stepped in close, grasping my arm gently in her hand just above the elbow, and spoke with such concern. "What are you saying? What is a Nidhogg and why does it want you dead?"

"The Nidhogg, what John called it, is a God who has worshippers and devoted followers still. It seeks our deaths because we were born to bring about its end, or something akin to an end for a God." Ru answered from the side where he stood drawing a quick look of confusion from Fade.

"How are you two- "

"Four of us," I broke in pulling Fade's attention to me.

"However, many there are of you John! How are you four supposed to kill a God?" She snapped. I could see her growing concern and frustration in her eyes and hear it in her voice.

I shrugged my shoulders and shook my head, "we don't know yet. We're not even sure where to find the Nidhogg at the moment, but by the end of this day, we will."

Now her eyes really opened wide as she stared at me for a long minute in silence before speaking. "What the hell is going on here John?"

"You wanted to talk, the truth, and I am finally giving you both. I should have been honest a long time ago with you Fade, but old habits and all." I answered letting my southern drawl pull at the words.

She finally smiled, that small grin which had made men's hearts stop, and sighed. "Yes, yes you should have. We're much older than the first day we met on the deck of that air ship. We've lost too much time on old habits."

"You're only forty years old Pirate Captain, there is more than enough time- "Ru began before Fade spun toward him.

"How the hell do you know how old I am?"

"We're shamans Fade, you ask the right dead people the right questions and you can find out anything you want to know about anyone." I responded and she turned back to me, smiling still which made me feel a little better.

"Oh really, and just what 'other questions' have you been asking about me to dead people, John Greywolf?"

"Not enough I'm afraid, the Nidhogg and his attempt to kill my sister Sara has taken much of my attention of late. The Nidhogg's threat to us had been foremost in my mind."

Fade stiffened just a bit at the mention of the threat to me. She quickly brought her emotions under her steel like control and looked at me without flinching. Her hand slid down my arm to take my hand as she spoke. "Then how do I help John? Tell me what I can do to be at your side."

I nodded as I saw the courage from the usually wild Fade. I could see the devotion in her eyes as I squeezed her hand. "There is nothing you can do to help us with the Nidhogg my heart, our fate is linked to it and only my sisters and my brother and I can face what comes. There is something though you can help me with, a necessary task."

Now her eyes squinted as her ears picked up on this new information. She looked deeply at me with her green eyes and whispered, "what task?"

"The one who poisoned my sister Sara, he has tracked us here to Chicago. I may have to journey to 'fix' what this client of Malus has stumbled into. While I help this person, I need someone to watch over me, to make sure this man can't hurt me if he shows." I asked, in my own way, which meant I really didn't ask Fade for her help.

An answer might have been forthcoming, but instead she looked to Ru and spoke, "you're not staying?"

"No Pirate Captain. I must find Zheng and the Tiānkōng so I can tend to something else, which came about when John intervened for the Weavers." Ru stated as he walked up, looking Fade directly in the eyes. She looked at him with a worried expression for a moment and my brother smiled reassuringly before turning to me. "Be quick my brother, time grows short for what must be done."

"I know," was all I said as we hugged and he moved off down the empty street. He stopped though on the edge of the shadows and called back. "I like your hat Pirate Captain. It shows your boldness perfectly!"

I chuckled as I turned back to Fade, who smiled while she shook her head, her long curly hair waving with her. Then she sighed and I knew the mood would turn serious yet again as she spoke. "You're still going in there, this obvious trap Malus laid out?"

"Yes, I have to. I can't leave an innocent to suffer if there is something I can do to help." My hand pulled out the folded paper Laken gave me again and I checked the address again. This was the place, funny how the numbers never changed, even after my eyes scanned the note for the twentieth time before looking up to a set of steps which led up to a stoop, a landing which had seen the worst of its many years recently I assumed.

"Well, you're not going alone John. I won't have that," Fade told me and I felt better for hearing her say it. There was a test coming for her I knew, a trial of trust, and I only wished I could help her when it came time for her to make a fateful decision.

I nodded as I put the paper away in my jacket pocket while thinking, if this was to be my end, here in the physical world, then I would meet it with open eyes and no fear. I led Fade and took the steps up one at a time silently, reaching the door to the building, and instantly noticed the portal was broken. Someone had opened it with a well-placed boot right above the knob shattering the jam and now the door was basically just leaning there. I chuckled before picking it up, letting Fade step inside. I was still chuckling as I put the door back its original position after stepping in, hoping no one come knocking very hard. They might break the door even more, though I was sure that was quite impossible. I turned and looked down a hall that led to two rooms which split off the west wall while a set of stairs ran up along the east wall to a second floor. The stair case had seen better days, and from what I could tell, about halfway up it had crumbled and fallen apart. No one was coming down or going up that way without alerting us.

The sound of feet scraping on the floor caught my attention. I kept my hands free and ready for a fight while watching as a man came out of the second room dressed in a nice suit, which clung to his slim frame *awkwardly, as if the tailor had sewn it for another larger body entirely. He looked frail and very old, sallow skin tone with sunken eyes, and yet when he spoke the voice was a deep and young baritone with a Maine accent. "Are you here for Madame?"*

"Yes, I'm here for Madame." I replied calmly. Now I was starting to understand why the suit did not fit. I heard Fade behind me whisper a word Pirates use to exclaim shock while the figure in front us shifted and turned back toward the room he had appeared from.

"Then follow me, she is this way."

The morning sun was bright and glaring, to some a gracious welcome to a wonderful day. To the men navigating the mighty Protectorate Battleship Maryland though the air, the glare from the blazing ball was a dangerous distraction on an extremely busy day. With her keel laid in 1919 and launched in 1921, the Battleship Maryland was based on the revolutionary British 'Dreadnought' design. The 'Fighting Mary', as she was called, was sleek and fast, powerful and deadly. She carried eight 16" main guns on four separate turrets, more than enough power to fight and down any enemy air ship. Her thick hull was just over 13 inches of steel and armor plating, all gleaming and sparkling in the morning sun as the latest in steam turbines and boiler tech kept her aloft, capable of air speeds no other ship could attain. The Maryland was the pride of the Protectorate Air Fleet and this day her captain meant to prove it.

"What is our altitude con?"

The young officer at the helm checked his gauges and then turned to the captain, who was standing by one of the many windows that circled the bridge. "We're just at 200 feet sir," the officer answered with a snap.

The captain lowered the modified binocs he was using to scan the horizon and looked to his con. "Wings at five degrees up, take us to 250 feet slow with a port turn, come to ninety degrees relative."

"Aye Captain," the officer acknowledged before turning to the crew manning the helm barking out the same orders, "up on the wings five degrees, port turn to ninety degrees relative."

Almost immediately the Maryland began a slow ascent to the higher elevation ordered, the ship swinging and listing into a turn just as slow to the left as it gained altitude, beginning to head west.

"Observation, how are the air lanes?" The captain asked with a loud yell.

A man out on a raised step on the weather deck, the lookout, responded almost before the echo of the captain's request died off. "The air lanes are full this morning captain, with all the air haulers and the personal whips, it's usually very full. Now, with all the Protectorate air ships up and patrolling, the lanes are dangerously close to capacity."

Well damn, that's not good the captain thought. Too many blasted ships were in the air this morning, slow moving air haulers and zeppelins and personal whips crowded the city's sky. The Fighting Mary was the most maneuverable of the Battleships, but even she needed a good bit of room to turn in. The captain yelled out an order to the lookout while also going back to his own observation of the horizon.

"Then keep a close eye out observation, keep the Mary out of trouble."

"Aye sir," the man acknowledged before going back to watching the sky all around the bow and side of the ship.

Why are there so many damn Protectorate ships in the air the captain thought silently? There had to be a complete battle group up in the air over Chicago. Why was there so much fire power up here? The captain couldn't think of an answer so he went back to making sure the Maryland didn't run anyone over during the patrol.

"Are we close to the Magi House yet?"

The question left Alice's mouth just as she appeared from inside the whip and stepped out onto the stern by the big wheel of the helm. She handed the glass of water she was carrying to the colored shaman Sara as her sister Marisol answered with her own question.

"Is it the big building with all the windows?"

Alice was about to answer when the question, the words making up the inquiry, clicked in her mind and she fell silent. There were literally hundreds of tall buildings, 'with all the windows' here in Chicago. Alice mouthed an inaudible response as Sara took pity on her before taking a sip of the water.

"Do not take offense with my sister. She is quite the playful one among us."

"Si," Marisol smiled turning the whip to Port with small spin of the wheel she gripped loosely. The personal air ship swung away from a slow and large zeppelin, giving the dirigible a wide berth. As they passed, a group of children stared at them from the long row of windows of the dining section of the fuselage. Marisol laughed and waved back as she continued. "I have always been the playful one, while Sara is our strength and Ru, our brother, is the thinker."

"Please my sister, our brother Ru is the faithful one." Sara chuckled before taking a second sip of water.

"And what is John, who is he?" Alice asked taking seat on the small bench by the wheel. She had changed while below, her tan pants were tucked in a pair of calf high black leather boots with thick soles. She wore a simple red shirt under a brown lace corset.

Sara smiled and sighed, "he is our North Star."

The simple answer caused Alice to blink for a minute trying to decipher the answer as Marisol added to the response. "Our brother John is our quiet leader, the one we follow even though he never has to ask or order us to."

"Our dear Grandmother, the shaman who raised us, told us we were all equal. She told us on several occasions that one of us was never greater than the rest, that we four were at our most powerful when we were together as one. And yet, from the day when we first started to practice our Grandmother's teachings, we all followed our brother John, as if he were our true North."

"It's easy to see why, with what he did yesterday in saving that Weaver's life, after she had been shot and all. But, why was he at Carlo's? How did he and you know about the Weavers?"

"Ah, ahora hay una pregunta que sólo puede conducir a más preguntas!" Marisol laughed again as she turned the wheel for the helm once more, sending the whip into a course to arrive at the Magi House.

Alice looked at the shaman flying her lover's personal air ship with a confused expression before turning to Sara asking what Marisol had meant. "What other questions?"

The eyebrow on the colored shaman raised just a bit as she smiled her beautiful wise grin. "My sister means your questions has a very simple answer, which you might not believe Alice."

"I watched John heal a bullet wound without any first aid. I think I'll believe whatever you tell me." Alice remarked leaning back from Sara, sitting up just a little taller and straighter.

The move by the young woman wasn't meant to be confrontational even, though one could have seen it that way. The shaman sisters though only nodded before Marisol answered Alice's question. "We made a bargain with the one who bound the Weavers as one, the Magi called Isaac. If we freed the two young senoras from the grasp of that mal hombre, the man who had them, then he would give us some information we needed."

"You knew Isaac before he was killed?" Alice asked leaning back in, intrigued yet again.

"No Alice, we never talked with Isaac while he was alive. We never met with the man at all while he walked this world." Sara spoke before sipping the last of the water Alice had brought her.

The remark made the young woman blink as she responded. "You never talked with Isaac while he was alive?"

"No senora, we never conversed with him while he was alive, but that has never stopped us from speaking with someone once they have crossed over. Once you begin to search for knowledge beyond the borders of this realm, then all the answers to whatever you may ask will lay before you." Marisol stated as she adjusted the wings on the air ship angling the craft into a descent into the city below.

The remark left Alice just a little stunned, and grievously shocked, right to the bone. They can talk with dead people too. They can heal the injured and talk to dead people, and apparently make deals with them as well. Alice looked to Sara who only nodded while smiling noticing the look on the young woman's face immediately.

"We're normal people actually, just blessed with certain extras that some find exceptional."

"I think what you do is more than exceptional," Alice whispered.

"Oh, you have not seen us cook yet." Marisol winked.

"Cook?"

Sara chuckled as her sister gasped and nodded. "Si, when this is all over I will cook us all a meal we will never forget."

They can heal the injured, talk with dead people, and cook a meal fit for a king, that is exceptional, but there was still one thing Alice needed to know. "You said Ezio is in trouble, how bad is it?"

Sara sighed and nodded, the smile on her face still showing and creating a weird calm for the younger woman. "Yes, he has put himself in a serious situation Alice, and I am afraid he is no longer a secret to the ones he pursues."

"Oh no, that means the Cabal he was looking into is after him, and it's because they want the Weavers?"

"Si, he and Miss Camille both." Marisol added.

"They're after Camille as well?" Alice asked with a gasp.

"Yes Alice, her as well. This Cabal, the conspiracy, is larger and more sinister than you or anyone can imagine. The conspirators are hidden deep, embedded in the very bones of the two houses involved, and the ones in charge will go to any length to succeed."

"Two houses, you mean the Magi are working with the Cabal?" Alice gasped a second time, her heart ponding in her throat now. If the Magi were collaborating with the Cabal then this was beyond dangerous, beyond what Ezio could do.

"Yes, which is why we must stop your love before he digs himself any deeper into this conspiracy. He has stepped into a pit of vipers I am afraid, and that is never good senora."

Alice looked to Marisol with fear in her eyes, fear for her Ezio, and she might have let that emotion wash over her entire being if not for a touch to her hand and gentle smile. She looked over to Sara who only nodded and spoke.

"Now do you think we would let anything happen to Ezio or Camille?"

No, Alice thought strangely as she shook her head, I barely know you and yet I trust you would keep my Ezio and me as safe as new born babes.

Part Seven

Lachlann Ceanandach was a tall Scotsman, wide at the shoulders, and as strong as an ox. It was these very traits which landed him the work down in the stockyards, handling the large and heavy sides of beef. On more than one occasion old Lach, as everyone called him, would carry two or three of those large heavy sides across the work floor to the cold rooms, the long awkward carcasses placed across his wide shoulders. Lach was a man among men, no one could work as hard or as long as the blond Scotsman, until the day the accident happened. A faulty piece of steam equipment, something Wally could have fixed in a minute if the foreman on the floor had wanted to stop work to do so. No one stopped working at the stockyards though, you see work never stopped on the floor except when accidents happened, just like what happened to the stout Scotsman. Lach lost his left arm from the elbow down that afternoon in a horrific scene, and just like that, the 'man among men' was no more at the stockyards.

The Scotsman wasn't finished though. He had lost his place and job at the stockyards, but Lach was not done by a long shot. Partly because he was too damn stubborn to give up, but mostly due to his sweet firebrand of a wife who wouldn't let Lach just curl up and stare as life passed by. Caitlin MacCuirc was all of five feet five inches tall, with long brown hair encircling a pretty face with blue eyes. She was as tough minded as she was physically strong, and she had fought too many other lasses back in Scotland to marry and call Lachlann her own. She wasn't about to let the best man in Scotland, nay the entire world in her opinion, just sit down and die.

So, she decided to find the next best man she knew of in this whole damn world, and ask him to help her sweet Lach. It took a bit of time but Cate, as everyone called her, found the man and when she did the fates for Lach turned right around. The greatest Technoist of the time, and a Scotsman by God, saved them both.

"There he is, Wallace you sweet man!" Cate called out as she spotted the engineer enter the small neighborhood grocery store she ran with her husband. She stepped around from behind the counter, her long dress sweeping as she did. Her simple leather corset was a dark brown matching her tan shirt, which was opened at the top to show off the large broch choker Cate always wore.

Wally entered through the wide doors smiling from ear-to-ear practically. To say he was happy to see his fellow Scotsman would be the biggest understatement of 1929. He walked up and into the strong hug of Cate as she laughed and shook him. "Ah, it's good to see you sweet Cate!"

The lady laughed even more and stepped back, looking into her dear friend's eyes with pure joy, "not as good as it is to lay eyes on you Wallace McAndrew."

The pair stood hugging in the center of the store, and gathering place for other Scots who had also found their way to Chicago. In truth, if you asked any of the other highlanders who stopped by the store every night, the establishment run by Cate and Lach was more of a welcomed and needed piece of home for those hearts missing Scotland than it ever was a grocery. Even as the two embraced like brother and sister, others in the store who were hanging about spotted Wally and cried out.

"Ho, Wallace!" A young man yelped before running over.

And soon it seemed everyone not shopping, which was almost the entire occupancy of the store, was around Wallace and Cate. Some clapped the renowned Technoist on the shoulder while others, the ladies, leaned in kissed his cheek taking care not to ruffle the thick sideburns. Wally nodded and smiled, greeted each hail with an equal enthusiasm, but really the engineer wasn't in his favorite element. He hated being surrounded by people, being crowded in. He had never fully recovered from what the Felton's had done to him, and Wally doubted he ever would be the same man again. Still, he didn't have the heart to hurt his friends, and fellow Scotsmen, so Wally moved among them with a large warm smile till a deep voice cut through the crowd.

"Wallace McAndrew, you no good foul smelling dobber!"

The crowd parted, not out of fear but anticipation, letting Wally get a glimpse of the large Scotsman dressed in work clothes much like his own, standing all alone. He was tall, wide at the shoulders, and his left arm and hand was a metallic piece of wonder. Gears and thin round shafts of metal, forged and mated as one, formed a near perfect appendage and shined in the morning light. Cate stepped a single small move away as Wally smiled and shook his head.

"Well you would certainly know Lachlann Ceanandach, seeing as you've been one your entire life."

The remark might have sounded nasty, but it was never meant to hurt, and Cate couldn't help but let out a loud cackle of joy as her handsome husband rushed over and literally scooped Wally off the ground and into his large arms. Everyone joined in on the happy mood adding their laughs as the two men hugged, well, it was actually more like Lach shook and poor Wally just held on for his live. It might have turned nasty if not for Cate stepping up and slapping her husband across his bicep playfully. "Let him down Lach! Let the man take a breath for glory be!"

Lach was quick to follow his wife's command, dropping the Technoist to his feet where the man gasped for breath. The large Scotsmen laughed and slapped Wally on the back, "are you getting a little soft there McAndrew?"

"Trust me Lach, if there was anything soft on me you just popped it!" Wally chuckled before turning back to Cate who was beaming with pride at the two men. "You know, your husband squeezed me damn near to death's door right now."

"And he'd have fought the devil himself to bring you back to us Wallace!" She laughed as the crowd around trio watched happily.

"Ah, I know he would Cate," Wally chuckled still before turning to Lach, "how's the hand working?"

Lach held up his metal hand smiling, "it's been doing fine thank you for asking."

"Oh no it hasn't, and don't you be telling him otherwise husband of mine. That thing has been clenching down so hard on things around here it's a wonder everything isn't broken or crushed." Cate spoke up suddenly, her eyes filled with a seriousness that made the crowd take notice. Cate was known for her jovial personality, but her serious side was even more famous it seemed as some chuckled and stepped back.

Wally laughed and looked to Lach," oh you married a feisty one here boy, pure fire."

"I know, and I love her for it." Lach chuckled as Wally pulled a screwdriver from his pocket, getting ready to adjust the gears on his dear friend's metal hand.

"Now you girls just go ahead and get out of those coveralls this instant and let papa and I take care of getting you dressed properly. Oh, and please do not worry, you may leave the collars in place."

Wells and Boles both stood in the center a large circular changing area in the back of the shop, complete with a long hanging drape from poles and a rolling step ladder with a platform at it's very top. Wells smiled as she started to undress, the image of the small man and woman standing there looking eye to eye with her made the Weaver happy, and quite comfortable, as she pulled the shirt over her head. Boles was doing the same as Inga giggled and moved the small ladder between them preparing to take measurements.

"And do not worry if I yell, papa is outside the drapes writing down what I tell him and I want to make sure he hears everything."

"It'll be fine," Wells smiled as she slid out of Wally's coveralls letting the garment fall to the floor. She stood perfectly calm without a stitch of clothing, as did Boles, and the situation wasn't one Inga was used to as she began to blush. The little lady smiled, embarrassed just a bit, and called out as kind as she could. "Oh, well, we will need some underthings papa, for both girls!"

"You can just add it to the bill Mouse." Wahkan remarked as he took a bite of the apple he had bought earlier.

"Ah, please my friend, there will be no bill." Mouse smiled as he prepared to write down the measurements his wife called out in a large book on the counter he stood at.

"No, there will be no bill, especially not for our John." Inga added quickly, getting herself back in a state of control as the Weavers slipped into a pair of robes set aside for them. She wasn't used to having her clients be so comfortable in all their 'altogether', and she was welcomed to have that 'altogether' now covered. Yet, as Boles slid her robe up over her shoulders, the little lady caught sight of a strange mark on the Weaver's skin just at the blade. "What is that, it looks like a brand?"

The question instantly embarrassed Inga even more, to be so forward and intrusive had never been her nature, and yet when she saw the mark it brought an instant response. For her part, Boles only smiled a meek grin and spoke softly. "My second Magi, he wanted to ensure everyone knew who his Weaver was. He wanted to make sure there was no mistake."

"He, burned you?" Inga whispered low.

"Yes, it's what you do when you want to make sure your property isn't stolen he told her just before..." Wells added, and when Inga turned to her with her mouth agape, the Weaver only continued with a sac expression. "It's the life of a Weaver and nothing will change this."

The mood in the changing room instantly went cold as Inga was left speechless for a moment. She had heard of the dark days of slavery here in the United States, when branding your 'property' was common place, but to see an actual marking of the skin, well that was so much more than a story. Outside the drapes, being free from the sight of the mark wasn't enough to be free of the audacity of such a thing. The Mouse turned to Wahkan with a look of horror on his face. "They put a brand on her, that pretty girl?"

"Unfortunately, Mouse, some people are born with holes in their hearts and never see the damage they cause." Wahkan replied before turning to look out the doors to the street outside.

"Ja, I have met men like that before, and I have felt sick for it." The Mouse whispered before turning back to his book, writing down the numbers his beautiful wife called to him.

Part Eight

The pilot guided his Curtiss P-6 Hawk with a slight push of the right pedal and turn of the stick back toward the city. They, he and his wingman, had been up all morning just circling the skies above Chicago trying to, simultaneously, avoid hitting another air ship or plane in the crowded air space while also trying to think about some old Chinese air ship, a 'Junk' it was called. Truth be told, he wasn't really thinking about that, whatever the air ship was called, while flying up here among the clouds. The pilot was too busy keeping track of every other thing he had to while airborne, the most important was the new P-6 Hawk. It was fresh from the technoist and engineers at the Protectorate, barely any testing time put into the design or performance. He and his wingman were handed the keys just two days ago, this flight this morning was only the fourth for him in the plane. The P-6 was far more advanced with the engine upgrades, with the precision handling, and add to that the steam tech and you had a beast ready to break its chain. He could tell. He was holding the P-6 back, making sure he didn't lose control in midair and slam this bright new beauty into a building.

The pilot finished his turn and checked his gauges to ensure everything was in the green. Seriously, how was he supposed to think of a, 'Junk' wasn't it, when he was too busy keeping this plane-

"Able6, this is Able7, I lost my pic of the, what was it called again?"

And there was another reason he couldn't keep his attention focused on any one thing, his wingman. Then man was truly beginning to step all over his last nerve as he spoke back into his Hertzian wireless. "It's called a 'Junk' and how did you lose the damn drawing?"

"I don't know, maybe it flew out of the cockpit on takeoff?"

Well, that could have happened. The Curtiss P-6 was an open cockpit Bi-Plane and the damn thing was so powerful that on takeoff anything not held in place or pinned down just might fly out. "You can get a new one when we land for fuel next time."

"Roger, going to fall back and trail. The sky is too full of civilian aircraft this morning to fly in formation."

"Roger that," the pilot responded as the matching Curtiss began to drift back leaving him alone, somewhat. The pilot had to agree, grudgingly, there were way too many whips and air haulers and blimps up this morning.

Just another thing I have to keep in mind the pilot sighed with a shake of his head. His long white scarf whipped behind him as his goggles with darkened lenses held back the morning sun light.

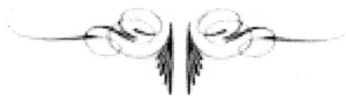

Nidhogg...

The Great Serpent...

The Eater of the Middle World...

The ancient God once claimed a vast and dominating presence in the Lower Worlds, so many domains did it touch one could count for a lifetime and never see the end of Nidhogg's reach. Shamans, and the others who journeyed in the old days, stayed clear of these realms, avoided the Nidhogg's presence when crossing into the Lower Worlds. The Great Serpent is a devourer, an eater of light, and any one straying too close would be captured and their life force drained to feed Nidhogg. Some say it was this insatiable hunger which brought about the prophecy, the curse on the Great Serpent. The Eater of the Middle World would finally be consumed itself, by the Four Winds from the Silver Mountain, from the Middle World.

Nidhogg would not go without a fight though, no, it had decided once the words of the prophecy were spread it would fight. The Great Serpent sent its agents to the Middle World to destroy the Four Winds, to rid this threat to its existence. It watched with fury as its most devout followers failed at each turn, each of the small babes slipping from its grasp, as if protected by some unseen force, and when the four disappeared from its sight all together, Nidhogg enacted a last plan. It drew in all its power and influence from all the domains it touched, it's very reach, to a single hidden realm in the Lower World. The Great Serpent pulled in its vast number of shadows to one domain of the purest, deepest dark, and there it stayed and waited, secreted from the Middle World. Quietly it watched, year after year, from its sanctuary of night, for any sign of the four babes, until just a few days ago when a single shade came to tell the Great Serpent it knew where one of the Winds would be. The shade would end this affront to Nidhogg it claimed. It would end the threat to the Great Serpent, only just as before, as always it seemed, the Winds were protected by something...or someone.

Where is the white hair?

The Great Serpent's voice boomed from the blanket of the dark that enveloped its realm. The force from each word hurting the one who had been summoned for an audience. The being who used Frank's body like a puppet floated in this dark, its incorporeal form shifting and spreading like oil in water with the blast of Nidhogg's thoughts, that was if one could see anything here in Nidhogg's world. This realm was nothing more than a void, a fathomless pit from which the Great Serpent existed.

"He has gone to a meeting with someone. I followed him my Great One, right to the building where he now resides." The shade replied, more with thought than spoken word.

He is supposed to be dead! You were supposed to destroy him! It is why you poisoned the South Wind, to bring forth the North Wind, the most important one!

"I know Great One, the intent of poisoning the South Wind was to bring the North out of his hiding, and it has worked! I know where he is and I will destroy him Great One. I will protect you as you have protected me!"

There was no answer for a long moment, just the dark which made seemed to smother any sound. The realm of the Great Serpent seemed to deaden any noise, just as it drained the light from those approaching too close, the dark stifled any sound or noise. Then Nidhogg was speaking again and the force of the words struck the shade like being punched.

Do not fail me my underling. Do not fail in destroying the white hair, the North Wind, for if you do the punishment will be beyond any pain you may imagine.

And then it was over, with a snap, the shade was back in Frank's body and both were standing in an alley just across and down the street from the building the North Wind had gone into. The shade shook as the last words from Nidhogg yelled coldly in its mind.

"No Great One, I will not fail you. I will destroy the white hair and I will protect you!" Frank hissed as he stepped out of the alley.

With careful steps the shade, and Frank with it, made their way to the building John had gone into. It was going to kill the shaman, it had no choice, and even if it did the shade would not dare to disappoint the Great One

No, it could never do that.

Part Nine

The abandoned building looked just like it had the day before I assumed, dirty and dashed, but then there was something that was missing from that notion. There is something every discarded and condemned building has, something that gives it that thrashed quality, which was missing from this one. I looked around trying to put my finger on it, and after following the oddly over-aged man-servant for a few feet down the hall toward the last door on the left, I derived that precise missing element. There was no trash on the floor, not a pile or a scrap or even a small piece of paper. The floor had been cleaned, as if someone had plans on using the dilapidated structure for a high-society party. Would the rich have those kinds of parties on this side of town I thought to myself? Whoever was here might be considering one from the way the floor looked. Odd though, pick up all the trash on the floor and leave a broken door and torn walls.

"Can you help Madame?" The servant asked as he walked through the last door, disappearing from my sight momentarily.

"I do not know what happened to Madame, or who Madame even is, so I'm not sure if I can help her until I meet her." I replied, following slowly while keeping my eyes open and sharp. Behind me Fade followed close, had her hand on my back as we walked. She sensed the same 'out of the ordinary' feeling I had. I could tell because she was busy biting her bottom lip, something she did when confronted with this type of situation,

something just slightly out of her control.

I turned back to the front in time to see the servant had picked up his pace and was well in front of me now. When I made the turn through the portal he was already at the end of another long hall. There were a set of doors on either side of this hall, right in the middle, but the man was waiting on me at the end of the passage by the last door again, on the left even. Whoever Madame was, she insisted on always staying at the end of the hall and always having clean floors. I walked down the hall, pausing at the doors in the middle to peer in, to make sure no one or anything was planning on trying to surprise me, and when I was sure I was safe I moved on cautiously. Fade did the same, her sharp eyes peering into each hazy room, scanning for any sign of an attacker in wait. She caught up as I reached the end of the hall, and the man servant who had waited so patiently for me. As decrepit and frail as the man looked, he moved surprisingly spry. He simply gestured for me to enter the door to his right, my left. If this was a trap, I was not feeling the cold press of impending danger or doom on my energy. I took a quick look inside the room from the doorway. My eyes caught sight of a girl of maybe seven years old sitting at a small table in small chair, facing the door, in the center of a room which was illuminated by candles all along the walls, numbering well into the hundreds. I turned back to the servant and his sunken eyes. His face, now in the low candle light, looked as dried as old parchment paper, like he was maybe four hundred or a thousand years old. HIs voice though made him sound like he was just out of his twenties.

"Is this Madame?" I asked.

With a cold stare from even colder eyes, and with a voice that sounded out of place in that old body, the servant answered, "Yes."

I stared at him for a second with a raised eyebrow. Why I'm not sure, maybe it was the feeling in the small room I was noting, a strange hint of betrayal. I had a thought as to the man's predicament, what had caused this contradiction in his appearance and body, but I kept my notion to myself. I turned back to look into the room realizing my answer lied with the 'Madame'. Whatever had happened to the servant had happened to her, and he was more than likely just an innocent who was caught up in a bad decision, the Madame's bad decision. As I entered the room the little girl didn't move or look up to greet me, instead choosing to sit at the table and draw on a pad with pastels and charcoal. I noticed now she looked small, even for a child, her legs and arms maybe half the size of a normal child of the same age. Fade suddenly reached up and grabbed my arm, squeezing the bicep, and I knew my lover was warning me. Fade wanted nothing of this room, of this place, and she was probably right. Still, I could no longer walk away, not yet at least, and as such I entered into this 'meeting'.

The Madame wore the clothes of one of the many orphans running the street or living in one of the many orphanages. A worn skirt half covered by a ragged grey apron and a white shirt which was more yellow than white was all she had to wear I suspected. I walked up slowly as the heat from the candles swirled in the room, and on the waves, was the smell of exotic sandalwood and lingering jasmine, a heavy hypnotic smell, along with other herbs. I knew this combination of incense, the purpose one used it for. I looked over the room a little more carefully and spotted a large circle of salt in front of the small table where the Madame sat. Inside the circle was an easily recognizable star with five points, the top pointed toward the Madame. All of it, the candles and incense and sigil drawn in salt, only helped to confirm what I had suspected had happened last night.

Well Laken, I thought to myself, I see now why this had to be so secretive.

The little girl kept sketching with her charcoal ignoring me, her head down, as if refusing to acknowledge my presence. I stood quietly refusing to speak as well. This was not my meeting. I came at a request, an invitation, which held me to no obligation to act. This may seem cruel to some, but a necessity in my life and my way. Only one who is willing to cross the bridge may seek your help my teacher told me several times, and right now at this moment, it held more truth then it ever had in the past.

"I see Laken found you." The little girl said in a voice that was as far removed from the age of seven as I was.

"Yes, they found me and passed on your note," was all I replied with, no emotion in my voice.

She still refused to look up as she continued to speak. "I knew you would come to see me Mr. Greywolf."

"How were you so sure he'd come here?" Fade asked looking around the room with cautious eyes, an expression of loathing on her face. She detested this place and Fade wasn't trying to hide it.

I let my lover's response be mine as well while noticing there was a second room through a closed doorway to the west. I wondered what was beyond that closed door. I knew it wasn't someone waiting to ambush me and Fade. One look at the man servant and the Madame and I could tell they needed my skills too much to try and kill me.

"Why are you here Miss Fade, Sky Pirate Captain?" The Madame spoke, still refusing to look up from her drawing.

"Where John goes I go," Fade answered quickly with an

inescapable hint of defiance to her voice as her eyes bore down on the head of the little girl, "and from what I see you're in no condition to 'ask' me to leave his side."

I continued to stare at the door which led west as the two women played their game of 'who-was-in-control', seeing which one would blink first. I looked around the room again, trying to discern what magic was being called on as Madame was the first to break in the contest of wills, or maybe she just felt the sudden need to answer Fade's question, though I doubt it.

"A man of Mr. Greywolf's honorable reputation would only allow himself one choice when an innocent soul is involved."

I had to grin at her attempt to stroke my ego as I spoke, "I can tell by all the magical components, and the lingering energy in the room, there was more to this evening than a simple rite-"

"I was simply dabbling." She responded quickly, cutting in between my words with a sharp tongue and the air of someone who had simply made a bad mistake and was now being punished far too harshly. Anyone with the training of reading people like I had, truly seeing them, could have seen through the statement, like a clear piece of glass.

"-into a world which you have no experience to walk." I finished with a hard tone, narrowing my eyes while looking at the west door again. Now I trusted what I had assumed had truly happened here, what was supposed to happen but obviously did not, and I felt a sudden sense of rage.

The sounds of her charcoal ceasing to move lasted for what seemed a minute before the small stick was slowly, purposefully, laid down on the paper she was working on. "I was tricked Mr. Greywolf, fooled into losing my very life essence," she said in the same entitled voice.

"And you wish for me to reverse what has happened?"

"I wish to be returned to my true and proper form."

"Then I have stipulations for my help, Madame."

"I know Mr. Greywolf, I am willing to cross your bridge. I am asking for your help Medicine Man."

The words, the term at the end, made me look down to her with a snap. Hearing another voice speak the same phrase I had just remembered my teacher telling me so long ago threw me for a moment, and then I saw she was looking up at me finally. Her face looked older then the servants, so much older. As if something from a dark realm had stolen a hundred years more off of her life than his.

"By all that is great and good, what the hell happened to her John?" I heard Fade whisper with surprise. She had seen much in her life as a Pirate, the endless blue sky above the clouds on a fresh morning to escaping certain death from battle, and even a form of reawakening from her friendship to Camille, but Fade had never come across something like this before in her travels. The withered skin of the little girl's face only added more tension to the 'strange' feeling Fade was experiencing. Her breathing was quick now, fast and strained.

"I told you. I was dabbling, and now I need your help." The Madame stated, blinking slow. She was obviously a calm and collected person in everyday life, not one to be shaken by a little trouble, like being a walking corpse.

"What's your true name?" I asked quickly, for no other reason than to wrest away the control the Madame had over the room.

The little girl turned away from Fade and sighed, "I was told you *would not ask for real names."*

"Laken does not set the rules here, I do, and I want to know your true name." I stated coldly while stepping closer to the west door, the same one which held my curiosity so tightly now. When the Madame didn't respond I shook my head, "I will only help you when truth is applied to this meeting. To cross my bridge, one must be true and honest, there can be no healing without both."

The little girl turned in the chair, not like a child of seven would do, but just like a woman of say fifty would. She kept her legs close together under the skirt, shifting only enough to point her knees in my direction, but never letting a fold on her clothes slip out of place. Then, with that same strange maturity so out of place here, the girl put her hands together in her lap looking as prim and proper as an English lady. Only the hiss of her voice as she spoke next assured me she was not very much of an English lady at the moment.

"Fine, Mr. Greywolf, my real name is Abagail Grouse. Is that enough 'truth' to garner your help?"

"May the devil take us all," I heard Fade whisper as the Madame only stared back at me. She knew the name just as well as I knew it, anyone in Chicago knew the name.

Miss Abagail Grouse was a known 'obtainer' of historic artifacts and a valued patron, or provider, for a list of Museums. She was also a dabbler in the dark side of the arcane it seems. No one was sure what country she was born to, and her only home was a large expensive airship docked just outside of town in a single large warehouse surrounded by an army of very large guards. On board said airship were said to be artifacts and treasures that would astound even the most experienced archaeologist. The money Abigail gave out seemed to have no end, and where it started was just as much a mystery as where she was born. She used her money to gain access to places, people, and all of it to further her own gain and ends. Abigail accepted nothing but 'yes' to her offers and woe to the poor soul who stepped in her way.

"It will, but I also need to know who you were communing with last evening when all of this happened?" I asked letting a grin slide across my face as I inched toward the closed door, my eyes staying with Abagail's to keep her attention.

"He never gave me his name, not a real one at least." The Madame answered, her eyes locked to mine. I made a mental note Fade had taken up a position between myself and the man servant. She had obviously sensed my intentions and was setting herself up to block the old man, or the young man who now had an old body, take your pick as to which.

"I doubt it would have given you its real name Miss Grouse." I remarked while acting as if the pentagram circle on the floor held my curiosity now as I looked down, all the while sliding up to that door. And quite accidentally, in the middle of my ruse, I saw where everything had gone wrong for Miss Grouse. It was a simple mistake in the construction of that sigil which would cost her everything by the time the sun would set this very day.

Across the room the man servant took a step toward me, his senses beginning to alert him of my plan. "Why does that matter to the Madame's condition?" He asked just as Fade stepped in front of him to block his path to me.

"Simple, beings from the Other Worlds are ruled by their true names. For someone to speak the name, properly, means the being would be under their control for a short amount of time." I said while looking at the man with a smile before turning to back to Abagail, the grin gone now as I let my anger roll forward in my presence just a bit. "What you attempted last night, the dark magic you tried to release, cannot be done without aid from certain special beings, Abagail. Who was it from the Other Worlds, who were you calling on for help with the rite?"

"I told you Mr. Greywolf, I was dabbling and that is all I was doing last night."

It would take more than anything this world could produce, a punishment harsher than anyone had ever seen, to get Abagail Grouse to admit complicity in her own predicament. She was like the hardened steel Wally made my knife and Fade's sword from, unwilling to break or bend, even when the truth was stronger than her will. Miss Grouse would never admit her fault in this, and it was pure delusion that caused this way about her I thought then. Now, I see it was pure stubbornness, but frankly I was done with it, whatever the name. I stared at her for a moment then turned and walked the last step to the closed door and opened it. I heard the man servant call out in a useless attempt to stop me.

"Sir, you cannot-!"

The low light from the candles of the main room barely illuminated the one beyond the door, but it was enough to still see what I had been assuming this whole time. What looked like a bed, a cot really, was setup inside in the middle of the small room, and on it resting easily, was a lady maybe a year or two older then myself. The woman looked as if she had passed to the other side, her body was perfectly still, not even the rise and fall of her chest from breathing, but looks can be very deceiving when it comes to dark magic. She was dressed in a long black skirt with leather boots, matching shirt, and a purple corset. Her hair was a dark brown, long, and touched with grey here and there and everywhere. She was quite beautiful on the outside, and to Abagail it was worth any amount to keep, even death.

"What is it John?" I heard Fade ask and the sound of her voice made me turn back to the main room.

"It's Abagail's true body." I answered simply while stepping back toward the little girl at the table.

Fade's eyes narrowed at the answer and she immediately moved toward the room to take a look. I was about to tell her not to disturb the salt lines of the sigil on the floor, but then with her acute awareness, the Sky Pirate easily dodged every flake of salt with precise steps. I waited quietly as she looked in the room. I noted Abagail never flinched once during this discovery. I assume she knew we would find her body and she had prepared for this very outcome. Abagail was smart, she knew what to say and when to say it. I had to watch my step here I thought, the request of my aid looked genuine on the surface, but then I always look deeper when it comes to helping people.

"Who is the child you now inhabit, Abagail?" I asked as I heard Fade behind me whisper another colorful curse at the sight of the woman lying on the cot in the room. My guess, the 'strangeness' of this meeting was still prickling my lover.

"She is a waif, a street urchin with no future, especially being as small as she was. No one is going to miss her Mr. Greywolf." She replied with a small shrug of her shoulders.

As soon as the words were out of Abagail's mouth, the intention of what was said, Fade popped back into the room with a roar. "Wait! You were going to end a young girl's life?"

"In a way, yes Fade. Miss Grouse, here, was going to end the life of an innocent child, one whose only crime was to be 'too small' it seems."

My answer wasn't meant to ease the anger or the shock Fade was feeling. I wanted her to know exactly what was supposed to happen last night, what should have happened, and when Abagail refused to explain I did. "Miss Grouse intended to absorb the child's life, take it and meld it with her own so she may live longer, only the tables were turned on her I think."

"I was lied too! I was betrayed and robbed!" Abagail hissed again, the veneer of control she liked to display finally cracking.

"You tried to kill a CHILD! You deserve to die!" Fade growled, her hand going for the hilt of her knife, by the handle of the long gun she wore in the large sash across her midsection.

She might have acted on her anger, and maybe Fade would have been justified, but with rage comes blindness and my lover had yet to see everything clearly. I reached down and grabbed her hand while speaking with peace and calm to her. Just like the day before, when I eased Wahkan's rage at the sight of Boles and Wells being treated so harshly, I used my voice to bring Fade back from the edge of the canyon you might say. "Easy my heart, we can't harm Miss Grouse."

"And why not?" Fade growled again, turning her head to look at me. I could see bloodlust there, and I must admit letting her hand go crossed my mind for a split second.

"Because, her body is in the other room. This person here, this is the child she meant to take in the rite."

"What?" Fade asked blinking abruptly, the anger in her voice and body ebbing as my words took hold. She was beginning to see what I had put together, that Miss Grouse had somehow been 'transferred' into the body of the child.

I smiled again as I felt her getting control of her emotions before turning back to Abagail. "From ancient times on there have been stories and myths passed down about those who have tried to cheat growing old, that long walk toward death we all must make. Tales told about countesses bathing in the blood of virgins to retain their beauty, of warriors drinking the blood of the ones they have conquered to ingest their vitality and courage. What you did last night Abagail, it's nothing new to this world, just a different form of the same foolish vanity. You thought you would hold back time, save yourself from that which we all must face, and in the end only found...old age."

"Yes, this was a very large setback, which is why I used my considerable influence with Malus to bring you here to help me Mr. Greywolf."

"You're a monster, why would John even consider helping you?" Fade snapped. She hadn't quite reigned in all of her emotion I noticed, and Abagail wasn't one to just let a slight or insult pass.

"You have no right to judge me, not someone such as you Fade the Sky Pirate! You've killed how many men and women in pursuit of what, some silly notion of freedom from the rule of law?" Abagail fired back, like a broadside from Fade's own air ship The Crescent Moon. The blow was sharp and harsh, but Fade has never stepped away from an argument or a fight.

"I've never taken a life which didn't deserve to be taken, in either self-defense of my own skin or a member of my crew. You tried to kill a child!" Fade spit with disgust.

"An orphan," Abagail hissed coldly, cocking her head just slightly to the right before carrying on, "who lost her future when her parents abandoned her to the streets. I wonder, how many orphans have you created with your pistol or sword Captain Fade? How many children have been left to fend for themselves in this world after one of your raids?"

The room went silent as I watched both of the women finish trying to bludgeon each other with their words. In all the animosity, both failed to see the simplest of things, the fact I still had no choice.

'It doesn't matter, if you are a monster or not Abagail, because in the end I have to rescue you to rescue the young girl you condemned by your actions." I said loud enough to bring both of the ladies' attention to me. As they stood staring at me I shook my head and continued on. "Whatever being you were communing with played you for a fool Abagail. It took the girl's soul, along with your life essence, and disappeared back to the Other Worlds to hide, but not before switching you into the child's body. So, now that we know where we stand, I think it is time to tell me the name of the being you were communing with, Abagail?"

""I see you're as smart as they say Mr. Greywolf, astute and good looking." The Madame said with a sudden wicked smile.

"I do a lot of push-ups." I replied letting the flirtations end right there, my face blank and emotionless. I wanted her to confirm my suspicions, and only that. "What is the name, Madame?"

The room stayed silent for a minute before the Madame sighed and spoke low. "The being was called Malfeus."

That name, Malfeus, I knew it too well, like a dreaded whisper from the past touching my ears. Of all the dark entities, evil beings, she could have been working with, this one was the harshest. Malfeus was pure malignance formed into a being of dark shadow, a feeder of the last bits of energy and the memories of those who were sent to his realm, to be 'cleansed' as they crossed over. Malfeus was one of the Grand Nightmare's, one of the original thirteen Nightshades who had no use for the living except to devour their energy when it suited his appetite. Coming here, to this realm to bargain with the living, that was not his usual method. The Nightshades can only influence as well, direct humans with subtle suggestions, which meant Malfeus could only hint to Abagail about the rite, never perform in or tell her how to do the ritual. This would never do for The Reaper, because if he could only watch and never touch, then Malfeus would be too bored to even talk with Abigail. And anyway, the dark one had a field to feed from on the other plane, easy prey for him, so why come to this place and play out a game with someone who was obviously less than skilled at magic, an unworthy challenge? There was something amiss here, a lie inside another lie maybe?

"But Malfeus wasn't the one who told you what was needed for the rite, what to say or do?"

"No, he was not. An Alchemist who I was pointed to after a delicate and secretive questioning of someone, who I will leave nameless here for certain reasons, told me what to do. And he simply steered me to an old tome in a far-off land. He told me if I was truly set in my intention to see this though then the instructions for the rite are written in the pages. All I had to do, he said, was to follow the instructions and my wish to remain young would be granted. I know now though it was all a deception, a machination to steal my very life!"

It must have been easy for Malfeus, if it was the Nightshade, to trick poor Abagail Grouse into going through with her plan. She was no sorceress or Magi or even a magician with the knowledge of card tricks, and she hardly had the morality to use magic. Yet, what she lacked in ability, Abigail made up with in sheer will and tenacity. If she had to court one of the darkest of malevolent entities to obtain some power then so be it, price was of little consequence to the end prize.

"Well then, we have the truth finally. I will help you Abagail Grouse, if you agree to my terms."

"Terms?" Abagail yelped, her head and back straightening with the incredulity she suddenly felt.

"Yes, I agreed to help and for my services I wish to be paid. Being a business woman, I thought you would understand this?" My last was pushing it, and I knew this, but I wanted Abigail to feel a little more than just the discomfort of having to ask for help.

The smile from a moment ago, was gone now as I saw the Madame sour instantly, her face scrunching inward as she replied. "And what are your terms, Mr. Greywolf?"

"The orphan girl leaves with me after I'm done, unharmed and free of all your intentions."

"Is that it? No monetary amount for compensation of your service? No 'favor' to hold over my head?" Abigail smiled suddenly, as if the last few minutes had not happened, as if she was winning in this agreement between us or her predicament was just a small thing to overcome.

"I have no need of your money or favor Miss Grouse, and it's not your soul I must go and retrieve, is it?" I asked, hinting I was being forced into action here.

And Abagail seemed to accept what I had said as she just nodded. "Oh, I understand fully and agree Mr. Greywolf, now what do you need of me?"

"The powder you made the circle from, do you have more?"

She looked to Michael her servant and nodded. The man reached into his pocket and pulled out a leather pouch, which he tossed to me. The throw looked like it took all of the servant's strength and the distance the pouch flew was just a few feet. This didn't concern me as much as the power emanating from the pouch when it touched my hand. It felt light, it felt weak and limited, not even strong enough to hold back a simple ghost. It was good I brought along some of my own dust to add to this one I thought while reaching into the vest pocket to produce a second leather pouch. As I mixed the contents of the leather pouch the servant gave me with the one I brought I spoke to Abigail. I wanted it to look like I needed to know what she had said during the rite, what Malfeus had directed her to say with that tome he placed in her path so nice and conveniently. In truth, I just needed a distraction.

"What did Malfeus have you say during the rite? Where is the book you read from?"

She only pointed to yet another desk where three large circular candles burned, on it sat a large book that from a distance looked rather old and worn. When I picked it up though, nothing about the tome felt old or worn, even calling it 'just off' in a way could not explain what I was sensing. I had hoped Fade would recognize the move for what it was, a chance to get her away from Abagail to speak confidentially, and as sure as the sun was going to rise, she walked over as I began to turn the pages in the book.

"What does it say, anything helpful?" She asked in a low whisper between us.

"I don't know," I whispered back still turning pages, "the words are from a language I've never seen before, maybe some kind of Sanskrit."

There wasn't a need to look over my shoulder at Fade to know there was a look of shock on the face of my companion. The tone of her voice was enough to tell me she was taken back just a bit. "Then why did you ask to see the book?"

"I didn't know it would be written in some language I had never seen before, and I was curious anyway." I whispered back with a smile finally looking up to see Fade had started a smile as well. I felt a bit of relief as I continued on. "Did you sense we were followed from Twylah's to here?"

She nodded, still smiling and carrying on the ruse for Abagail and her man servant. "Yes, but the man stayed in the shadows so I was never able to see who was following."

"I never saw him either, but I am sure the one we sensed was the man who poisoned my sister Sara. You will need to be extra careful while I journey."

"I will,' she pledged.

"Also, when the child's soul is retrieved and safe, we will need to take her to Mouse and Inga." I added.

"Why?"

"Simple," I shrugged, "what better loving parents are there than those two, and the child is a dwarf like them? It is a perfect match."

Fade only nodded. She understood, she would be my guard, my protector, but she wasn't ready to end our conversation. Before I could think, she leaned in and kissed me sweetly leaving words in a loving whisper as she pulled away. "Be careful John, wherever it is you need to go, please. Come back here to me in one piece."

"I promise Fade, my heart. I will come back."

And with the promise between use set, I turned back to Abagail and the sigil on the floor. "How did your servant end up like you?" I asked as I walked to a part of the pentagram where the third corner met the circle, or should have. There was a noticeable gap where the three lines should have overlapped and touched but did not. It was an opening, a small one, but enough to allow Malfeus or whatever to slip free of the prison Abagail had tried to construct.

"Michael stepped in, like any well-trained servant, when he saw my obvious distress. Malfeus did not like the interruption, and thus, my dear servant was attacked as well.".

I poured the mixture of crushed crystal and salt out to connect the lines as my mind whirled with thought. This was most definitely not the work of Malfeus I told myself silently. The shade would not have left either of them alive, and for trying to stop the spell, Michael would have suffered like none before. No, this was something else entirely I told myself as Abigail watched my every move intently.

When I was done I stood and walked over to the side, over by the small table so I could prepare for my journey. As I did I was peppered by a last set of questions.

"How do I get my life essence back, my body too?" Abagail asked quickly, and it wasn't hard to miss the fact she had no concern for her servant or the girl.

"I am going to journey and retrieve the girl's soul. Once that is done you should return to normal." I replied taking a seat in a normal sized chair just out of reach of the small table. From the arrangement of the furniture, I assume Abagail's plan was to keep the child busy with coloring while she stole the girl's life.

"Will that help us?" she asked, the first time I heard concern in her voice that night.

"I can't say for sure, but it is the only choice you have at the moment." I answered getting comfortable in the chair.

"I am not fully vested in this plan of yours Mr. Greywolf."

"Your concern doesn't matter right now Miss Grouse. Trust in me and my plan is all you have now Abigail, all which is left so maybe you should get comfortable. The wait will hopefully be short."

I started to control my breathing, focusing on my heart rate. I used the teachings of my teacher and my path to begin to concentrate on the necessary steps to journey to the other plane. I closed my eyes and let the darkness cover me. As I did, as the world around me began to fade away, I gave one last command to Abigail.

"If something appears in the sigil, leave it be. And under no circumstance, do not make a bargain with it Abagail."

I am sure she had a caustic reply to my last, but I had slipped from the room by the time Abagail spoke. I was no longer in the Middle World, but on my way to the One Tree.

Part Ten

The inside of the tunnel instantly reminded Ezio of the subways back home in Manhattan, the BMT and the IRT, both which ran to certain parts and sections of New York's underground transit system. He noticed the arched ceilings with intricate iron and stone work, the walls were part stone from the floor up, and then white marble tile taking over from one's midsection to rise to the ceiling overhead. Ezio looked up to the electric lighting, a soft yellow which soothed one's soul, and thought about home, about Alice. He missed his lover, his precious one, and for a moment the tall Umbra felt his heart hurt. The thought of his sweet Alice flying away this morning brought a fresh pang of wanting, only eased as he thought she was at least safe from what was to come. Ezio sighed and continued to wait with his friend Daniel, waiting for someone to open the doors which led to hidden stairs, and the secret way into the Magi House here in Chicago. The tall Magi looked to his right, to of all things a message board hanging on the wall. Why would a secretive escape tunnel have such a thing he thought? Was someone, in full flight, going to stop and take time to read anything posted here? A secret tunnel was just that, a quick way to egress from the House above, not a library where you stopped to catch up on the local news.

"You know Ezio, I hate meeting like this, takes away from any 'cordial' feeling I could offer."

"Why is there a message board down here Dan?" The tall Umbra asked, ignoring the last remark. Ezio understood the chance his friend was taking, even more now that he was being hunted by the Cabal and its people. Still, he just had to know about the message board.

The question brought the smaller man, dressed in a very nice coat with tails, face to face Ezio. He was obviously older with his blond-grey hair was held firmly in place, a stylish cut, by pomade. "The Umbra use the tunnel here from time to time to leave the House unnoticed. Most of the messages down here are for them, for what I can only assume are operations they are conducting."

Daniel's accent was pure Maine, and it made Ezio smile. He read the first note and sure enough it was a directive to all Umbra to be aware of a certain establishment where a woman from Europe sold things and held rituals, someone named Twylah. Ezio turned to his friend and chuckled. "We do the same in the House in Manhattan, just with notes passed through the front desk."

"Doesn't that drive the clerk mad?" Dan asked back with a shake of his head.

"It does," Ezio nodded turning back to read more of the notes, "which makes me wonder, how many notes are 'accidentally' lost to the waste bin by the front desk? Say, how many Umbra are here in Chicago?"

"Usually the same number you have New York, a small enough group who conduct business out of sight of the other Magi. Though, because of all this calamity from yesterday in your neck of the woods, Absalom has tripled the number of hunters here in the city."

"Tripled?" Ezio snapped, turning back with shock. That many Umbra here in Chicago, it was pure overkill.

"Yes sir, triple, which means whatever you're into Ezio, your right up to ears my friend."

"I know, which is why your sneaking me in here is so important Dan, more than you want to know."

The smaller man nodded and smiled, "oh I have no interest to go where your gong Ezio. You understand, once I get you upstairs, you're on your own. I can't help you anymore."

Ezio nodded and smiled as well. "I know Dan, you get me in and I get myself out."

"And if you get caught?"

"I won't, but if I do, I haven't seen you in 5 years or more."

Dan nodded turning back to the large doors which led to stairs and the House above. "Make it seven, sounds better, and safer for me."

A small laugh slipped from Ezio as he responded, "seven it is my friend."

The pair stood waiting in silence in the ornate tunnel when those large steel doors suddenly clanged, then popped. Ezio winced hoping no one upstairs would hear just as the door on the right swung outward toward him. Amazingly, the large portal made no sound as it moved, not a squeak or even a ping. It was pure silence as a woman stepped into the tunnel. She was not dressed as a mage, but more of a worker employed here at the House. She wore a long skirt and a plain corset over an even more plain white shirt. Her dark brown hair was held back in a pair of braids and she smiled with perfect white teeth within a pretty face.

"Have you been waiting long Daniel?" she asked with a sweet Irish accent. She might be in her late twenties Ezio thought as Dan next to him answered.

"Not long Maggie, not long enough to make us worry anyway."

"Ah, good, now come on while the coast is clear." She replied while stepping backwards quickly.

The two Magi followed her into the stairway, then waited as she closed and locked the doors to the tunnel again. Then all three quickly, and quietly, climbed the three flights of stairs up to the House where Maggie went through another smaller door. Daniel and Ezio waited till they heard Maggie hiss, the signal all was clear, before moving through the portal and into a secluded hall in the main floor. Daniel looked around then turned one last time to Ezio and nodded.

"Be careful my friend, and may luck walk at your side."

"Thank you, my friend. Now go and get as far away from me as you can." Ezio smiled before watching his one-time mentor turn and leave, ushering Maggie with him.

The tall Umbra waited just long enough for the pair to get away before moving onto the real reason he had risked his life, and Alice's as well. Truth be told, Ezio had calculated his chances in his head earlier and the outcome was less than enthusing. Still, the Umbra knew if he could make the stairwell behind the west corner door he had a better chance of success. All he had to do was cross the lobby, the main area where the Magi met with visitors, the one area always bustling and busy at the House.

And it was certainly busy this morning, even now this early.

So, with a deep steadying breath, Ezio started out heading deeper into the Magi's House, going for another set of stairs which would take him up to the third floor of the building. Ezio moved with a steady gait, his long legs propelling him as he kept his head down in an attempt to keep from drawing attention, which was hard being he was over six foot tall and well known. So, he kept close to the walls, hoping by staying away from the center of the lobby area of the House he would have some cover and stay unnoticed.

And it worked, to Ezio's somewhat surprise, and small relief. He found the stairwell he needed to and ducked past the door with not a soul noticing. Without a care to his usual impeccable appearance, Ezio took the stairs as fast as he could, climbing the flights in leaps. When he reached the landing with the door to the area he needed, Ezio stopped and caught his breath. As he did, he straightened his coat and vest before stepping out into the hall beyond.

Empty, just as he knew it would be.

The Magi were anything but not predictable, and as a group there were very few among them who had an inclination or ambition toward the mundaneness of simple office work. Ezio knew there would be no Magi here where the true 'magic' of the Magi happens. There never was as this floor was considered 'low' to most everyone but the staff. While the Magi studied and experimented on the floors above, the people here in these offices kept this place running, with things like money and records and other essentials. The life sustaining coin was brought in, balanced in the books, and accounted for which meant the Magi were paid and were able to pay the bills. All the activities and operations of the Magi were documented, transcribed, in files and journals, which was then used when those Magi were to be judged for 'Ascension'. Ezio knew most of the men and women upstairs didn't even know this place even existed in the House, which meant he was safe for the moment as he silently passed empty offices and unoccupied desks, till he reached the one he was looking for. Just as before, with the door to the stairs below, Ezio slipped in quickly and shut the door silently. He turned hoping to greet the men he come to meet cheerfully.

Unfortunately, that was not going to be the case.

"Good morning Fausto," Ezio said to the man who sat behind an extremely neat and well-ordered desk. There wasn't a thing out of place, and when the older man replied with a short snap of an answer he put his pencil down in exactly the right spot by the blotter.

"Do not 'Good morning' me, Mr. Ezio!"

"Oh, I'm sorry Fausto, maybe just 'Morning' then?"

The man stood up quickly from behind the desk, and as he did, Ezio noticed there wasn't a wrinkle anywhere on Fausto's clothes, not on the waistcoat or the blue shirt underneath and certainly not on the dress pants, which billowed slightly at the thigh then squeezed in tightly just at the calf and down to his shoes. Well, this was Fausto Ezio thought as he watched the man stride up to him, as exacting with his clothes as he was with his duties as head of the Administration offices. Even his salt and pepper hair was perfect, held in place with the same exacting eye. It was all very mental the tall Magi ended his thought with, because just at the moment a finger was thrust in his face by the smaller man and Ezio stepped back into the door trying to retreat.

"You sent a man to my personal residence las night! Do you even know how boldfaced a move that is? How do you even know where I live"?

"Yes, I did, but- "

"How impudent you are Mr. Ezio, to wake me at my house at such an ungodly hour as 3 AM to deliver a message! How impertinent and garish you are Mr. Ezio!"

"Now wait a minute," Ezio replied with a small whine as stepped away from the door, trying to gain a small foothold in the conversation as well a safe spot in the office. "I am neither of those, not that much anyway, and I did say in the note it was an emergency Fausto."

The small man of Sicilian decent only shook his head, "and what kind of emergency have you gotten yourself into Mr. Ezio that requires waking me at 3 AM?"

Ezio sighed as he straightened his coat before answering with as much solemnness as he could muster, hoping the show of calm would bolster the truth of his words. "The kind of emergency which you should never hear a word of Fausto, for if you did then your life would be in as much danger as mine."

The tension in the room disappeared almost immediately, and for that Ezio felt some relief tinged with just a bit of pain. He hated to treat Fausto like this, to be as blunt as he had to be, but in the end, it was for the best. Then the tall Magi spotted a folder resting on the edge of the Administrator's desk, the corner of the file perfectly even with the corner of the desk. "Is that the file I asked to see?"

"You know; I was of the notion to tell you no Mr. Ezio. I came to the decision the moment the messenger left my doorstep."

"Then why did you pull out the file Fausto?" Ezio asked with low tone, questioning all that had happened in the last minute.

Yet, the Administrator only carried on as if the question had never been uttered, every syllable seemingly ignored. "Then my curiosity got the better of me. I've been working here at the Magi House since its formation. I even wrote the check to buy the building, Mr. Absalom watched me sign it himself. In all that time, I have never been curious with what happens on the floors above me. I have never been curious as to where the Magi come from or how long they have been around. My only duty was to this office and its functions, first and foremost."

The tall Magi watched as Fausto turned and picked up the file off his desk gingerly, almost with reverence. If there ever was a man more dedicated to the Office of Administration, more zealous about the necessary documentation being signed in triplicate and filed away in its proper place, Ezio had never met. The Administrator handed the file to him as he spoke on.

"And yet I could not understand why you would ask me to look at the file of another Magi, knowing full well it is not allowed. Why would you ask me of all people Mr. Ezio to see the file, someone who follows the rules so closely I asked myself at 3 AM? So, with my curiosity nipping at me uncontrollably, I came into my office early and pulled the file. I was struck numb when I found the folder completely empty."

The last words of Fausto hit Ezio like a thrown brick, it actually took a few seconds for everything to coalesce in his brain. Empty, that's impossible the tall Magi thought as he opened the file and noticed it was completely empty, not one single sheet of typed paper. "How...how is this possible?"

"I don't know, but someone has defiled the sanctity of my office and worse yet, my files. Someone has committed more than a transgression against the House Laws, an atrocity has been perpetrated against me personally!"

Well, that might be taking things a bit too far Ezio thought as he closed the file while hoping he might find some light at the bottom of this pit which had opened suddenly beneath him. "Who has the authority to empty a file on a Magi?"

"Only Mr. Absalom sir, and he would never do something as heinous as this." Fausto answered with a wave of his hand.

"And why is that?" Ezio asked quickly, just a bit confused.

"Because he's Mr. Absalom of course, the Head Magi."

"Oh yes," Ezio replied with a raised eyebrow still trying to think of something, anything. "Of course, Mr. Absalom would never do anything such as thing to you Fausto. Only, now I am left without the information I desperately need, the information I so rudely woke you at 3 AM for."

"What about the Umbra, want they have the info you need?"

Ezio shook his head and sighed again. "No, if your file has been purged then I can assuredly assume the Umbra's have been purged as well. I can safely assume I may be at an impasse here Fausto."

The smaller man only huffed, shook his head, and turned walking back around his desk. "As if I would be without a backup of my own files Mr. Ezio. As soon as I found the file empty I went to my secret room and pulled the second copy of the contents."

And just like some street magician, Fausto pulled a stack of papers from the drawer he opened in his desk. Ezio was struck numb a second time, only this was a good numb. He walked over quickly and almost kissed the smaller man on the forehead, but instead took the papers from him. The tall Magi flipped the first page over, a very neat and efficient title page, and began to scan the second page. It held the information he needed, a well-documented personal history of the Magi he was locking for. And there, halfway down in a box marked as 'Family', Ezio found the name of a sister in Bowling Green, Kentucky for the Magi. He smiled and noted the address before carefully turning the title page back over, handing the stack back to the Head Administrator.

"Thank you, Fausto, for all your help and personal eccentricities."

"And that's all you needed, a quick glean of the first page?"

Ezio only nodded with a smile.

"Then go with all the luck I can wish for you Mr. Ezio. I think you will need it most definitely." Fausto sighed taking the stack and putting it back in his desk.

The tall Magi nodded and added one last request, or bit of aid. "I was never here Fausto, and needless to say, you need to put the empty file back where it belongs along with the same for your second copy."

"Because whoever took my files might come back?"

A small nod was all Ezio offered as an acknowledgement before turning and leaving the office without looking back. Fausto looked down at the stack of typed papers, for a minute or more, then decided that Mr. Ezio was right. It would be for the best if he put everything back and let his curiosity finally quiet itself. It was never good to look past one's station in life.

No, it was never good at all.

Well, the hastily conceived plan from last night surely did not call for him to be trapped in the Magi House, which was just the latest gaff he had walked into with said plan. Cooper had left the hotel just behind the four Magi he 'recruited' to help him complete a daring infiltration this morning of the Magi House. They were going to help him by getting caught by the Protectorate, drawing all the attention to themselves, and thus giving him ample time to climb the stairs to the third floor Administration offices. Cooper knew General Samuels would have the Umbra and Protectorate guards looking for him, orders to take him into custody on sight. He knew the Umbra would find out he rented the room the four went to this morning and they would pass on the information to the Generals. Cooper was counting on it, the discovery of the four Magi and all, because that meant he had the perfect diversion. He wasn't naive, not after last night, when both Samuels and Hamelin made sure he understood his place in the hierarchy of this foul Cabal. It was actually the 'Why' of why he had decided to try and extricate himself from this thing. Cooper knew it was time to get out of this secret conspiracy and he actually came up with a good plan.

Or so it sounded on paper, or in his head.

The proverbial train started leaving the tracks just after the four Magi from this morning went in a different direction from the Magi House. Yes, you heard it right, the four went in a direction completely in the opposite direction of the House. Cooper stood in silent, motionless thunderstruck shock, as the group disappeared in the crowd while traveling down the street away from him. He even heard a woman, a very polite and gracious lady he was sure, mumbled something under her breath about rude young men taking up too much damn space on the sidewalk. Where in the hell we're they going he thought in a panic?

His mind didn't respond, which might have scared Cooper if he hadn't just let go and let pure instinct take over. He swallowed and turned back toward the Magi House. All right, he decided quietly while still standing in the middle of the sidewalk, drawing more and harsher looks, no turning back and no stopping now. You can do this he told himself, those four are just taking a not-so-direct route to the House. They'll get there in just a few minutes after you do, and before you throw a fit, yes, you're going in by yourself Cooper.

By myself, the young Magi heard his mind answer back with a small yelp. Even with the question lingering in his mind Cooper was off and walking toward the House without hesitation. This strange and abrupt bit of courage was now in total control of Cooper's body, sending commands for him to walk right toward the lion's Den. There might have been, probably would have been, some hesitation if the young man could have given his legs any kind of direction or mandate. No, for the foreseeable future, Cooper was just along for the ride as they say as his body went into a strange kind of trance guided by this sudden show of bravery from who-knows-where.

A few minutes later, to his utter surprise and slight horror, Cooper went right past the guards and Umbra at the front desk. He just knew he was going to get caught, promenading by the people at the front doors of the House as if there wasn't a care in the world. Cooper even screamed at his own mind he was going to get caught, look, it's about to happen. Then, with a shower of pure luck Cooper never knew could exist, a group walked in with him. He meshed right into the mix of Magi and others so perfectly the desk people never even looked up. He was in and no one was the wiser. He made the third floor with no effort, moved past the other offices and desk with silent efficiency. Cooper was sure now he was going to succeed, going to pull this off!

That was till he reached the door to the Head Administrator's Office, a man by the name of Fausto, who he had been told was quite austere and taciturn with his duties. Cooper was hoping to convince the man to let him see the file on Eleanor, to find the name and location of her sister who was living somewhere in the Southern United States. If he could find the sister then he could find the niece, and he was one step closer to finding the alchemist who could create the vessel needed for the Philosopher's Stone, one step closer to freeing himself and his father. Only, as he reached for the door knob to turn the ordinary looking metal handle, his ears picked up on two voices inside having a rather testy one-sided conversation. Cooper knew the higher pitched voice was Fausto's, because the other lower one belonged to the tall Umbra Ezio, the second to Camille.

He stood there, motionless yet again, as the trance provided by that abrupt bout of courage seeped right into the floor through his feet. There Cooper stood as still as column, listening to the men on the other side of the door talk.

Hey, where did you go? You can't leave me like this!

Cooper screamed in his mind as his parched lips moved not in the slightest. Where did the courage go? It was just here, moving me along, where did it go? His mind, let loose of the restraints now, raced in terror. What the hell was he supposed to do now? And then his ears, miraculously still catching the words the two men were having and deciphering the syllables, picked up on the fact the file for Eleanor was empty, not a piece of paper inside.

What, the file is empty? Well now, that was it, Cooper went into a full-fledged tidal wave of panic. He couldn't breathe, couldn't move, and he sure as hell was close to passing out. The conversation from behind the door was lost as his mind reeled while he stood with a hand just an inch from the door handle. Then, before Cooper could think of it, as if he could have a single thought at the moment, he spun and quietly trotted over to an office which was open but unoccupied. He ducked inside the door and closed it to the point where there was just enough of an opening to look out into the hall. He stood there quietly, inhaling slow breaths, trying to think of what to do now. With the file empty he had almost no choice on what do next or where to go. The Generals had the file purged, had to be the ones to have done the deed, or have someone under them do it. So, what next Cooper? With no niece of Eleanor, the one who would construct the vessel that would become the all-powerful Philosopher's Stone, he was up the creek without a paddle.

Cooper was still looking out into the hall, still trying to think of anything that might help, when Ezio suddenly appeared stepping out of the office and moving quickly toward the exit. The tall Umbra was by Cooper's hiding pot without a glance, his face a mask of stone as he was thinking about whatever he and Fausto had talked about. Cooper knew the look well. He may have only been with Camille's Umbra troupe for a short while, but Cooper had taken in as much as he could about the others, especially the older Magi. He knew Ezio was now in deep thought, turning something over and over in his perpetually moving mind, and you can make a safe bet that something was a bit of information from Fausto.

There you go my boy, right there, that's how you get yourself out of this nightmare. You follow him and you get whatever information out of him you can, by any means necessary. Cooper heard the voice in his head, felt the assurance the thought gave him, and he decided to do it, to move.

Unlike before though, Cooper was in total control of his body this time. He was the one who told his legs to move, to follow Ezio. He moved like a shadow after the tall Umbra, trailing Ezio from a safe distance, always keeping the man in sight but not so close as to draw a look from him.

The pair made a quick exit from the Administration offices, through the empty realm, and out into the halls of the House. Cooper felt the sharp bite of fear and concern as he noticed the home of the Magi here in Chicago was starting to 'fill' up. People were coming in, Magi and visitors and workers, which meant soon someone was going to spot him and raise the alarm.

Yet, Cooper never swayed from his current plan. He kept Ezio in sight as the tall man was heading downstairs to the main lobby, the very place where everyone would be this morning. Cooper was starting to think he might have to cease this idea of getting the information, whatever it was, from Ezio for the time being. Getting caught would most certainly not help him or his father, but then Cooper noticed Ezio took a quick route to the back of the main lobby, away from everyone and the guards, especially the guards. It took all of a second for Cooper to stay with his plan and follow the tall Umbra. He even took the same route, which is why Ezio was waiting for him when he rounded a corner. The smaller Umbra walked right into the taller one, even bounced off him a bit as he heard Ezio whisper coldly.

"Morning Mr. Cooper, may I ask why you're following me?"

The small umbra stepped back, felt his mind go completely blank like a piece of white paper with no words, and only gurgled something that was not close to an answer.

"Umm, ah, what?"

His eyes narrowed, his brow furrowed, as Ezio looked down on Cooper with suspicious intent. "I know what you've done Mr. Cooper, how you've betrayed myself and Camille."

"What are you saying, betrayal, of you and Miss Camille?"

"Yes, Cooper, of me and Miss Camille."

In an instant Cooper's mouth was dry, like a pile of sun bleached bones one might find in the desert. His mind was scrambled, flipping around like a fish out of water as he tried to come up with something to say. See, the real problem was the simple fact Cooper was trying to decide if he wanted to punch, kick, or try to talk his way out of this and at the moment he wasn't sure which one was the best option.

Maybe I should try all three, and not in any certain order he thought dry swallowing. Or maybe I could-

Before the thought was done, hell it was barely formed, the loud clang of bells and the ear-piercing shrieks of whistles echoed off the white walls of the lobby. Both men knew it was the sound of the alarms, both turned to the source, and immediately Cooper noticed his four Magi, his diversion, had finally shown up and completed the first part of his plan, just really late.

Well, not the best timing in the world, but they did show up and distract everyone perfectly Cooper thought just as a voice yelled over the din that was once the quiet lobby.

"Ezio and Cooper, how nice of you both to be in the same spot at the same time. This saves me a lot of time hunting you fellas down, so be smart and give up quietly."

Both Umbra turned to see a Protectorate guard standing with three others, all rather large and brutish looking. Cooper recognized the man talking from the night before, at the meeting with the Generals. He was one of the men from the dark watching them, one of the personal guard. If they went with him, quietly or not, it would be the end for both Magi.

"I think we need to run Mr. Ezio, very fast and very far from here."

Hey, look at that, I formed an actual sentence Cooper thought, just as the three men started toward them.

Part Eleven

"Why do they call you the 'Mouse'? Is it because of your size?"

Before the words were even out of her mouth, Boles was regretting each and every one. A sudden wave of guilt washed over her for being so discourteous to someone who was being nothing more than the most gracious of host. Yet, she couldn't contain her own insatiable interest about the nickname, was it because he was so small?

The shop was abruptly quiet at the inquiry, which only deepened the feeling of guilt Boles was feeling. The sewing machine Otto sat behind came to a stop just as quick and the Weaver began to feel she had truly insulted the small tailor, but then Otto began to laugh deeply turning to his wife with a broad smile.

"Mama, she is too lovely, no?"

"Ja, she is," Inga replied with a giggle while working on the seam of a shirt, one that Wells has just tried on.

The immediate sensation of relief was as sweet as a kiss from Wells Boles thought, and yet her curiosity was still an itch that needed a scratch. She smiled and opened her mouth ready to try and ask again, only with a little bit better tact this time. The deep voice of Wahkan though beat her to the punch you might say, the baritone sound seemingly filling the store from floor to the very ceiling.

"Otto is called the 'Mouse' because of Heinrich."

"Who is Heinrich?" Wells asked with a smile, her joy apparent on her face.

"Heinrich is our kostbares." Inga declared with just as much joy in her voice as the Weaver displayed in her smile, the last in German though leaving both Wells and Boles a little confused. As they stood in the small shop literally lost in translation, Otto reached under the counter and a second later produced a cage holding a large white rat.

"This is our Heinrich!" Otto called out as he sat the cage down before beginning to open the small door. In anticipation of being let free, Heinrich began to squeak and hop by the door. The Weavers both giggled at the sight as the portal opened and the rat jumped out and into the hands of its loving master. As soon as the animal was in the tailor's hands he laughed with a happy mirth.

"From the time when my papa was a small boy to now, he has always had a mouse. There has been a Hilda, an August- "Inga said as she looked to the ceiling thinking of all the name of her Otto's past pets.

"And Else and finally Heinrich here." The tailor finished before rubbing noses with the large rodent. Boles giggled again, the sound infectious, as Otto sat Heinrich down on the counter. In a blink, the rat ran off in a scamper to attend to an order of business only he knew of. The mood of the shop was happy again, light enough that Wells spoke up still smiling.

"I thought Heinrich was your son."

And just like Boles moments before, as soon as the green haired Weaver spoke the words and noted the reaction in the shop, she wanted every syllable back. The happy mood changed in an instant to a somber tone, Inga sighing with the smile on her face slowly fading, and it might have slipped even farther into a deep solemnness if not for quick action of the small tailor and his wife. As if he knew what would happen, how dark the atmosphere might become, Otto quickly acted with a warm compassionate smile hoping the Weaver would not feel one bit of guilt.

"Our son's name was Maximillian, or just Max as we called him. We lost him to the war, it is one of the reasons why we left our homeland."

"I'm sorry," Wells whispered wishing she could roll back time and take back every word she had spoken. "If I had known- "

"No Miss Wells, do not feel guilty. Thanks to John and Wahkan, we were able to speak with him once more and we have been at peace ever since." Inga said with a wide smile and a shake of her head. A calm began to rise in the Weaver's heart as the smile eased her anxiety.

Yet, Boles wasn't sure what to say as the shop drew quiet again, only that she should say something because civility demanded it. She breathed in ready to speak when Wahkan was talking, taking over again. "John helped more than I did Inga."

"Ja, but if not for your words we would not have believed John could help. If not for your honesty and veracity, we would not have taken John's help." Otto responded and the tone, the very feeling, in his voice made Wells gasp just a bit.

"Yes Wahkan, John let us visit our Max again, but you were the one who made us believe in him." Inga added with a nod.

The large IP looked at all the eyes locked to him, stared hard for a moment, then down to the apple he had been eating. He was perfectly set to let the conversation go right there and then, but Inga needed to pursue something just a little father. "You still feel guilty, don't you our dear Wahkan?"

There was no answer for ten or twenty seconds as Boles felt her heart being squeezed by the tension she was feeling. She felt like she was standing on the edge of a steep cliff, the anticipation was so strong. Boles watched with an earnest nervous twitch of her fingers for a response, and when Wahkan spoke she damn near jumped out of her skin.

"Hard not to, after seeing what war is and all. It's hard not feel guilty when you live and a man standing just five feet away dies from a stray bullet bouncing off a wood post just at the right angle."

"Do not feel guilt for living Wahkan, it is not right. What does John say, that we all have a purpose in this world and will only leave when that purpose is served?" Otto remarked, asked after petting Heinrich, who had scampered close enough to be touched, like a little puppy dog.

"Ja, Wahkan, do not burden your heart with such a heavy weight. You still have things to do here with John, with everyone. Your purpose is still incomplete." Inga added looking at the tall IP with such grace it touched even the walled off heart of Boles.

The Weaver with the dark hair turned to her love Wells and noticed even she was being swept away in this sudden surge of emotion sweeping the shop. Then Wahkan was talking again and Boles snapped her head in his direction.

"There was this kid, lied about his age to get in the war the damn fool, who was in our regiment. He was all talk, usual for his age, till one morning he starts to cry because he's as sure as the setting sun he's going to die when we go over the trench wall the next time. He's crying and pleading with our Sergeant whose as tough as a piece of steel. The man just looks at this kid and tells him to do his job, do it right with courage, and everything will be fine."

Everyone was deeply invested into the large man's words now, hanging on each one breathlessly. Wahkan, leaning up against the door still, looked down at his apple for a long second or two then out to the street and the passerby's before continuing. "The kid quiets down after a minute, more from those cold eyes the Sergeant stared at him with than what he told the kid probably. And the quiet, it lasted just about as long, because not five minutes later the kid is crying again, that was till this fella named Jones told him he'd look after him, keep the kid safe."

Wahkan kept his eyes out looking on the street. The memory was still so fresh. He could still smell the gun powder floating on the breeze from the large artillery guns just west, the smell of earth from the trenches mixed with human sweat and blood invaded his recall like the tentacles of some monster. He looked back to the people in the shop and grinned sadly as he spoke.

"We get the word we're going over the top a little later. We get our gear ready, rifles loaded, and get to our spots next to the ladders. I remember looking over and the kid is as calm as you could be before being told to run headlong into a storm of bullets and mortar fire. He's stopped crying but I could see the fear in his eyes. The kid was just like the rest of us, scared but just strong enough to hold it together to do your job, to do it right with courage. Then the order came, a whistle blew, and over the top we went."

He stopped again, had to for a moment. Wahkan looked down to the apple noting he had eaten about half of the fruit. It didn't look right to him suddenly, didn't feel right in his hand, like it wasn't an apple at all. He knew why too, because he wasn't standing in Otto's shop with the others anymore. No, Wahkan was back over there, on the Western Front, going over the top of the trench using an old rickety ladder. Then he was running over dead and broken ground that was once a field of beautiful green grass, right toward the Germans.

"What happened?"

The words were sweet, filled with curiosity and plenty of fear. He looked up to see Wells, her small pretty face filled with a mix of eagerness and dread. He sighed, went this far he thought, might as well go the rest. "We jumped out of our trench and ran like a mess of screaming mad men toward the enemy and their trench. Those of us who weren't shot or shelled had to fight a regiment of men we had never met or knew to the death then. You fired your rifle till it was empty, went to your pistol and used it till it was out, and finally hand-to-hand with anything you could use as a weapon. It was bloody. It was a bad way to die and that's all I want to say about it."

The air was thick now, quiet again, and the shop seemed more like a tomb than a place where one could buy a suit from an exceptional tailor. And the worse part, it was still to come Wahkan thought as he breathed in than continued. "The kid, he made it, and never fired his rifle once. As far as I could make out he ran like hell for the other trench, dropped in, and then covered up so no one could find him till the fighting was over. Later that night he took off, deserted us, and I can say I wasn't too surprised by it."

"Why is that?" Boles heard herself ask, almost as if the question just leapt out before she formed it in her mind.

"Because when someone told him Jones was dead, shot while crossing the field, he didn't even blink. He just asked who Jones was." Wahkan answered just before tossing the half-eaten apple into the trash bin. "A lot of men died, good men who could have done who knows what to better this world. I feel angry because I can only imagine what could have been. I feel guilty because better men than me are buried over there, taken instead of me."

"And I say, 'a better one' one is standing right here, in my shop." Otto quickly shot back, the little man leaning in to express his dissent with Wahkan's last. "You should never feel remorse for surviving Wahkan. Ja, good men died, but that is the nature of the beast we call war. Men, like you and my Max, you are the ones who keep us, me and mama and these ladies, safe from the beast. Without you and your purpose we would never know the sweetness of life we have,"

"Ja, without your protection and friendship we would not be the happy little ones we are. Please, do not feel the way you do Wahkan." Inga added once more, her words lifting the spirits in the room just a bit as always.

"Maybe," Wahkan nodded as his grin picked up just a little, "I'll have to keep that in mind."

"Please do," Inga huffed before giggling and going back to sewing on the shirt for Wells.

The two Weavers stood in stunned silence watching with wide eyes. Boles was shocked to her very core. She would have never guessed the gruff exterior of Wahkan hid a soul like that. He was always so stoic, at least these few hours she had known him. He was just like Isaac, a sweet soul hidden away from the world. Boles looked over to Wells, noting her love was staring back. Even before they were bound together in Isaac's ceremony, the pair had unusual mental connection. One mysteriously always knew what the other was thinking and with just a glance it seemed. Just like now, Wells only nodded and Boles knew instinctively they were thinking the same thing.

Suddenly, and surprisingly, they wanted to know even more about the large man named Wahkan.

Major General Thales Hamelin

The man charged with conducting, and thus controlling the dissemination of, all intelligence gathering operations for the Royal Guard. There wasn't one scrap of information, not one word of one paragraph from one document or cable, that passed through the Guard Thales did not eye personally. He read everything, sometimes twice, which was to be sent up the chain of command to the Generals at Operational Command. Thales had reached his current rank with lightning speed becoming the youngest man ever to obtain the rank of OF-7, Major General. He accomplished this feat by displaying a masterful touch with military politics, an indominable work ethic, and an ever-watchful eye of all things around him. Much like his counterpart in The Protectorate, Major General Silas Samuels, both reached their rank of Major General through a long career of vigilance and a steel like loyalty to only a few. Thales and Samuel were no fools. They built this alliance because one day soon both would oversee everything in their respective militaries, and when that day arrived it would be nice to have friends in high places like they say.

At the moment though, he was busy checking more communiques and dispatches, making sure he and Silas were always one step ahead of any news making its way up the military chain of command. He was also keeping a close eye on the Magi sitting in the chair across from him and his desk, one Addison from the US. Yes, she was a colleague in this covert mergence between the Protectorate and the Royal Guard. Yes, she was a necessary cog in the wheel of this engine, which was steadily moving toward completing the endeavor to create a Philosopher's Stone. Still, as said before, Thales was no fool, and he knew any engine would come to a crashing stop if one component failed, or if it betrayed the engine completely.

Was Addison planning to deceive, and ultimately forsake, the Cabal? Thales was not sure, and whenever he was not sure he doubled his vigilance accordingly. Like right now, he could tell Addison was thinking, stewing, on why Cooper had turned rogue after the failure in Brooklyn. Of course, he and Silas knew what the young man was trying to do, what he was attempting. It did not take a great amount of intelligence to see what Cooper was up too, especially when presented with the fact he had contacted four other innocent Magi. The young man was seeking a way out of his 'circumstance' and the four from the hotel room were being setup as a distraction. Cooper wanted the Cabal looking one way while he went the other, obviously, which left only one question.

How much did the young fool truly know?

Thales had an idea, the fact the room was just a few blocks from the Magi House was the giveaway. Cooper knew about the Alchemist who was going to make the very object which would be the Philosopher's Stone. Or, at the very least, who the Alchemist was related too. He figured that out the moment he saw Eleanor's name on the list of four Magi from the Hotel room.

Thus, the reason Thales was watching Addison so closely for was simple, if she did not see Cooper's actions for what they were and speak up, well then, she was more than likely hiding her true allegiance. Our faithful Magi might be up to something he thought just a second before Addison stood up abruptly and called out.

"I know what Cooper is up to?"

"You do?" Thales asked quickly, his astonishment and concern pure pretense, and a damn good act he thought.

"Yes, I do," Addison remarked walking up to Thales desk and holding out a paper in one hand while pointing to a name on it with her other finger. "Here, one of the Magi Cooper contacted, Eleanor. She's the aunt of our Alchemist."

"She is?" Thales gasped, still playing the astonished fool.

"She is, which means Cooper is trying find her niece, our Alchemist."

"Yes, that does makes solid sense."

Addison smiled and nodded quickly. "We need to send our people to Kentucky as quick as possible. Cooper may have a lead on us already."

Oh, he doesn't dear Addison, Thales thought coldly while grinning with just a touch of malice. He was about to reply and tell the Magi he would see to it personally, dispatch a contingent of Protectorate and Royal Guard to ensure the Alchemist was kept safe. Yet the door to his personal office opened and with a rush Silas Samuels entered with a red face and fast gait.

"What is it Silas?" Addison asked before Thales could, that was if he was going to inquire why Samuels burst into his office. In truth, he had a suspicious idea as to why his fellow conspirator was rushing about for.

"The Magi house, Ezio and Cooper just showed up, about three minutes apart."

The gruff answer shocked Addison into a gasp, but Thales just kept his calm as his mind started to chew and rip into what Samuels had just told them.

"Together?" Addison asked with a shake of her head, to clear it obviously, Thales thought as spoke up.

"Probably, maybe our Mr. Cooper felt an alliance was in need. He does seem light in the experience bucket when it comes to espionage."

"I would have to agree, maybe I should go down to the house and help Corrine?" Addison asked and Samuels smiled back.

"I already have a car down on the street ready to run you over to the House. Make sure the First Magi is kept informed on just what he needs to know for now."

The remark seemed just a little out of the normal for the General and Addison froze for a moment. "Are you telling me to lie to the First Magi Absalom?"

"Absolutely Not," Thales interjected with a quick word, "we're just asking you to ensure the First Magi does not worry over things we have handled, like the Alchemist."

The answer seemed to quell the suspicion Addison was having as she nodded and left the room without looking back. Just after she did Samuels turned to Thales. "Did she finally figure out what Cooper was up to?"

"Yes, but it took her all bloody morning to do so." Thales sighed walking over to a small cart where he kept his best single malt Scotch. He poured two glasses as Samuels behind him spoke.

"That's not the Addison I know. She's whip smart, quick to the deduction, know what I mean?"

The English Officer turned and handed one of the glasses to Samuels and nodded. "I got the same impression, which is why I have been watching her carefully all morning."

"Is she still with us you think?"

"What I think my friend," Thales started after drinking a portion of his glass, "is it was a very shrewd move to take the Alchemist out of play just as Isaac began his work."

Samuels nodded drinking a bit of his Scotch before replying. "it was, a very prudent move now that we have rats on board the ship, as they say."

"We have the Alchemist hidden away. I'm confident we'll soon have the Weavers as well. I say we keep our Addison under a watchful eye and if need be, we retire her from our ranks."

"Sounds good to me my friend." Samuels agreed with a nod before drinking the rest of Scotch.

Thales did the same, nod and all, as the two men easily agreed to rid themselves of a partner, smiling without a bit of hesitation.

Addison made the first floor of the building in no time, her gait long enough to chew up the distance in chunks. To say she was moving with purpose was an understatement as she flew through the doors to the outside, bumping past two Protectorate soldiers. She saw the car Samuels had mentioned was for her, walked toward it in three steps, and then moved past the automobile without looking back. She crossed the street, walked on some more past several other cars, and stopped finally at one that was as non-descript as possible, which was the idea. The car had no markings, no dents or scratches, and nothing to set it apart from any other car on the street. It was the perfect vehicle to ride around in, if one wanted nothing to be remembered of your passing through. Addison quickly opened the door to the back and got in, taking a seat next to the other person sitting in the back of the car.

"Go, to the Magi House, and make it quick." She ordered the driver up front with a snap.

"I thought they only said that in the movies," the man next to her said with a bright smile as the car pulled out into traffic.

"Since when do you watch movies, Eloy my friend?" Addison asked with a shake of her head.

She is nervous, the Spanish Magi thought as he shrugged his shoulders while pulling the receiver for the Hertzian wireless from his ear. He had been listening to the device, conspicuously hidden in the arm rest between them, noting all the action of the morning, or lack thereof. "I like watching movies when I have the chance, which is not enough these days I am afraid."

"Yes, not much time for anything personal, has there been any word from Corrine or the First Magi?"

Eloy shook his head, "no I am afraid. There has been nothing but silence so far. Why are you here by the way, and not with the Generals?"

The female Magi shook her head and sighed, "it seems Mr. Cooper made his move last night. He contacted four other Magi in what I can only imagine is meant to be a distraction to us."

"Sacrificing four other souls to garner a distraction, that does not sound like Mr. Cooper. What does he hope to gain by having the Generals look the other way?" Eloy asked rhetorically, shaking his head now while staring out the window.

"It will make more sense when I tell you one of the Magi he contacted, she is the aunt of the alchemist the Generals recruited. He reached out to Eleanor." Addison added.

"Oh, so he thinks he can free himself by getting to the alchemist and stealing her away, like the shaman did to the Weavers?"

"Obviously, only the young fool overestimates his prowess as a spy, and the fact the two men he is up against are masters of that particular field completely eludes him." The female Magi sighed, looking out the window as the car moved through traffic, heading toward the Magi House.

"It is a foolish plan, but maybe we can use it to our advantage. His failure at subterfuge might be used to cover our attempt, do the Generals still believe we are with them? They still believe the story I told about the shaman letting the Weavers go?"" Eloy asked.

Addison nodded, turning back to look at him. "Yes, they filled the air with Protectorate ships and the streets with Umbra and soldiers. It looks like they still believe the ruse, though they have to be getting suspicious. Too many moving parts in this lie, and I knew the moment I saw Eleanor's name as the one Cooper contacted what he was up to I kept quiet all morning and Thales must have started to grow weary of me. I tell you Eloy, those two men are not to be trusted, not one inch."

"No, they cannot."

"The Weavers, has there been any word?"

"No," Eloy sighed with a shake of his head, "and I think we will have a hard time finding them after today."

"Why is that?" The female Magi asked with a raised eyebrow.

"I am very sure the shaman is going to give them their freedom, if he has not already. Once that happens, the Weavers will be able to go anywhere they wish."

"And we will hunt them down with the Umbra, as planned," Addison started before realizing the man she was talking with was never this straight forward. Eloy was a grand Magi and an even better tactician. The man played chess like a shark, circling his opponent and nipping at them before finally moving in for the kill. "I think you have more to say, my friend."

"I did hold back a bit," Eloy whispered with a smile before taking in a breath and finishing finally, "the Weavers will be free, but they will not leave the shaman's side. They know their chances at staying free are best with John Greywolf, so both will join him and his crew, on board that fabulous air ship one can only see if they are thinking of it as the craft passes by."

The thought finally set off the lights in Addison's mind, what Eloy had said making full sense. The Umbra could track the Weavers magic, just like a Joris stone, if they knew where the pair were using their stored magic. And when it's being used while in the air, aboard an invisible air ship for all intents and purposes, it would be impossible to even get a trace. "Yes, that would make finding them very hard indeed."

"Yes, very hard, but not entirely impossible." Eloy said with a smile before putting the cap of the receiver back to his ear to listen in on the Protectorate communications.

Now what was he thinking, Addison thought for a second before turning to look back out the window of the car.

'It's a long road that's not got a turn Wally, but all come round soon enough, you best remember that.'

Wally's dear brother used to repeat the old Scottish saying every time he would get frustrated with some crazy project. It meant don't lose heart in times when the dark seems to go on forever, there's always a turn up ahead, or light at the end of the tunnel Wahkan would say with his deep voice. Damn, Wally sure wished his friend was here at the moment, he might be able to stop what was coming.

Men, eight by the quick count, were standing by the entrance to the store and all were armed with double barrel shotguns cut just short enough to make it easy to carry concealed. Lachlan and Kate recognized the men and both knew instantly why they were here. Wallace, standing by his friends, had a vague but sure idea what was happening, a kidnapping. He had been talking with a young lad just to his left about the boy's new banjo, a special hybrid thing you know. The boy had built the instrument by hand adding a special new piece to it, a bottle of steam. Wally had been shocked to see it when the lad brought it up to him to see. The technoist had been mulling over doing the same to his own banjo, and when he picked the strings the sound the banjo emitted, combined with the steam, was a mixed amount of reverb and amplification. It was the actual sound Wally imagined would come from such a setup, a real beauty he knew, and then the men pushed their way into the store and the newly created banjo was soon forgotten.

"What do you lads want?" Lachlan demanded, his voice short and strong. It was more than easy to discern he was not letting a mob run free in his store.

"Oh Lach, how can you speak such an inquiry. We came to see our old friend Wallace here of course." A voice called out from the back, behind the armed men. It was thick with a Scottish brogue, a gravely sound, and everyone knew instantly who the man was.

"Glory be, no." Kate whispered as Lach took a hard swallow. Both, though shocked, knew Wallace had to be struck cold to the bone as the man with the voice moved past the eight armed men holding court at gun point, an unsettling smile across his face.

"Aonghas Felton, you bastard." Wally whispered with shock as his mind practically exploded with realization. The man who had damn near crushed his life into small unfixable bits just sauntered in like he was going to church. Felton, he went by his last name because he never liked his first one, still looked like a haggard farmer. He wasn't dressed in fine Victorian clothes or even the work clothes others around here wore. He was dressed in a ragged pair of canvas pants and a dirty denim shirt with scuffed work boots. It didn't help his long hair looked like it could have fought off a comb single handedly.

"Morning Wallace, it's been dunky's since ah last saw ye." Felton replied with that smile which looked like pure evil.

"Get out of my store Aonghas Felton!" Kate shouted, and the command drew an instant reaction. All at once the men with the shotguns reacted, the business ends of their weapons coming up and pointing right at Kate, which snapped Lach into motion as he stepped toward the men threatening his precious wife with a loud growl.

The other poor souls caught in the middle of the unfolding confrontation cried out and the noise seemed to bring the emotions down just a bit. Cooler heads, though, hadn't prevailed as Felton laughed a little while never letting his eyes leave Wally's.

"Leave Lach be Felton, he's only protecting his own." Wally stated calmly and pointedly.

The man named Felton shook his head while sucking on his bottom lip, the sound disturbing and annoying all at the same time, before speaking again. "Where's ye lads Wallace, eh? Where's the big Indian and the man in that great big black hat, eh?"

"Your here for me Felton, and no one else. You don't need to be hurting my friends." The technoist replied, still in a tone of defiance.

"I'm here for me due Wallace. I'm here for what you failed to do for me in Dublin." Felton whispered with a snarl, the crazy dripping off each word. "Those two Wallace, ye mates, they embarrassed me back in Dublin, you know? I hate being embarrassed Wallace, it makes me quite mad, you know?"

"You killed Innes! You murdered his brother in cold blood you-"Kate screamed again, in pure contempt and rebellion, and this time Felton fired back with his own spite.

"Haud yer wheesht woman or else!"

"Damn you Felton, speak to my Kate like that again and I'll kill you!" Lach bellowed, approaching the haggard looking man just as the barrels of a shotgun touched his neck. Felton licked his lips, and for the first time his gaze left Wally and turned to Lach. His voice was madness, anger, and the God's honest truth.

"You step into ma business again Lachlan and I'll have my lads cut yer heart out and show it to you." The threat wasn't a threat at all, it was the simple truth. Felton then turned back to Wally and those crazed eyes bore into the technoist as he spoke. "Innes stepped into ma business Wallace, and I killed him for it. You know I'm speaking the truth and nothing but."

If the words were meant to intimidate, to put fear into Wally's heart, every one failed. There might have been a day just after Dublin, just after John and Wahkan had found him, that Wallace would have let Felton scare him, but he would never let the man own him. Innes dying made sure Wally would never be Felton's puppet and he told the crazy Scotsman so. "I will never give you what you want Felton, you mad dobber. When you shot, and killed my brother, that was the very second you failed."

"Really Wallace, are you willing to risk all these innocent lads and lassies? You see, I know ye McAndrew. I know ye too well. Look me in me eyes, tell me I won't kill them all to get what I want from you!" Felton responded with a sneer.

That's when Wally heard them, all these innocents, for the first time. There was a lady crying while her husband held her. A lad just a few feet from them was having a hard time breathing and the young boy who had come to see the great Wallace McAndrew to show off his one of a kind banjo was reciting a prayer for the Lord to watch over him and the others. Yes, Felton knew Wally very well.

"All right Felton, I'll go with you. These people though, they go free with nothing to fear from you or your band. Promise me that and I'll go with you."

Felton stared back, his expression unchanging, for what seemed an eternity. Wally could hear the others in the store cry more, certain the mad man would have his men kill them all. Only with a sudden move Felton laughed and nodded. "O' course Wallace. You come with me and I'll have the boys leave these people all alone."

"I got your word on this?"

The question hung in the air for a second before Felton stepped forward going nose to nose with Wally, the sneer from before back. "Are you trying to anger me Wallace, because you know what I do when I get angry?"

"No Felton, I'm not trying to anger you. I'm just trying to get these people out of here and away from you." Wally answered calmly, even though his insides were churning.

"Good," the mad man whispered before turning to walk back out of the store, "then let's get going. I have a new life to get to."

Kate had been watching in disbelief as the negotiation was carried out. Her fire and anger at the men with the shotguns, at Felton and his crazed hate, was being replaced with confusion. She stepped forward, just a small step, and Felton stopped immediately. He pulled out a large handgun with a long barrel, pointed it right at her, and was stopped short of anything else by Wally's commanding scream.

"Kate, just stop," the technoist pleaded while holding up his hand to her hoping she would cease her movements, "please, let me go with Felton so these people can go home."

"But Wally- "Lach whispered with the same confusion his wife was feeling.

"No Lach, the lives of these people mean more than mine. Now, let me go and deal with this, please?"

The last hung on the air of the shop. Felton held his gun on Kate just a minute longer before lowering it. He smiled again at Kate, spoke no more words, and left the store. Wally stared at his friends, nodded just slightly hoping they wouldn't try and stop him, and then he was following Felton with heavy steps. The eight men with shotguns filed out then slowly, backing out keeping everyone in sight.

Wally watched Felton get into a beat-up truck and was about to follow when a blow from the butt of a shotgun to the back of his head put him down. Before he could hit the sidewalk though, two other men caught him and tossed his unconscious body into the back of the truck where the men with the shotguns jumped in. Lach stepped out of the store and onto the sidewalk feeling helpless as he watched the truck with his friend speed off into the Chicago traffic.

"What do we do now?" Kate was asking by his side, a calm but frantic sound to her voice.

"We have to follow that truck somehow, or we'll never see Wally again I am sure." Lach said back just as one of the others in the store called out.

"Felton's staying down at the abandoned warehouse, the one by the end of the neighborhood."

Kate gasped with a smile and turned to her husband. "We know where Felton's going."

"That we do my love, and with a little help we're going to put that crazed bastard Felton down!"

"What help?" Kate asked just as Lach was pointing to the boy who had been talking to Wally.

"Alick, run over to the tailor shop, the one run by the Mouse, and get a man named Wahkan. You bring him here as fast as you can lad! Go, get moving!"

The boy took off running down the street toward the shop as ordered while Lach looked down into his wife's eyes. "I figure me and Wahkan can put a good hurt on those dobers. We'll get Wally back and get some revenge while doing it."

"You're not going with just Wahkan my love and if you try and stop me I'll hit you I swear." Kate replied and all Lach could do was smile.

Damn, if he didn't marry the sweetest, bravest woman in a l the whole world.

Part Twelve

I remember my first journey, my first travel across the veil that masks the Other Worlds.

The breeze, its gentle fingers caressing my young face, was the first thing I noticed, the first sign I was no longer in the Inipi, or sweat lodge. The sweet smell on the air was such a drastic change from the thick sage smoke it stirred me awake from my trance. Tall stalks of long prairie grass swaying above me came into focus, twisting slowly around me in the gentle breeze. It was relaxing, so much so I laid perfectly still enjoying where I was for a second.

I made it, after three days of fasting and two in the Inipi I had crossed over to-

Then suddenly two large yellow eyes were staring down at me from behind a maw that looked like it might swallow my entire head with one bite. The words of wisdom my teacher had passed on to me just before going into the sweat lodge came back as I heard heavier, larger, feet approaching me. The whip sounds of wings touched my ears as well as I stared back into those mysterious eyes,

"Do not fear what comes to you John. They are only curious to see the one who calls to them."

"I call to them?" I asked Grandmother with a wrinkle of my face.

"Yes, your guides will be there when you wake in the Middle World. They will always be at your side John, from this moment on. Even *though you must walk your path alone my little white hair, you will never truly be alone."*

So, I laid there in the tall grass, still looking up into a perfect blue sky as the others came to see the one who called to them from across the universe.

I cannot count how many times I have been asked what it is like to Journey, to travel to other worlds through the Astral highways. Each time I simply smile and say it's kind of like dying, slipping away into the dark of the void, and then reappearing in the field by the Gol, the One Tree, the sacred place where all life begins, ends, and returns to start again. And It was the same this time as it has been with all the other times, I fell into nothingness and floated on emptiness in dark until I felt a familiar tingle on the back of my hand. When I opened my eyes again I was sitting in a large open field of high grass, the stalks swaying with the push of a gentle wind, a flat warm land that is always so beautiful. I had come to the valley of the beginning, the place where all spirit energy enters and gathers. The sun above rained down its warmth and bright light on a world few visit and remember. The sweet smell of sage drifted on the breeze, juniper and jasmine intermingled with it, and off in the distance was the One Tree. I stood up and adjusted my nat before starting off toward the Gol, but as I walked along letting my fingers just touch the top of the high grass, I felt a pair of unseen eyes watching my every step.

I knew who, or what, was keeping such a close observation. I also knew he would not stop me here, so far from the One Tree, but once I was close enough my friend would try and keep me from my decision. So, with each step, I felt more mystical eyes follow me, and with each step the high grass inched lower till my fingers felt nothing. As I approached, the One Tree grew taller, larger in girth and height, to the point it would dwarf any tree on any world I have walked on. The trunk was large enough for eighty men to stand around holding hands, and the branches numbered more than you could count in one day. Some spirits come here to be judged, some to seek a path to another realm like I was doing, and some to meet with the ones who help guide them and teach them, their Spirit Guides. As I walked on toward the Gol two ghostly spirits, a mother and her daughter, whom were walking across my path holding hands and humming a soft tune, came toward me. What happened to them to bring their spirits here to this other world? I do not know, but I could ask, only that would be intrusive to the pair, unfair to ask such a thing, even if they had just passed. I then accepted they, this loving family, will never walk the Middle World as mother daughter again, and that saddened me a little. The daughter looked to me, and I nodded, tipping my hat. Both only smiled back then, and as I stepped past the pair, another spirit appeared suddenly between me and the One Tree.

The sight of her froze me to the bone. She looked just the same as the day Grandmother described her to me. Her long blond hair flowed about her face, fell down her back like a waterfall, and disappeared into the high grass. He white tunic was open from the neck down to mid breast and her long grey coat seemed to accentuate the whole scene. She was so beautiful, just as comely as the day she passed. I smiled, and after a moment, she smiled back. I could feel, for just a second, her love for me, and her worry. Then, as quick as she had appeared, she was gone, and disappointingly the feeling of love disappeared with the breeze.

I was so lost in her sudden appearance the ones who had been watching me finally made their presence known. I never saw them before they wanted me to, and only after I was ready.

"She still looks after you, even after passing she will not leave your side, such is the way of blood."

The voice was male, close to my age, and echoing in my mind. I didn't need to turn to know it was the voice of the Wolf Spirit that guides me on my path. "I know, even after I told she could go and find peace." I whispered looking to where the spirit had stood just a minute before.

"She is devoted and loyal John, as any sister would be, and she sees what you plan to do as a folly, as do I." The voice said harshly.

I was surprised to see he had waited so long to talk with me about this, but not in the tone he used. "And why do you say this?"

""She questions your intentions John, as do I, with the Nidhogg so close. We do not see an end which is hopeful."

"You know why I am here and what I must do Wahna. I must try and retrieve the child's soul. I have no choice but to." I answered turning to my left, South, to see my totem animal just a few feet away in a spot that was empty just seconds before.

A large wolf, Wahna stood as tall as my chest with fur that was black as the darkest night and eyes that were as yellow as the sun above which stared at me. He stayed back, eyeing me hard as the words sounded in my head. "Malfeus is not one to humor fools John, so what happened to the human woman Grouse was what she deserved. To travel to the Lower World of the Nightshades now, with the prophecy so close, is to tempt the darkness which comes to consume you and the other Winds."

Before I could answer another voice entered my head, deep and wise. "Wahna speaks the truth John Greywolf. Malfeus has seen his plan to fruition and giving back the girl's soul will not he do. You face the danger of Nidhogg and its followers coming for you being this close to its realm if you do this."

I turned around and there was the Great Bear Ursu. He was over Twelve feet tall with paws that were as round as my waist and a mouth that could swallow me whole. His fur was dark brown, thick, and it rippled as he breathed. Ursu walks with the Spirit of the North as Wahna does with the Spirit of the South. They each represent one direction on the great Medicine Wheel of the Universe. Each has special medicine and each has its own personality. Where Ursu is gentle but firm Wahna is direct and forward. I looked up to Ursu and spoke to him with my mind just as I had with Wahna.

"Is it right for me to walk away then, Great Bear? Is it right for me to turn my back on the little one?"

Ursu knelt so we could see eye to eye. "No John Greywolf, to walk away from an innocent such as this would darken your spirit. We, Wahna and I, only wish you to understand where you must go. To retrieve a soul from the Nightshades world will not be easy, not with Nidhogg looking to end your spirit. To journey to the realm of the Nightshades is far John, maybe too far for you to risk this time."

I nodded and spoke. "I understand Ursu, but Wahna taught me well. He showed me, that on my path, dangers cannot keep me from helping those in need. You Ursu, you taught me to keep the ones who could not defend themselves safe from the ones who threatened them."

The Great Bear turned to the large wolf letting Wahna speak. "Yes, you are strong with our teachings and medicine John, but where you must go, you will need to be quick. You will need to walk swiftly, but carefully, or the Nidhogg will find you."

"I know Wahna, and I will be as fast as I can." I agreed.

The pair looked to each other just as a screech split the quiet of this wide valley. I looked up to see the great Eagle Wanbli descend on the thermals from high in the sky. She came to a soft landing just to my right, out of the East, standing proud and as tall as I am. She clawed at the ground with her large talons while looking into my soul with her black eyes, almost through me. Wanbli is graced with vision to see over the horizon, to see the future with her powerful sight, and she has never been one to be blunt with speaking about what she sees.

"You go to confront the Nightshade Malfeus John Greywolf. I can see you crossing into their Other World, but be warned, the dark spirits of the realm know you are coming."

"How do the Nightshades know John Greywolf is coming Wanbli, unless the spirits have the power to see the future as you do?" Ursu asked the Eagle Spirit.

The Eagle never turned her eyes from me. "The girl's soul is not with Malfeus, but he can set you on the path to her. You will need to be careful though John Greywolf, the Nightshade will lie to you, trick you as to where the little girl's soul is now. And there is the Nidhogg, it seeks your death on the Middle World while you are here."

"Thank you, Great Spirit of the East. I am thankful for your sight. I have one looking after me. I am protected." I praised and assured her.

The Eagle closed her beak hard twice and then nodded her head quickly with a snap. "He will not be swayed from this path my brothers. Let him go, let him try and save this little soul."

"Yes, go and try to bring back the girl's soul John, be swift and be careful." Wahna said, and from the look of his eyes, he was not happy with finally letting me go.

"I will Wahna, I will."

I started for the One Tree again, and as I did, I felt Wanbli and Wahna slowly fade, but Ursu stayed and watched me form his spot on the field. "She also watches over you John Greywolf, and she approves of the one who keeps watch over you."

I stopped and looked back over my shoulder toward the Great Bear, and there just a few feet behind him, stood my sweet teacher, my Grandmother. Her face was hidden in the dark of a cowl pulled over her head, but I knew it was her and I could feel her concern as well. "Fade is a good soul Grandmother, as compassionate and as beautiful as yours."

There was no answer from her, no words in my mind. She only nodded, and I knew back in the recesses of the dark of the cowl, my teacher was smiling. Then Ursu was speaking again, taking over with his knowledge. "Walk three times around the great tree as the sun sets John Greywolf and you will be shown the way to the Other World of the Nightshades. The path will only stay open for a short time though, be fast of foot Shaman."

"Thank You Ursu." I answered. Even though I know the way to the realm of the Nightshades, I will never turn down the knowledge of Ursu.

As I approached the One Tree, I could feel its power, and I started to harmonize with it. I felt my soul start to meld with the Tree's energy, to be one, and I could sense all the other worlds those branches and roots touch, thousands upon thousands of worlds. I chose a spot on the trunk with a knot as large as my head as my starting point and headed west, around the tree, as the sun sets, and on my third pass I had not seen the path Ursu promised yet. I knew better though to be impatient with the words of the Great Bear and I kept walking west slowly. As I did, I saw a spot among the tangled roots at my feet, a soft glow that stood out. This was the way, down through the ground and the roots, to the Nightshades realm in the Lower World.

　　　To some it might seem crazy to look down at a glow on the ground and think a path might lead somewhere, but they have never stepped into the Other World. And to make it even more confusing, one must 'know' the way to the Other World they wish to visit, and by that, I mean one must have the knowledge of where the World they seek is. To travel the astral path to a realm you have no knowledge of can be dangerous sometimes, can lead one to be lost among the pathways of the universe. Think of it this way, if someone says meet them at a certain address, and you have never been there, then you would need a map to find your way. Well, in a round-about way, it works the same way when I journey, for if I do not know in my center where I am going I need a path to follow. It is for this reason my brother and sisters and I have not been able to confront the Nidhogg. It has hidden itself among the infinite realms of the Lower World and we have no way to find it, not until the other part of our plan comes to fruition at least.

　　　I knelt and reached out for that soft glow knowing full well what was going to happen, and when my hand dipped below the ground like the very dirt wasn't there, I was not shocked. I kept reaching, kept moving forward, and soon my whole upper body, all the way up to my hips was in the ground. I know it sounds like I had entered some magical tunnel, and in some way, I did, but this was no tunnel. I was passing through what you *might think of as a conduit, an energy flow that runs down through the ground. I could see through the dirt, to the roots of the One Tree leading to other worlds, and everywhere the energy of all the paths. The conduit pulled me down, drew me in, and even deeper than I had expected. I wasn't falling but floating and when I came out in the Nightshades realm, well, it was what I was expecting.*

I was home, in a strange way circular way.

"There, at three o'clock, I just spotted the target!"

The Curtis P-6 was running fine, purring like a kitten actually, so the pilot for the Protectorate only had to worry about keeping the plane from running into the other air ships. Oh, and he had to keep that damn 'Junk' in his mind-

"Are you sure it's the Junk?"

Now, amazingly, the one pilot who seemed to think of anything and everything but the Junk spotted the damn thing. The pilot looked just to his right and down like he was told, his eyes scanning the roof tops of the buildings below. At first, he didn't see a thing that looked like an old Chinese water craft, then he saw it, moored up against the side of a tall tenement in plain sight. He didn't even need to look at the picture tacked up on the control panel in the cockpit. Hell, it was pure luck they stumbled on it, what with the sky as full of air ships as it was.

"Damn, it's the one we've been looking." The Pilot stated with controlled excitement as he reached over and clicked the switch to set his Hertizian to a set frequency. "Citadel, this is Able 6, we have the Junk spotted on the West side of the city. I say again, we have spotted the target, do we engage, over?"

A second or two passed before the radio crackled again and a voice answered. "Able 6, Citadel, are you saying affirmative to sighting the target?"

The Pilot locked back over to the building ready to tell the controller on the other end of the radio that hell yes, they had found the damn Junk. Only the craft was gone, lifted off and away from the wall of the tenement now. He felt a bit of panic, just a smidge of a touch, before he spotted the Junk climbing skyward now. "Citadel, Able 6, that is an affirmative to the sighting. It's on the move now, heading northeast across the city."

He turned the P-6 into a slow climb and turn, following the Junk while keeping a safe distance. He went high over the nose of a zeppelin as his wingman went low under the tail of the same blimp. The twin planes kept an easy track on the Junk as the radio crackled again.

"Able 6, Citadel, you are to tail the Junk for now. I repeat, only follow and DO NOT ENGAGE, do you copy?"

"Citadel, Able 6, copy the orders. Will keep the Junk in eye sight for now."

"Able 6, Citadel, send along any changes in course. We will need a sitrep every ten minutes."

"Copy Citadel, Able 6 out."

The two pilots fell into a tailing formation and for the first time the Pilot noticed there wasn't a turbine visible on the Junk. How did the damn thing fly without a turbine? Forget that, how was it turning left and right with no wing or rudder?

"I think the Protectorate has found us Zheng."

Ru could see the sleek pair of airplanes following now. He had watched as both turned from the course of bypassing the Junk to slipping into a tailing position. He had called to Zheng to pick him up off the roof of the tenement and now, it looked as if the move had brought a bit of attention.

"Yes, we have been found. Do you want me to elude them?" The Master of the Gāi Gōng De Tiānkōng asked. He appeared out of the thin air next to the shaman with a blink, the usual way the ghost moved about on the air ship.

"No Zheng," Ru replied not affected by the abrupt arrival of the ghost by the rail, "let them follow us if they want. As long as the planes do not interfere then we can keep their eyes trained on us and off the others."

The ghost only nodded watching the planes closely. "Agreed, so we are not needed yet?"

"No Zheng, not yet, but I am sure with our loved ones scattered as they are, we will be soon. Until then, we need to pick up two more."

"The Onmyoji and the Druid, I know where both are." Zheng responded just as the Junk changed course, slipping past a whip and an air hauler.

More friends for the fight, Zheng thought silently, we will need all we can muster I think.

Part Thirteen

"I'll ask you again, once more, to come peacefully Mr. Baird."

The woman giving the order in a calm, but brutally hard tone, was a Magi and more importantly, was a high raking Umbra. Baird knew her, not personally, but by reputation and it was one of pure seriousness. She was very good at taking 'into custody' those Magi who found themselves in the cross hairs of the Magi who hunt from the shadows. He locked eyes with the woman trying to analyze why what was about to happen was actually going to happen. Behind him, Eleanor and Tomo watched every move between their friend and the Umbra leader, who hadn't come alone it suddenly dawned on them. Both heard the careful and purposefully silent steps of approaching feet and when Tomo glanced backwards he noted at least four more Protectorate soldiers and three other Umbra waiting silently. Eleanor looked out to the lobby and took note of four more bodies moving slowly, like crocodiles stalking prey on the river bank, through the morning crowd at the House.

"And just why are we being detained?" Baird asked with a snap, the frustration and suspicion easily detected in his voice.

"Come peacefully and I'll tell you everything once we're behind closed doors." The woman replied, calmly, trying to keep the four Magi from starting anything that resembled a move toward the exit.

Adelaide, who had been quiet since the beginning of the stand-off, finally spoke up. Her accent was a strange contrast to the tension, like a beautiful bird flying across a battle field. "Why are you blocking the doors? What have we done?"

"Stop acting all innocent Magi, you know why we're here."

The voice was harsh and without one ounce of empathy. It came from one of the Protectorate soldiers from behind Tomo and Eleanor and it was exactly what the Umbra Leader didn't want. The woman in charge sighed as she realized any hope of getting the four out of the lobby quietly was gone now due to the oaf with the gun.

"I'm not going anywhere with you, or anyone, and especially not to some back room." Eleanor hissed turning her body just slightly to face the group closing in from behind. She was deadly serious. She was not about to go to any backroom, because Eleanor knew too well, if that happened then she would never leave that room as a free woman.

Damn, well, there went our chance for a-

Suddenly, and quite abruptly, a short woman of Hispanic ethnicity appeared between the Umbra leader and Baird looking up to the male Magi. She wore a wide brimmed hat with a colorful beaded band around the base of the crown, which seemed to fit her sweet face, and which was filled with a broad smile. "Ai, Senor Baird, there you are. I have been looking for you!"

The tension, so thick it was like a fog, dissipated with the arrival of the strange woman. She claimed to know Baird but he wasn't sure who she was, evident by the confused look he gave her while speaking. "If I may ask, just who are you?"

"Oh, no one special mi amigo. I just met your father and grandfather, and both were concerned you might be in trouble, so I had come to check on you." The woman replied, which confused Baird even more as he looked over to Eleanor. She only stared back wide eyed, the look meant to elicit an answer from her love as to what was going on, who just shook his head in return. Baird's father and grandfather were both dead, passed on some years ago, back home in Australia.

"Excuse me Madame, your interfering-"the Umbra leader began before being cut off by the very person she was trying move along.

"Solo un minuto por favor," The strange woman broke in, still smiling and still blocking the Umbra Leader, to her growing annoyance with the whole situation. Everyone in the cluster, and that included the four Magi who were supposed to be detained, looked on with open mouths at how everything about this 'detaining' had gone off the rails.

The Hispanic woman turned back to Baird with a twist, just in time for the Magi to ask a question. "My father and- "

"I know Senor," the woman broke in again with a shake of her head sending the feathers in hat band waving, "your padre and abuelo are no longer with us, but that does not mean they cannot watch over you and worry when you get into trouble, which seems to be frequently they say."

There was a long moment of silence, not really weird if one thought about what was happening, before Baird knew the woman wasn't lying about talking to his father. "You actually spoke to my father, didn't you?"

The woman only smiled letting the look sink in, just as the patience of Umbra Leader behind her finally snapped, like a dry twig. The leader reached up and put her hand on the woman's shoulder ready to spin the lady round to face her, only with a swiftness, the Umbra wasn't prepared when the strange woman turned back to her.

"Madame,"

"Ai, I am so sorry, but can you hold her for me, por favor? She gets so excited at the worst times."

And at that moment, on top of the very hand the Umbra leader had used to touch the woman's shoulder, the largest black spider anyone had ever seen just popped right out of the very air itself to sit down with a plop. The bristly hair of its legs was the first thing the Umbra felt just before the weight of its body set in. Her eyes went wide with horror as both orbs locked with the spider's many small ones. She drew in a long haggard breath in terror just as the woman turned back to Baird, still smiling broadly while yelling.

"I think it is time to go my sister."

"I agree sister, time to depart with our friends." A voice called out from behind the Protectorate soldiers. The men turned to see a beautiful colored woman staring at them. She was dressed in a blue Protectorate dress coat complete with tails, which made no sense because she was also wearing a stoker top hat adorned with feathers and a beaded band, just like the strange Hispanic woman.

No one, and that was not a soul mind you, knew the Umbra leader was deathly afraid of eight legged arthropods, spiders in common tongue. She stood there frozen, staring in horror at the beast on her hand, her mind screaming to shake it off but her body refusing to move a single inch. Then the spider hissed, made a noise like a growl maybe, and that was it, all that was needed. The Umbra leader shrieked, flung the spider away with a snap, and literally ran into her companions behind her. She knocked one over while sending the other spinning.

And that was how the entrance to the Magi House became a war zone on this bright morning.

Who made the first move?

It's a valid question, a great starting place in the conversation about that morning, and if you asked Cooper the same just before all hell broke loose, well, all you'd get was a small shrug of his shoulders. The Magi wasn't sure who started the whole thing, maybe the Protectorate guard, the one who had growled menacingly at him when the large man spotted him. Or maybe it was Mr. Ezio, who grabbed his coat collar and with a hard shove moved Cooper a foot or three to the right, a good head start for the entrance. And he needed it, because before Cooper knew it, the whole lobby of the Magi House descended into chaos complete with screaming, broken furniture, and explosions.

Yes, explosions.

"RUN FOR THE ENTRANCE MR. COOPER! RUN AS FAST AS YOUR LEGS CAN GO!"

The command from Ezio, echoing in his ears, was enough for Cooper to continue his movement toward the entrance. Just as he did that, break in a run for the doors leading to the outside, one of the Protectorate soldiers drew a very large hand gun. It wasn't one of the automatic types with flat sides, no, this weapon had a large round cylinder just back by the grip. Cooper knew this because his eyes locked right to the large barrel on the gun as he imagined the thing probably used a really large bullet.

Then the man squeezed the trigger. Cooper knew this too because the front of the gun exploded with a large fiery gunpowder burst. A micro second later something, more than likely the bullet, whizzed within an inch of Cooper's left ear. That's it, I'm dead, he thought as the soldier brought the gun back down from the hard kick it gave when fired, down to point right at his forehead again. It was at this instant that Cooper realized he had stopped running for the entrance, a bad thing he guessed.

The soldier took aim, ready to blow Cooper's head right off, when a bolt of lightning hit him square in the face. All at once there was pain, overwhelming and debilitating, which caused the soldier to drop the gun just a moment before he was flying backwards, spinning like an unconscious rag doll. The attack from Ezio left Cooper alive for now, but it also left the tall Magi open and vulnerable, which is exactly how the large Protectorate soldier got a hold of him.

In the short time it took the tall Umbra to throw an arc of energy into the solider trying to kill Mr. Cooper, the soldier was on Ezio with a flash. One of his large hands grasped into the lapel of the fine coat of the Magi while the other drew back and hit the Magi with a solid rabbit punch right to the jaw. Ezio felt his legs wobble just a little as the blow scrambled his brain for a second, just long enough to watch the man to draw back his hand again and then land another solid punch, about an inch from where the first one hit. This time his legs really wobbled and Ezio had reach up and grab the soldier's arm to keep his feet as his brain seemed to short circuit.

The Protectorate soldier smiled, an evil grin, as he had every intent to beat poor Ezio clean into a puddle on the floor. He drew back again as his comrade, the only one left standing, ran to help his other fellow soldier. Oh, I am going to-

Something large, and really heavy, slammed into his face just then. Now it was the soldier who had to fight the scramble going on in his mind, that loss of cognition. He shook his head to get his senses back, more than enough time to feel Ezio reach up and place the flat of the Magi's hand against his chest. A second later pain hit like a wave swamping the large muscular soldier, his consciousness of the world blasted away. He was mercifully out cold as his body went flying backward just like his smaller comrade, only the large man went a lot further across the room.

With smoldering hands, Ezio looked down to see the remnants of what at one time was a very nice vase. It was probably very expensive he thought as he looked up to Mr. Cooper, standing by the table the vase used to sit on. Ezio gave a small wave in thank you and was about to add some words to the gesture when a woman's voice cut above the din of the fight going on up front.

"BADU! BADU!"

"Alice," Ezio whispered with a look of pure befuddlement as he watched his love running toward him, past arcs of Magic energy and people throwing punches. "What are you doing here?"

The Gal Golomt

The 'Great Smoke Hole in the World'

The first time I came across it, I was journeying through the Middle World, the one we live in daily but hidden away from our eyes. It was just my third-time Journeying to the One Tree, and it was by pure accident I found the tunnel. Smoke, acrid from Sulfur, made breathing hard as the small clouds rose in long yellow snaking tendrils up to the blue cloudless sky above. The feeling of foreboding coming from the hole was so strong, it made me stop a few steps away from the portal to another realm in the Lower World, with a touch of concern for my safety.

What is wrong John Greywolf?

I turned to see the yellow eyes of Wahna, my totem Wolf, standing suddenly beside me, appearing without a sound. He was just my height those days, when I was younger, and he spoke with his gruff voice only in my mind. I hadn't fully realized the fact I could hold a conversation with him in my mind yet, but at the time I had no care to ask a question about it. I think it was because, at that age, the fact I was talking with the spirit of a large black wolf was more exciting than the how of it all.

"That hole, it feels strange to me, like something bad is down there at the bottom, waiting for me to fall in. Is that 'Hell' Wahna". I asked the question with concern, and more than a little curiosity. A few nights before, a man had come to our home seeking Grandmother's help, suffering from an ailment I had never heard of. And strangely, he seemed more frightened of what would happen to his soul more than what this ailment might do to him physically. He kept crying, screaming that he was going to die, and that his soul would surely go to a place called 'Hell'. It must be a truly terrible place Ru whispered, this Hell, if this man was so scared of going there after dying.

The hole is just a path John Greywolf, a simple passage to a realm in the Lower Worlds. Where it leads, what Other World the path touches, is only known to the one who opened it. The Gal Golomt is nothing to fear John Greywolf, it is but one way to visit and return from the realms which are below the One Tree, just as flying among the clouds

above or climbing through the branches of the One Tree is a path to the
Upper Worlds.

"Then 'Hell, it doesn't exist?"

Wahna stepped closer to me, his nose touching mine almost, as he
explained what my mind had failed to understand. **Heaven and Hell, those**
are just ideas from convictions John Greywolf, images born from tenets
brought about belief and faith. There are realms in the Upper Worlds
born of fire and lava which would burn any who are not prepared to
visit, just as there are beautiful forest and mountains meant to heal
those who visit in the Lower Worlds. There is no good or bad, no injustice
or righteousness here in the Other Worlds, unless one brings it with
them.

"If there is no Heaven and no Hell, then is there Good and Evil in
the Middle World? And why, if there is no good and evil, are there places
like that one, places that scare men so?" I asked, my head tilting to the
side just a bit.

And why does one so young wish to see the Worlds in such a
stark manner, eh John Greywolf? I say wait my young one, grow and let
your eyes see more before asking that question of me again. For now,
just know every act you do while walking your path in the Middle World
has a cost, a weight you could say, which your soul keeps.

"A weight?"

Yes, every soul bears the cost of the path it chose to walk. If a
soul takes a life, betrays a love, or acts with hatred, then that soul is
weighted down. If the soul acts with love, kindness, and with forthright
intention, then that soul is lifted. This cost, a weight, is added to every
soul for every act it takes. When one goes before the One Tree, their soul

is set to the scale, and it is decided where that soul must go to be restored.

I began to see what my spirit guide was telling me, his medicine altering my knowledge and helping me to understand. Still, I was confused from the other night. "Then why was the man so scared Wahna? Why was he so certain he was going to Hell?"

Because he fears death John Greywolf. All men do, for they know not what comes next once their time is done in the Middle World.

"Grandmother says death is just a transition, a change of our energy from one form to another. She says there is nothing to fear when one dies."

Yes and no, John Greywolf. Men, from woman to man to child to old, all tally a debt while they walk the Middle World, and when they cross, those souls must be held accountable. That place at the end of the Gal Golomt, the one you feel fear from, it is one of the many places where those souls must go to have the scales balanced and their energy cleansed. What you feel, it is the fear all have for such places, in both the Upper and Lower Worlds.

"Why do we have to go to those places when we die?" I asked, turning to Wahna with a little touch of fear if I remember correctly.

You know all men are just energy John Greywolf. When their time comes to an end they must travel to one of the Other Worlds and be purged, and you know that the energy is used again once it has been freed of its shell and cleansed. This is the way of the things, always and forever.

I nodded looking back to the Great Smoke Hole. "How many Lower Worlds are there Wahna?

As many as there are Upper Worlds John Greywolf, too many too count. Each one is ruled by its own master, its Grand Spirit. The Worlds are different but alike, separate and unique but intertwined and inseparable. You will journey to many of them in your life John Greywolf, journey to bring back souls who have ventured too far or are too sick to return, and you will learn which Other Worlds will not tolerate your presence and which ones will.

I nodded again understanding where Wahna was taking me, or for those who don't understand, explaining to me.

"So down there is where we're freed of our physical shell and restored for a return to the Middle World?"

Wahna eased forward and nudged my hand with his nose, the usual signal he wanted his ears scratched and I was willing to oblige. He let me run my fingers through his thick coarse fur while finishing.

Yes, and it is where you will go one day too John Greywolf, though alone you will not be.

Those words from Wahna, spoken so many years ago, have stayed with me all my life and even brought me balance in times of contemplation and need. Truth to his wisdom, it wasn't till many years after that fateful journey did I come to know and accept what he was telling me. I could spend hours and hours talking of the Other Worlds, how the One Tree is the path between the Upper and Lower, and how we, the ones who walk the physical path, make our own 'Hell'. That discussion my friends, those are words for another time.

I thought of Wahna and his teachings as I glided down the tunnel to the Nightshades Lower World. I moved along toward a bright light, blinding and scorching at the same time, and then in a blink I was out, free of the tunnel. There was no exit, no hole to emerge from, just the end to the path. Even blinded by the bright light, I knew from past trips down the Gal Golomt to this realm that I was standing at the foot of a sheer wall made of dark slate, the base of a large mountain that stretched forever skyward and spread out from that point right or left for just as long.

I grew up in what people call with a certain awe 'The Badlands', a northern section of New Mexico. I was raised among the craggy sandstone and shale buttes, the scrub brush and the cactus, where the sun shone down baking the ground till was hard and fired. It was a harsh land, but beautiful beyond words, and strangely so was the realm of the Nightshades. Before me there would be a rolling desert of scorched and burnt bad land lay stretched out, red packed sand and dunes as far as the eyes could see was the only way I could go. I didn't need my eyes to tell me I was at once home and also in the realm of the Nightshades, one in the same almost. The only difference is this realm, it has a special spirit waiting for the newly arrived, and I readied myself to meet this unusual guide, a dark shade which greets all who enter.

Though, 'greet' might not be the appropriate word.

The Faceless One, a dark spirit with no discernable facial features except for a small hole in the center of blank flesh which was supposed to be a face, has the appointed the task of meeting all who touch the ground here in the Nightshades realm. It has no nose, no lips, and no eyes with which to see, hear, or smell. It dresses in a nice Victorian gray suit with black shoes that buckle up the side, the look of a perfect gentlemen. And yet it has all the temperance of a mad dog and would lie to you as soon as say hello. It berates and tortures every poor soul sent here with a list of the horrid acts the person has committed, true and false acts, while alive, reveling in the torment the reliving of the deeds cause, and yet there is one thing it cannot do...lie when asked for directions.

I know, I laughed when I found this out as well.

So, when my eye sight returned, I was ready to be called various names and be told my soul was damned. Only, the Faceless One wasn't there, and where my feet should have settled on hard-packed red sand there was grass and soft dirt, a simple four-foot-wide section that looked like someone had rolled out a green rug. I looked up and for a good distance I saw this splurge of life in a place of death run on down the slope of a dune then back up the rise of another. I stood for a minute taking in the sight, letting my mind process what was occurring. I made some mental notes and then made a fatal decision.

I didn't need to ask for directions it looked like.

I started off in a light jog, using the grass and dirt as my guide, and as I topped the rise of second dune and the grass flowed down, I found the Faceless One finally, doing battle with a mighty foe it seemed. The shade was standing right where the grass and soft dirt ended. It was fighting the grass, blade by blade, in the only way it knew how as I approached.

Damnable Fungus!

The shade screamed at the grass. It didn't actually speak with an audible voice, but more with a grating sound in your mind that made you cringe, like glass breaking as nails scratched across a chalkboard.

I smiled watching the shade's distress over this foreign intruder to its world, and then I noticed why it was having such a hard time. The grass was trying to grow inch by tireless inch, and the Faceless One wasn't having any of it. As soon as single blade popped up the shade was barking *at it.*

Treacherous Parasite! Away with you!

And each time, at the attack, the grass would dip below the dirt from the harsh words, for a minute, before another green stalk would make a try setting off another barrage of hate. It was quite entertaining to watch I must admit.

"You're not winning the battle," I pointed out, speaking with my mind while stepping off the grass. I could instantly feel the heat from the ground through my moccasins, and with the temperature as high as the sun, there was no relief in sight.

The shade looked up and I am sure if it had a face it was sneering at me with hate. **Your responsible for this, I know it!**

"No, I have nothing to do with this. I could no more change this place then you could change the One Tree."

I do not believe you shaman. You lie when it is convenient to you, one John Greywolf. You, who tread with liars and thieves and whores, you will soon be ours!

The shade spat its words with venom. Its voice was like needles stabbing my brain and pain blossomed all through my skull, but again I knew it would happen. I just smiled and responded. "You have no power to see the future Faceless One, and I have seen where my end comes. Your words don't scare me."

They do not, do they? I can see your darkness John Greywolf, deep and buried, but I can see it as I see it in every soul that comes here. You have a tally like all who pass me and it will be cleansed like all the others. You know this. You have seen this too.

"Like I said, you do not scare me Faceless One, not with words I

already know are lies. Now tell me, where is Malfeus?" I asked politely while smiling smugly under my hat.

You seek the Reaper of Souls, eh shaman? Well John Greywolf, go to where I point, and with luck, your time here will begin. The Nightshade hissed holding out a long bony finger in the direction of a rise, and then further off into the desert.

I only nodded knowing the Faceless One could not lie when asked about Malfeus, though using the Nightshade's old name was a little much, and as I started off I pointed to the ground and spoke using my voice one last time. "You missed a piece."

The Faceless one turned its featureless face down and yelped in my mind while taking three quick steps back. The grass had come back with a vengeance, almost reaching the Nightshade's foot. I could still hear him screaming at the green wisps, driving them back with his vitriol as I left the area.

Away with you insect! Away with you I command!

Part Fourteen

"I think they're still onto us lad"

Ru had to agree with the deep voice, a British baritone an equal match to Wahkan's low vocal tone, as he watched the pair of shinny bi-planes slide back into a tailing formation behind the flying Junk. After picking up Megumi the Onmyoji and the Druid Gabriel, both literally leaping onto a moving air ship from the roof of a building as Zheng refused to stop the Junk, the Tiānkōng took off quickly heading into the full skies above Chicago. Even being as large as Wahkan, in stature and weight, Gabriel managed the jump with ease, the tails of his long dark green coat snapping from the sudden movement. Megumi, being just above 5 feet and slight, could have tumbled and fallen onto the air ship and still looked as graceful as a dancer. Her colorful Kimono, which looked to Ru to be about half the full length of a traditional robe, whipped around as her boots landed with silence.

Zheng had tried one last maneuver to throw off the planes, a quick dip in altitude followed by a second quick slip to the right, around the corner of a building. He then had the Junk climb quickly, with a jolt of speed, taking the flying ship up and behind an air hauler. Zheng moved the Tiānkōng so close to the engine of the hauler Ru and Gabriel could see the engineer driving the flying train had spilt something on the front of his overalls. The shaman damn near lost his lunch, what with dropping, taking a sharp right, and then gaining altitude again. Ru was reminded why he hated flying, and somewhat sharply at that. Next to him, the druid cursed aloud all the changes in speed and direction, his stomach twisted in knots as well. And Megumi, well, she just giggled as the wind whipped through her clothes and hair, the priestess obviously enjoying the ride.

Ru, and the others, watched calmly from the aft tail of the Junk as his stomach began to settle down. The planes, at first, were nowhere to be seen and Ru was happy with that, but then as he scanned the full sky behind them he spotted the pair following still. The pilots were good he thought, they had plotted a quick intercept course and with some deviousness were now trying to follow unseen. They're using the other air ships and zeppelins as cover Ru told himself as he turned back to Zheng with a small smile.

"You almost lost them."

"Yes, these two are very persistent, and now it looks as though they are not alone." Zheng replied.

"Zheng is right," Megumi stated pointing to the sky, "the Protectorate are growing in number."

"I guess they intend to try and board us, as if they could!" Gabriel huffed, his contempt for the Protectorate clearly on display.

The shaman looked back to the trailing planes, assuming more planes should appearing now, grouping up. Yet there wasn't a third or a fourth plane and Ru wondered just what the master of the Tiānkōng had seen. Then he spotted the trio of whips, small fast-moving air ships, flying in from behind the planes. Two of the new air ships did a small dance, one above and the other below, to get around the cars of the very air hauler Zheng had almost hit. Damn, Ru thought, it looks as if the Protectorate are going to be a thorn in our sides for the remainder of the day.

"Do you want me to try and lose them again?" Zheng asked

"You do Zheng and I promise you I'll leave something nasty on the deck of your precious air ship here, not to mention my beautiful clothes!" Gabriel snapped causing Megumi to giggle again.

Ru chuckled and shook his head, "like Gabriel, my stomach may not take another attempt at eluding the Protectorate Zheng."

Zheng nodded before closing his eyes. He stood still for a second, the wind literally whipping through him, not disturbing a stitch of his ghostly clothing, and then he opened his eyes and spoke quickly with a sense of concern. "John has crossed into the Nightshades realm, why would he go there?"

"I'd think it would have to be a very important reason Zheng." Megumi answered before turning to Ru.

"It is Megumi, he went to save the soul of a child Zheng, taken there by one of the Nightshades. He will be busy for the foreseeable future, so we must help the others." Ru answered watching the whips and planes creep in closer.

"We can do no less while John is preoccupied." Zheng stated while also watching the tailing craft close in. "We may have to move quickly in a moment. The Protectorate are getting closer."

"As long as you keep the dips and dives to a minimum Zheng. My breakfast is still in my belly and I'd like to keep it there please." Gabriel remarked, which seemed to have no effect on the ghost.

This was because there was no answer from the shaman and Zheng turned to see what Ru was doing, which was what he had been doing just a minute earlier. The shaman was standing with his eyes closed, peaceful and relaxed. Then he abruptly opened his eyes and looked to

Zheng with a sigh, "Sara and Marisol are in trouble. We need to get to the Magi House as fast as the Tiānkōng can fly."

"Why, what is wrong with my Marisol? If something is wrong with my delicate flower I'll be taking some heads!" Gabriel growled, his words instantly raising the eyebrows of everyone. Even Ru, who looked at the Druid with incredulity while speaking.

"Marisol, my sister, a delicate flower?"

"Yes, my Marisol! She is the sweetest, kindest person I have ever met!" Gabriel barked.

The Onmyoji priestess looked on in shock for a moment before turning to Zheng. "He and Marisol are together, correct?"

"Yes, very much in love." Zheng whispered back, his eyes still on Ru and Gabriel.

"Then he should know Marisol is no flower, correct? She's broken the bones of more men than I can count."

"He should, but it seems love does blind."

The priestess only nodded as Ru leaned in and spoke calmly to Gabriel, "then we better hurry to help her. Who knows what danger she is facing right now."

"Your bloody right! Zheng, get this ship moving and get us...where was it again?" The druid snapped.

"The Magi House," Megumi pointed out with a nod, "Ru said the Magi House is where they are."

"Yes, yes, get us to the Magi House at once Zheng!"

The ghost grinned finally turning away from watching the druid and shaman to the approaching planes. "At once, and I will show the ones who follow just how fast the Tiānkōng can fly!"

"Wait Zheng- "Ru began just before the Junk leapt practically, jumping with a sudden burst of speed, which pinned the shaman and the others against the aft rail of the Junk. With his breath gone, the shaman held onto the rail with one arm while holding his skull cap in place with the other. He glanced back to see the Protectorate planes and air ships also speed up, going into a pursuit mode to catch them. Then he turned to see Megumi laughing while the druid screamed out.

"Damnable ghost, I'm going to lose my breakfast all over myself because of you!"

Now the shaman joined in with the priestess, letting loose howls of laughter.

"What do you think he is doing?"

The question, much like the voice which carried the words, was annoying to Fade. The Pirate Captain had knelt next to John, looking at his face with concern, and wondering exactly the same thing Miss Grouse was asking about. What are you doing John, my love? Are you safe, wherever you are? Then the inquiry from the maniacal mistress sitting at the child's desk broke her trance and it upset Fade, just a tad.

"He's risking his life for you Abagail, so keep that in mind when you speak of John."

The child, which looked to be a hundred and fifty but was actually not a young one at all, only smiled back with a shake of her head. "It bothers you that John is going to save me, doesn't it?"

Fade had been able to keep her anger in check, even after John had slipped away to wherever he slipped away to, with the Lady Grouse, but it was getting harder every time the woman uttered a word. She stood up, her one hand resting on her cutlass while the other she placed on the butt of her gun.

"It bothers me when one of my crew makes a mistake. It bothers me when the wine I prefer has run out. If something happens to John while he is trying to save your black soul, well Abagail, I will be so much more than 'bothered'."

The child-older woman just stared back at Fade, the weird contrast between the wrink ed face of an old woman and obvious child with eyes which had seen so much was unnerving for the Pirate Captain, and yet Fade only locked eyes with Abagail and kept her glare as Abagail spoke. "You obviously care for him, what with all the worry I've seen you-"

"I do worry about him, never question that."

"-show, and yet, with a wild guess, I'd say you more than likely keep him at arm's length. Why is that Miss Fade, afraid to commit? Are you afraid John will try and cage your rebellious spirit?"

"We're not talking about my life Abagail, or my feelings for John. and both will never be a topic of conversation between us, ever."

A sly smile crossed the face of Miss Grouse, again, unnerving as hell just like before, as if the devil were smiling back at me Fade thought. "All right, a little close to home I see, but there is something else bothering me. I thought all Pirates drank Rum."

"Oh, we do, and on the very day I hear your no longer with us Abagail, I'm going to drink a very large glass of the best Rum I can find." Fade replied, cold and with her own cruel smile.

The retort brought an instant reaction, but not from Abagail, who only sat at the desk quietly, calmly. Her valet, shuffling and wheezing, stumbled forward and called out the Pirate Captain with a raised finger. "You cannot speak to the Madame like that!"

Loyal to a fault, eh Michael the Servant? Fade thought as she was about to respond, but then her ears picked up the faintest sound of feet walking on the floor above them. She looked up to the ceiling while holding up a hand and hissing to shut up the servant. Fade listened carefully for a second, then another, and all the while Abagail and her man Michael stared with her wondering what the Pirate had heard and what she was going to do.

"You didn't invite anyone else to this party tonight, did you Abagail?"

"No," the child-woman whispered as another creak from another footstep on the floor above sounded, louder now.

Fade looked down finally and without turning her attention to either Abagail or Michael she stepped over to the table with the book used in the rite. She took off her special hat and laid it on the book carefully before turning back. "Then John's special friend has finally come calling."

"I thought you were John's 'special friend', Pirate Captain?"

Fade smiled and nodded, "yes I am, now and for a very long time to come." Her cutlass slid easily and quietly from its scabbard as she got ready to greet the man who had been following her love.

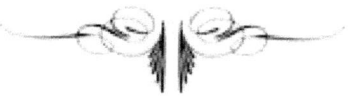

Otto finished up the last stitch to take up the hem of the brown dress Wells had chosen, a rather nice look for her. It was a simple design with brown lace over the cream base material, the sides of the hem higher than the front or back creating a nice 'V' shape. She completed the cress with an Ivory colorec shirt w th short sleeves and open neck exposing the collar she wore. When Inga had inquired about removing it, both Weavers stated emphatically they couldn't and wouldn't remove the things. So, Inga and Otto both worked around the leather straps. As Otto stood up, his wife finished the ast of the adjustments to Wells whale bone under-bust corset, a nice red color with a striking gothic design to the clasps and eyes where it was tied. The small tailor stepped back and sighed with a large smile.

"I think we have done it again mama!"

"Yes papa," Inga smiled watching Wells turn a tight circle in front of the trio of mirrors while smiling from ear-to-ear, "your work is always exceptional. It makes the girls look so beautiful."

Wells came to a stop staring at herself in the mirror and whispering, "do you really th nk I'm beautiful?"

The question was something a child might ask a parent, seeking for the joy of approval, but this was not childlike in any way. It was serious, coming from a young lady who had never once had such pretty clothes to put on. She looked at herself wondering who the striking woman was staring back. As she did Boles spoke up standing just off to the side of the mirrors.

"You look so beautiful Wells, you take my breathe away."

The small Weaver turned to her love and smiled, a small tear forming in her left eye. "I do?"

"As beautiful as any princess,"

The voice was low and it immediately grabbed the attention of everyone in the shop. Wahkan had been quiet since talking about the war, so when he spoke it was nice to hear. Boles turned to him and nodded, "that she does, even prettier than any princess you could pick."

Before Wahkan could answer, smiling broadly, Wells broke in walking over to stand by her companion. "And Boles, she's so striking dressed in such pretty clothes."

The dark-haired Weaver was striking Wahkan thought. She was dressed in gathered one piece dress made from dark rich grey, the edges of the hem embroidered with the front taken up to her, and short sleeves just like Wells. A black leather under-bust corset set was a perfect match, something Inga had pointed out and offered to the Weaver to try, but instead of hose like Wells had picked out, Boles chose dark leggings. Both had chosen boots which ran calf high, lacing up the side with low heels. Yes, both looked so sweet Wahkan was sure every man in the city would be staring at them.

"Oh, your both heartbreakers, take my word for it."

"And he would know, our handsome Wahkan!" Inga cackled as she stood by her husband, looking at the Weavers with a proud smile. Wells and Boles stared at each other for a moment, taking in how they looked as a glow touched their faces. Then Wells turned and looked at the small pair of tailors, that tear in her eye still.

"We can never repay you for what you've done, the both of you. We've never been graced with such...beautiful things before."

The small declaration was more than just words to Otto and Inga, both chuckling with joy. They were used to making and selling clothes to people who never truly seemed to enjoy what they had purchased, who never seemed to respect what they had in their very hands. These people never seemed to understand the craftsmanship that went into making such beautiful garments, and yet here were two who were truly in awe of what they were wearing If you asked Otto at that moment what he was thinking, he might say he felt a new inspiration in his heart at the words from the small Weaver.

"As long as you are happy my friends with your dresses, then that is enough to make me happy and joyful." Otto remarked with a laugh before kissing Inga on the cheek.

Inga laughed as well, which made Boles and Wells laugh just before she spoke up. "Yes, we are so happy you like the dresses, so much so we could never ask for money."

"No, no, we would never charge John for doing this. We are the ones in his debt for what he gave us." Otto added quickly.

"So are we, for helping us, for..." Boles whispered, smiling while holding Wells hand. The green-haired Weaver only smiled back squeezing her love's hand knowing exactly how Boles felt. Words just didn't seem to large enough to express what she wanted to say about John saving them from that terrible place in Brooklyn. But he wasn't alone Wells suddenly realized, the shaman had help. From the brilliant technoist Wally to the stalwart and steadfast Wahkan. Just the thought of his name caused the small Weaver to look over and catch him staring back at them both. It was then Wells realized Inga was speaking and she turned her attention to the little lady.

"Yes, without the help of our wonderful John, Papa and I might have closed the shop and stopped making these wonderful dresses."

"Really, why?" Boles asked with true surprise.

"We were lost, not so sure of ourselves after we lost our Max." Inga started before pausing, letting Otto step in.

"Ja, we were not even sure if coming all the way here to Chicago had been the right thing to do, but then John came into our shop and from then till now, it has felt right."

"So, he saved you too, in a word." Wells giggled feeling strangely happy and just a little giddy at the moment.

"Ja, he did, by letting us talk to Max again." Otto said and this time it was his turn to pause to let Inga take over when the Weavers looked just a little shocked.

The little lady stepped forward and explained while still smiling warmly. "Oh, I know it is hard to understand my new friends, and yet it is the truth. He came through those doors, and without a single pause, told us he had come to see us at the behest of our Max."

"Your son, but he was dead you said, killed in the war." Wells replied in a low, and hopefully, respectable tone.

Inga only nodded as her husband took over, switching in the conversation with ease. "He was, and yet here was John telling us that he wished to speak with us again. And before you ask, no, we did not believe him at first, that was until he told us something only Max would know."

"What did you do?" Boles asked speaking in the same low tone as Wells had.

The tale paused again as Otto let his wife speak and continue, drawing the Weavers in further. "Well, he told us he would return the next evening and if we truly wanted he would help us to speak to Max. So, the next night John came back to the shop and, well, we spoke with our son again. He gave us back our old selves, the purpose to make such wonderful clothes, for people such as you."

The shop was quiet again as Wells and Boles stared at the little tailor and his wife with blank expressions. The story seemed a little far-fetched, and if you asked Otto and Inga, the pair would agree, but both would stand firm that it was the truth. They had talked with Max, felt his presence surround them, and even stepped into a dream world to see him, standing in a beautiful never-ending field of tall grass. No, as crazy as it sounded, Otto and Inga felt their son Max that night, and that is why they were so devoted to the shaman. And this 'truth' wasn't lost or one of the Weavers as Boles only nodded and sighed.

Yet, just as Boles was about to speak, a young boy ran up to the locked front door of the shop screaming. As Wahkan unlocked the door and the child, speaking quickly with a Scottish accent, entered, Otto knew nothing good could come of this message.

Part Fifteen

She stoked the flames, building and teasing its flames to head higher and higher toward the night sky, forcing the cold away from the ones who sat around the fire. The shaman who taught us, we Four Winds, this path of Shamanism was one with nature, with the desert we lived in, and endlessly filled with old stories and myths. It was the way she taught her children those days, passing along old tales with whispers on nights like these. Tonight, was no different as she sat down by the fire, by us, on a blanket outside our hut and covered up with a heavy fur. I smiled as the fire warmed me, my imagination ready for what I knew was coming.

"Do you remember children, the story of the dark ones called Nightshades which I told you all?" she asked in a teasing manner.

She knew better.

She knew we knew, memorized her every word, but it did not matter. We wanted to hear the tale again so much, from her, that all four of us played dumb to her inquiry, leaving Marisol to speak. "The Nightshades of the Lower World, the Thirteen Nightmares? You told us a little."

"Well then, I will need to tell you the myth again." She smiled.

Oh, what such wonderful words to hear. These were the happiest times I remember with her. After this, maybe a year later, the training of my Path took on a more serious note. Even with the need to ensure we were ready to face what would come for us in our later years, she never once treated her children with anything but love. She smiled and leaned in ready to transport us along with her tale to a mystical and dangerous world.

"Some say long ago there were angels, great beings of light and love, who floated from land to land here in the Middle World bestowing happiness and gifts on those people they found living in villages and tribes. These angels were kind and gentle to the people and they were honored with gifts in return. There was one among these angels though, an old one, who held the greatest of their power, the most majestic of all these angels on high, the Exalted One. And this angel ruled the others with a gentle but firm hand, thinking all under its wings were loyal and trusting. Yet, there were some who were not so devoted my children."

"Who hated the Exalted One?" I asked cautiously.

Her eyes opened large as the image of the fire danced off the whites. "There were thirteen angels John, thirteen who wanted no part of helping those they found on the lands they visited. They felt this power they had was for them and them alone, helping others was not their calling. They disliked anyone but their kind, hated the lowly beings they helped, and even more, these thirteen angels wished death on any being more than aid."

I shook my head making the tumble of hair I was growing fall into my eyes slightly, it was stark white even then. Ru took over then and I was happy to hear my brother speak. "But you teach us that we should help those in need because it is the Path we walk."

"Yes, it is Ru," She answered leaning away for a moment and poking the fire, "that is our Path and it is a hard one to walk. There are others who think they walk it with us by giving money or gifts or words to those who they think need them, but they are fools my children. These people do not understand what someone needs, that there are times when a gentle hand must be put aside for the hard one. When you four are older, and have walked the Path for a longer distance, you will see the truth of what I say."

"Yes Grandmother," we answered together. It was all she would take for the wisdom she bestowed on us. Then Marisol asked a quick question, her accent adding to the speed of her words it seemed.

"Where did the angels come from Grandmother? Did they come from magic?"

Our Grandmother chuckled and smiled with a shake of her head. "No, my little one, not magic, just belief and faith. It is what gives birth and power to the Spirits of the Other Worlds. The power of belief is strong Marisol, for without it there is no path to walk. Without faith, one is blind and can only wander, understand?"

We all nodded as she smiled again, leaned in, and started her story once more. "And what do you think these angels who were against the old one did children?"

"They tried to kill the Exalted One, but they failed." Sara answered quickly, the melodic sound of her voice like one of the very angels were talking about.

"Yes Sara, they tried to kill him and they failed, but in the end, that was their very plan. The Exalted One cast them down into the darkness of the Lower World never to leave and that is where they wished to stay. When I teach you to Journey children, you will find the path to the Lower World and you will find the Nightshades realm. You may have need to go there. Just remember, tread carefully there for it is the Thirteen's home now and they will not accept you, understand?"

"Yes Grandmother,"

Her words have always been with me, safely tucked away in my heart and mind, and there has never been more truth to the last ones then now. As I made my way down the small rise to the field where thousands of white energy masses were shaped like men and women, I knew all were trapped by invisible chains which kept them secured here. These souls were making the final transition of their world, as Wahna had said, the necessary removal of the energy that made them who they were in their Middle World. This is where only a small portion of the men and women come to meet the end, and I passed among them quietly, but they still could tell of my presence. These souls could sense my energy and longed for the freedom which it teased them with. They turned to look at me with their white faces, and in my mind, they cried for help.

Help me!

I do not deserve to be here! This must be a mistake!

Please, I have children who will miss me! Let me Go!

There was no pleading, no begging, and no mistakes. To come to this field meant one's time in the Middle World had ended and there was only one step left to be done. There was one last entity to see, and he was Malfeus. I spotted his form just as his name crossed my mind, as if by chance, but I know, down here there is no such thing.

The Reaper...

The Angel of Death...

Some call him a Memitim...

Malfeus is all of those, and more.

He looks like a simple man, well built, standing about six feet five in a tight black suit with tails, and a tallow colored shirt with a red tie. His black hair is combed back and held in place with oil, just like his long goatee. If you were to pass him on a street you may not give him a second glance, but then the chills would start to roll down your spine. The smell of burning brimstone, and flesh, would touch your nose making you sick instantly. Then you would turn to see what caused this and there he would be standing, just out of reach, smiling with such evil and malevolence from solid black orbs for eyes your legs would threaten to give out. I have seen the strongest warrior falter when confronted by him, and this is what Malfeus lives for, the fear and revulsion one has when seeing him.

"Please, tell me your time has finally come to an end, shaman."

He spoke using his voice knowing it would send fear through the trapped souls around him. Malfeus's voice was deep, from some dark pit where light never touches, and it hurt your very bones when he spoke. I only smiled hiding this and replied keeping myself calm.

"Good day to you Malfeus."

In a blink, he had crossed the sandy floor of the desert field and was in front of me. I could see the black ichor drip from his hair and goatee, sliding down his suit and tie, and wondered what would happen if I touched it just in the slightest. Lose the end of my finger maybe, to some type of acid?

"Why are you here Shaman?" He glared while standing over me. Out in the field the trapped souls trembled and moaned.

"I came to retrieve a soul Malfeus."

"A soul, from my field?"

"No, she is not here from what I can sense."

His right eyebrow rose just ever so slightly before closing his eyes. The Nightshade concentrated for a second, just a moment. Then with a snap, he looked back to me with his solid black eyes. **"You look for a girl, a young and innocent soul."**

"Yes, she is the one I have come for." I replied, to the sudden empty space where the tall being had been standing just prior.

In another blink Malfeus had moved away from me, smugly, to stand by a certain soul in the field. He looked to me, then with slow move, he reached out and touched the soul next to him with his index finger, who was cringing and trying to avoid that long slender finger but unable to flee. In the end, it could not save itself, and with a shrill scream it disappeared from the field with a wisp of red dust. Malfeus sighed with such pleasure. His eyes closed and he looked up to the cloudless sky speaking with an almost a sinister laugh.

"A defiler of the young. A true monster, oh how I long for these souls to feast on. How could an innocent child compare to one with such darkness in his energy. Why would I waste my hunger on sweetness when I crave decadence and depravity? Why waste my appetite on innocence when I yearn for evil and cruelty?"

All the souls bound for the Nightshades realm come to this field, even the pious and forthright. Why they end up here, what brought them to this place, would take too long to tell my friends. Just know, Malfeus chooses when you leave, and if your soul is not clean or just, well you may wait a while in this purgatory. **"And that is why I need to know who among your brethren used your name when contacting a human in the Middle World. They took the girl when they tricked the human and I must bring her back."**

"What do I care if my sister or brothers used my name when tricking a human?"

"Because the girl's soul is not supposed to be here, and your home, this realm, suffers for it. Right now, the Faceless One deals with life that springs from the lifeless, a bed of grass that could turn this place into, something nice."

Malfeus just waved off the warning and the news. He took two steps to his left, attending to more important matters on his agenda. This world and its look was the domain of the Faceless One, and Malfeus had business which was more important to him. The Reaper stopped by another white soul, but then sneered his face and moved on mumbling how he hated Priest and their piety. As he walked on I called out.

"And what if your name is associated with a disastrous misstep, a defeat that brings you embarrassment Malfeus? In your family, a name means power."

"There is no power in a name shaman, none that I care for anyway." The Nightshade called back, stopping by another soul, and this time he grinned with malicious intent before reaching out quickly, like a cat snaring a mouse on its claws. The soul screamed loudly with a female voice as Malfeus hissed twice with the sudden flood of its energy. He looked skyward again and screamed.

"Yes, what a wicked, wicked soul was she! Many a man called her 'lover', used her bed as a pleasure palace, but in the end when she was done with them, she was done."

I watched as Malfeus looked back down and back to me. "She poisoned them shaman, cold and ruthless to the end, so many men to have killed, so dark a soul, and so tasteful to me."

"She may have asked for forgiveness at the end?"

Malfeus curled his lip as if I had thrown a stinky piece of food at him. **"I would tell you the name of my brethren who used just after granting forgiveness, and I never grant forgiveness."**

"Then I will take what I need to know by force." I quickly retorted. The ploy was as dangerous as trying to grab a poisonous snake in mid strike, and Malfeus knew this.

The Nightshade looked shocked, surprised even, as he turned back to a soul next to him and laughed. **"I think the shaman has succumbed to heat stroke."**

"I know your true name Malfeus. I can speak it." I countered. I hoped the threat would catch his attention, and it did.

All at once the Nightshade was across the field and standing next to me, directly in front of me. His teeth gnashed just an inch from my face. **"You know what will happen if you say it wrong."**

"My soul will be yours- "

"I will feast on you John Greywolf, feast like I have never eaten before!" Malfeus hissed with pure evil stepping back a single foot.

We stood staring at each other, like a pair of gun fighters outside some old west saloon. To speak the true name of a Nightshade can give one control over the Nightmare, enough control that is to ask for one favor or question. And that is if one can say the name right, with perfect inflection and intonation. If even one letter is spoken wrong, then the ultimate price is paid and the Nightshade will take the soul of the one foolish enough to misspeak the name. I took a breath as Malfeus stood and grinned eagerly, his mind already thinking of what he would do to me.

Then, with an exhale, I spoke the name of the Nightshade Malfeus.
I inflected and intonated at the spots I had learned from another spirit, and
as soon as the sound of my voice faded, I knew I had spoken it right. The
souls around us screamed in fear and pain while Malfeus glared at me with
pure rage.

"See Malfeus, there is power in a name."

"This means nothing! You have won the right for one question
shaman, but know this, one day you will come to my field, and I will
avenge this indignity you have set on me."

"I know you will Malfeus, but for now, which Nightshade
bargained with the human Abigail Grouse in your name?"

The Nightshade chewed hard on the bitter taste of defeat for a
moment then spoke in a low hiss. "My sister Enyo dealt with the human
Grouse. She is the one you will need to see next John Greywolf, and by
that, I mean she will find you."

I did not offer thanks to Malfeus. He would only spit it out. I simply
turned and started for the end of the field thinking of how I should be
ready for Enyo, the Lustful One. As I walked away I heard another scream
from a soul the Nightshade fed on and ahead of me, the souls still trapped
waiting to be released, begged for their freedom. I closed it all out. There
was only my Path and the little girl who I had to bring back.

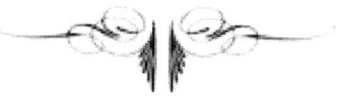

She stopped and carefully looked out from the corner of the alley
she had ducked down just a second before. Camille immediately noticed
the man and woman following her, Umbra both. In just the time it took for
her to leave Ezio, maybe an hour, all travel in the city was becoming more

dangerous and more locked down. The Umbra and the Protectorate had agents and Magi scouring the streets, looking for the Weavers, and her and Ezio as well. Camille leaned back into the alley and sighed. Yesterday, she was an Umbra just like the pair out there in the street, a hunter, but today she was the hunted. And as such, she had to use her knowledge of how the hunters from the shadows acted, how they worked. Camille had to use what she knew from years of being an Umbra to now escape the closing trap which the city of Chicago had become.

With a quick glance around the corner of the alley, she noted the pair following her had stopped and taken up position on the street to view people moving in both directions. The man covered the north direction while the woman covered the south. Perfect, Camille thought, they followed the protocol for following a target to the letter, which was going to make getting out of here and to Wallace just that more involved. Still, she was going to find him, and there was nothing these two could do to stop her.

As Camille stood there thinking of where she needed to go, what street she needed to look for to find this clothes shop of 'The Mouse' he second Ezio said to look for, she spotted the chance for an egress from the alley. A man moving a large wooden box on a dolly was just passing the woman looking in her direction. I have one chance at this she thought as the dolly rolled closer, because the Umbra have very sharp eyes. As the man moved closer Camille looked up the street trying to gauge what her next move would, could be, just as she spotted a truck with an open bed. Workers were just finishing up loading the vehicle with crates and boxes, it was going to be leaving in a minute, and sitting next to it was another car. The man inside reading a large paper, maybe a newspaper or map?

"All right Camille, time to see if you can truly be a shadow."

Her words were barely out before, with a quick long step, she flew out of the alley and right in front of the box. It was tall, high enough to block her, as Camille's gather skirt whipped around her feet from the sudden movement. She kept walking, just a little faster than the dolly, using it as cover as the truck and the car were just up ahead.

"First part done, now for the finale."

Then, with another leap, Camille dove out from behind the crate, and away she hoped. Unfortunately, she hadn't been a complete 'shadow', as much as she had hoped for. The female Umbra, Samara as she was named and called, wasn't a new recruit to the shadow hunters. She had trained with Camille some years ago, even. And Samara had a very suspicious nature, sometimes a boon when it came to her duty as an Umbra hunter, and that little tingling voice in the back of her mind at the moment, it was telling her a proverbial story.

"There Lucas, I think we just found our traitor."

The man looked over to where Samara was pointing, at a tall crate being pushed by a worker on a dolly. A first he couldn't see anything, just the man pushing the dolly which held the crate, but then he saw the hem of a black skirt swish just past the bottom edge of the crate, a very familiar hem.

"It's her, it's Camille."

"Yes, and she's not going to get away!" Samara hissed as she broke into a run, intent on catching the former Umbra Magi.

The dolly kept rolling, first by a group of people hanging out on the street having a conversation about something, and then it rolled by a truck parked by the sidewalk. Samara watched carefully, the dolly bounced as it hit something on the sidewalk, which caused the crate to shift, and behind the create...was nothing now.

"Damn, she's gone already!" The lady Umbra spat. She stopped with a skid of boots on the cobblestone sidewalk, began to look around for Camille, and then the truck parked just near where the traitor Umbra had disappeared came to life with a loud pop of its rudimentary, and barely running, engine. The noise was enough to immediately snatch Samara's attention, and oh, did her suspicion take over.

"There, she jumped in the back of that truck!"

"Are you sure?" Lucas asked

"She had to have, there's no time for her to do anything else!" Samara snipped as she leapt out into the street, putting herself in direct contradiction to the path the truck was heading in. She held up her hand signaling the driver to stop, and as the brakes squealed on the truck bringing it to said stop, her voice screamed out. "Stop, in the name of the Umbra and the Protectorate!"

"Hey," the man behind the wheel of the truck screamed back with a wild wave of his hands, both jerking off the wheel of the truck at the same time, "what the hell are you doing? I have to get this load to the air haulers at the airport!"

"You're going to be a few minutes late this afternoon." Lucas snapped back, walking to the rear of the truck and hopping up into the bed to search around and through the boxes and crates.

"Hey, I can't be late! The boss will dock my pay!"

"Would you rather spend the night in Protectorate custody?" Samara asked as she walked around to the driver's window.

"What's that, this 'custody'?" The driver asked, his hands still waving wildly at each word.

"It means I take you to jail for the night if you speak again." Samara sneered watching her partner search and, frustratingly, come up with nothing.

The Umbra bit her lower lip, also in frustration, wondering how in the hell Camille had slipped them a second time. The driver watched Samara, who watched Lucas reach the end of the truck bed in his search, nothing to show for it. "Hey, can I go now?"

Where did you go Camille, Samara asked herself? You only had this truck and-

A car, sitting and running just a few feet away, suddenly pulled out into traffic heading away from the Umbra. Like a bolt from the sky, Samara knew the traitor Umbra had jumped into the car instead. She just knew it, but could only watch helpless and angry as the vehicle swung into mass of other cars.

"She's in that car!" She screamed as Lucas hopped down from the back of the truck.

"You saw her?"

"Hey, can I get going now?" The truck driver yelled.

The lady Umbra just ignored both men and spun looking for, searching for, a cab and there, just coming their way, was one. She did the same with it as she did with the truck, jumping in its way to get it to stop. As the cab stopped, Samara flung the door opened and jumped into the back. Lucas followed just as the driver of the truck gave the pair of Magi a suggestion, something about self-gratification with a very large animal, before pulling away with his load headed for the airport.

The cab sped up and gave chase to the car, the Umbra in its backseat guiding it. As it did, one of the men in the group watched it leave then turned back and spoke to someone in the middle of huddle on the sidewalk. "They're gone now."

"Thank you, gentlemen," Camille smiled standing up and nodding to each one before speaking, "thank you for the help."

"Our pleasure, we hate those dark Magi types." Another one replied and Camille almost laughed at the irony. I used to be one of 'those dark Magi' she thought.

"Yes, so do I now, but can someone show me where the tailor shop of The Mouse might be?"

Another man laughed and pointed, "yeah, it's that way, about three streets over."

"Ah, yes, well thank you again!" Camille nodded before walking across the street in the direction the man pointed. She dodged a car with a quick start and then was walking as fast as she could on the sidewalk, hoping she could catch up to Wallace.

The truck Felton rode around the city in pulled up to the old abandon warehouse with a shaky stop, the vehicle shuttering as it did. Before it had even stopped shaking though, the passenger door opened and out stepped Felton. He looked around, making sure no one was staring too hard as they say, as his men began to pile out. They yanked a semi-conscious Wally out and dragged him into a side door by the large entrance to the warehouse.

An evil smile crossed the face of Felton as he started to let his imagination run a little wild. He had been waiting on this day for some time, waiting and waiting and waiting. Wallace had embarrassed Felton with his escape, and he was not one to take such a thing lightly.

Well, now it was time to get a wee bit of revenge.

Part Sixteen

"I do not believe that worked a second time my sister!" Marisol cackled as she ducked behind a table, which was now a convenient barricade after being thrown over on it's side. She hunkered down just as no less than three bullets slammed into the heavy top and splintered the thick wood.

Right at the moment the distraction started, right when the lead Umbra screamed from having Marisol's pet sit on her hand, Sara was moving, striking at the first two Protectorate soldiers with a right cross to one followed by a spinning back kick to the other. Both soldiers dropped from the blows, one where he stood and the other skidding backwards before going over a chair to land on the clean tile floor. As she finished her attacks, Sara moved with a swiftness dodging bullets and people, moving with a purpose and ending up by her sister after leaping over the upturned table.

"I think, dear sister, that your sense of 'worked' needs some refining."

A soldier reached over the table suddenly, his hand darting down and grabbing Marisol's poncho in a solid fist. Before he could do anything with his hand though, the shaman reacted bringing one of her sticks up and slamming it into the solcier's unprotected head. There was a thick 'whack' followed instantly by the man going limp from being knocked straight into an unconscious state. Marisol laughed pulling the soldier's hand free, turning to her sister, but then her smile turned into a frown as she spoke up.

"Where is senora Alice?"

"I thought she was back here with you?" Sara answered with a snap of her head, her expression abruptly changing to a concerned one.

"No," Marisol answered with a shake of her head, eyes wide. "I thought she was with you, hiding."

"She's not with me!"

The shaman from 'The Land of Shaking Earth' looked up from behind the overturned table and instantly spotted the one she and her sister were looking for. "Oh, there she is, right over there by those soldiers."

Sara looked up instantly, her face still locked in an expression of shock, as she spotted the woman running for her love Ezio. "Alice, what are you doing girl? Get Down!"

The prophetic words were barely out before a string of bullets slammed into the table again, causing both shamans to duck for their lives. As they did, behind them, Baird and Eleanor both lashed out sending arcs and bolts of magical fire into Umbra and Protectorate soldier alike, holding back the enemy for the moment. Adelaide and Tomo both retreated away from the fight, taking refuge behind a column, as two Umbra sent their magical energy into the large marble post with a missed strike. Chunks of stone broke and flew away from the pillar as the lightning smashed into it, and then Tomo leaned around and let a large arc of magical energy fly from his hand hitting one of the Umbra in his shoulder. The man spun off his feet and hit the floor with a crunch, a second later his partner reached over and pulled him to safety, both hiding behind a couch which was burning from being hit by a Protectorate explosive round. The stunned Umbra's body barely made it behind the burning furniture before Adelaide struck it with a bolt of her own magic, sending the oblong couch sliding back into the Magi hidden behind it.

"Well, this could have gone better!" A male voice called out, the Aussie accent easily recognized, which is why Marisol responded without looking to Baird.

"I think it is going very well, better than some of the situations I have found myself in lately."

"Is she serious?" Eleanor yelped as a spread of bullets sent splinters flying past her head. The table they were hiding behind was quickly disappearing, being decimated inch by inch from each round that struck home.

"Oh yes, my sister may have a wicked sense of humor, but she always speaks the truth, in her own way." Sara answered, her bright smile causing Eleanor to feel a little, comfortable, as hard as that may be to comprehend.

"Ai, thank you mi hermana!" Marisol gushed, a second before something looking which like a metal ball flew over the table. It hit the floor with a loud clank, just past everyone, bounced once, and then came to stop.

Baird, and everyone else, instantly identified the metal contraption as a grenade, what the Protectorate called it anyway. The Magi grabbed the shaman and pulled her away from it with a burst, getting to a safe distance he hoped just as Eleanor and Sara did the same, bolting over to the column Adelaide and Tomo were hiding behind. The grenade then popped instead of exploding, releasing a thick noxious gas from its inside. Marisol was instantly reminded of Wally's stink bombs, the ones he fired from his special gun, only the technoist must have a stronger recipe. His smoke smelled so much worse, it actually burned your eyes!

"Alice, what the hell are you doing here?"

That's a rather rude question, the woman who it was directed at thought as she ran past a chair, just a second before it exploded into a few different sized pieces. Alice gave a yelp, a small dance of her feet as she ducked the flying debris, and then growled loudly as she felt her lover's hands grab her arms.

"I'M HERE SAVING YOU MY LOVE, YOU FOOL!"

Two rounds from a rifle, fired by who knows which soldier, went screaming by making the tall Magi duck while he pulled his love behind one of the few remaining couches. "How did you know I needed saving, which for the record, I do not!"

Before Alice could answer, she felt a body slide behind the sturdy piece of furniture next to her, and she looked over to see a younger version of her Ezio. He was obviously a Magi, an Umbra from the color of his clothes, and probably up to his neck in this trouble just like her Ezio. She sighed as another explosion from a magical blast reverberated through the hall of the Magi House while turning back to her love. "I think the evidence proves otherwise Badu-"

"No it does not, I was in perfect control-"

"Wait one second, are you trying to say-"

"Until Mr. Cooper stumbled-"

The young Magi popped up at the mention of his name and screamed back, joining the surreal argument. "I never stumbled into 'your' plan Mr. Ezio!"

"Then why are you here?" Both Alice and Ezio screamed just as half the couch shattered from another magical bolt of energy. As fuzz and cloth floated down around them, Ezio half listened to the answer by the young Magi and half spotted an ominous figure stalking down the stairs towards them.

"I was here of my own intentions when Mr. Ezio stumbled into me and set off this whole debacle."

"Oh no, don't you try to play all angelic Cooper. I know all about you!" Alice snapped back as her love behind her gasped.

"It doesn't matter who crashed into who's plan anymore. We just need to get out here as fast as possible, as far as possible."

Alice turned to her love with raised eyebrows, the sound in his voice stirring even more panic in her heart. "Why do you say that?"

"Because," Cooper answered for his former Umbra counterpart, "we have roused the one Magi who can kill us all."

"Who," Alice asked just as her eyes caught sight of two people coming down the stairs from the upper floors. The person behind, a female Magi, the one walking in front didn't grab much of Alice's attention, not near as much as the older male Magi in front. He was tall, dark skinned, and her instinct told her this was a man not to be toyed with. Her breath caught in her throat as she locked eyes with him, the fire and fierceness of his gaze snatching the very air from her lungs it seemed. She felt a long chill run down her back as her Ezio whispered his name, an ominous moniker.

"Absalom is here,"

His eyes scanned the room, what was left of the lobby of the Magi house, his 'House'. At the sight of the damage, of the fighting going on beneath the roof of his very home, Absalom took each step with a slow conviction and growing rage. He spotted Ezio and Cooper first, and some strange woman stared back but Absalom cared nothing for her, then his gaze moved up and down the length of the lobby. A bullet whizzed by causing the Magi behind to duck, but Absalom never even gave the round a glance. A second later the firing and fighting ceased abruptly, all combatants now realizing who had come to see the fray. His anger boiled his blood as he spotted the four rogue members of his House, Baird and Eleanor and Tomo and Adelaide. The four conspirators had dared to return home, and from the looks of things, they had not come alone. Oh, Absalom recognized the dark-skinned shaman as she looked up from behind what was left of the receptionist's table, and his anger exploded at everyone around while he stared with rage at her.

"HOW DARE YOU ALL DEFILE MY HOUSE!"

Sara's eyes narrowed, to slits, as she slowly stood up and met the hard eyes of the First Magi with her own contempt. "I see you still hold a grudge Absalom. I remember telling you once that was not a wise thing to do."

The First Magi dropped down another step, his face a snarl and his voice a growl. "You fight in my house, destroy my things, and then try to counsel me! You were always an arrogant little girl Sara, so much arrogance."

"How does she know the First Magi?" Eleanor asked, her face a mask of confusion.

Baird didn't look back, just whispered over his shoulder as his accent punctuated his response. "Do I look like someone who would know what was going on?"

Point taken Eleanor thought as she watched Ezio grab the young Magi by one arm and the woman called Alice by the other, and then with a shove begin to guide both toward the exit. It was best to get away row, given the fact everyone was engrossed in watching the woman called Sara and Absalom trade words like thrown knives. No one tried to stop the trio, hell, no one even cared to step in their way as they trotted for the front while the First Magi took another step down the stairs.

"What you call arrogance Absalom, is simple knowledge, gained from meeting men and women who were just like you." Absalom refused respond, his eyes still locked with Sara's, so the shaman kept talking. She watched as Alice and the two men drew closer with each second, so she kept the powerful First Magi's attention locked on to her. "I told you Absalom, power is a fruit that never fills the stomach. It clouds one's mind and heart, fills you with lust and anger, which only makes you cling to negativity, like holding grudges. Nothing ever good comes from a grudge Absalom, just deeper emptiness."

The First Magi reached the last step, dropped down from stepping off it, and grinned with pure maliciousness. "Oh, but there is a reward for holding ones enemie's accountable shaman. There is a very nice reward for being so resolute."

"If you are going to say revenge Absalom, please do not." Sara suddenly yelled just as the First Magi finished. She shook her head slightly, the feather on her hat swaying just a beat with the motion as she continued. "It is a useless thing to seek and try to obtain. Revenge is even more useless than power, more destructive than any other path one could take."

The lobby was quiet then, not an echo of a word could be heard as everyone held their breath. What was going to happen next? Were they going to fight? The question ran through everyone's mind, from Baird and Eleanor who stood behind the desk watching with fearful eyes to Ezio who pushed his love and Cooper a step faster. They were almost out of the Magi House he thought as all three scurried past the overturned desk, and the shaman who was confronting one of the most powerful Magi in the world.

As for the First Magi, he only smiled on while raising his left arm and hand. He only smiled as he spoke, a glow from the large crystal he was holding enveloped his hand as the power was drained from the stone. He only smiled as the crystal cracked then turned to dust in his palm, the draw of magical energy so fast and complete from its structure the stone disintegrated.

"Then the speaking of words is done, and all that remains between us is action!"

The First Magi finished his sentence with a howl as his right arm crossed his chest, reaching down to the left. Then, with a grand sweep of the arm, he released his magic attack, a literal tidal wave of pure energy sweeping down the lobby with a bright blue aura. Ezio had enough time to see the wall of magic energy coming, and knew it would destroy everything in its path, living and material alike.

Part Seventeen

The shadowy being inhabiting Frank's body, the devoted fo lower of Nidhogg, stood silently in the hall, watching the room at the end of the passage with its eyes intently. It had crept down here, to this point n space and time, as silent as Frank's body could, and it hoped that was enough. After tailing the North Wind for the morning, all the way from the old witch's shop to here, this run-down structure, the entity had decided it was time to make its move. It had waited, patiently with growing ar gst, while listening as the North Wind talked with another human in the room it was watching now. The being had come up with a fool proof plan it thought would bring about the chance to deliver a final, fatal, blow to the shaman. It could strike down the North Wind and thus end the prophecy and save the Nidhogg.

It could do what it had promised the Great Serpent it would do, to stop this ancient plot to end its life.

The North Wind then suddenly told this human it was going to Journey, to travel between the Other Worlds, and the shadow had to hold back an evil wail of joy. This was the perfect time to attack, when the North Wind would be away from his body and thus as vulnerable as a little kitten.

Oh yes, it would most certainly strike down the shaman now.

So, the shadow being took Frank's body and headed up the rickety stairs easily jumping the gap, up to the floor above. It slinked down the dirty hall, past trash and debris, until it found the room right over the North Wind's. It slid into the space and with slow, gentle steps, started to cross the weathered and broken floor. Through the many holes and cracks in the wood, it could see down into the room below. There were candles everywhere, so many light actually beamed through-

On its fifth step, with a sudden loud crack that echoed in the room, and even more audible 'pop', the tip of a cutlass sword ripped through the floor right by Frank's foot, an inch over and the blade would have pierced the appendage causing great pain. The being froze instantly, not moving one muscle or even breathing, as a woman's voice called up.

"I know you're up there, the one who followed us from Mother Twylah's, and I know just where your next foot step will fall. So, take it at your risk, or leave and I'll let you keep everything intact."

Oh yes, the woman with the large hat, the one who followed the North Wind here as well. She's his protector the being thought, the perfect chance to strike was nothing more than a ruse. The shadow slowly slid its foot back, toward the door to the room, and the tip of the cutlass disappeared with a second 'pop'. The woman didn't say another word, but the being could imagine a sly smile on her face as it took a second and third step out of the room. It could see the smugness in that grin and the being felt frustration and anger tear at its mind. It made Frank quietly step down the hall, back down the stairs, and then stand in the dark corner staring at the room down the hall.

What now, what next? The words echoed in its mind, or Frank's, just as the sound of the sword punching through the floor did a minute ago. It was busy thinking when the woman called out again.

"I can see you're a stubborn one, are you not? Well know this, whoever and whatever you are, that I will not let you go near John. Whatever deviousness, however evil, you had planned will not be happening this day to him. Go away, slither away snake and hide in your hole, or else I'll come out there and take care of this myself."

Damn this woman, she will not stop me, the being thought with a hiss. She will not keep me from ending the shaman's life force and saving the Great Serpent.

However ill Abagail felt about the Sky Pirate Captain, and it was a deep and passionate despising, she had to admire the woman at this moment in time. Fade at this very minute was the gallant protector, the knight ready to sacrifice herself on the altar of all that she loves, and there was no mistaking it now, Fade was in love with John Greywolf. Every movement and word reinforced it to Abagail, even when the Sky Pirate Captain pulled her cutlass free from the ceiling where it punched through to warn off the intruder. It was all to protect the one her heart had taken in, probably the only one in her lifetime.

Grouse watched as Fade's thumb lowered the hammer on her long pistol, the click just barely audible as it was set. The weapon, at first, look like a pistol the infamous Blackbeard might have carried and used, with a high polished wooden frame housing the barrel and inner workings, but then old Teach's guns weren't of a modern design the way Fade's was. His old cap-n-ball musket was no match for what she held, the barrel made of some specia steel alloy to aid in accuracy and firing. And his gun surely was a single shot, whereas Fade's held a clip, just forward of the trigger guard, which held who only knows how many rounds. Abagail was no marksman, no expert with guns, so she had no clue about how many rounds that marvelous looking long pistol could fire before having to be reloaded.

Yet, she knew swords.

Abagail was a historian of some repute, and of all things she loved the sword held a special place in her heart, had since her father showed her his collection. From that day on, Abagail studied and learned about all there was to know about the weapon, and taking one look at the cutlass the Sky Pirate held, she knew it was as special as the pistol. The blade was the usual shape of a sword carried by the brigands of the skies, long and lean till just before the end where it tapered to a slightly wide curved point. The cutlass was also strong, whoever created the weapon knew a good bit about metallurgy, enough to know how to combine two metals into one increasing the durability and strength of the sword. The spine of the blade was a dark metal, thick until it began to change as it thinned into the blade, which was razor sharp, shimmering in the candle light. The handle and basket, which covered Fade's gloved hand, were obviously forged with the blade to give everything strength, and both were decorated with an intricate weave and engravings. The cutlass was a beautiful, and certainly deadly, weapon Abagail thought as she whispered.

"Is it gone?"

Fade only hissed signaling for Abagail to stay quiet as she watched the ceiling intently. As for Miss Grouse, well she hadn't been shushed in a very long time, and she felt her anger rise from it, but at the moment she was willing to let the slight go. Never poke a bear, her father had told her, the thing just might turn and take a bite out of you, and Abagail was sure Fade could take a very big bite if poked hard enough.

The Sky Pirate Captain took a step toward the door, a very quiet one, while still watching the ceiling. Her long boots not even creaking as she moved as silent and deadly as a tigress stalking prey in the jungle. She took another after a second, and then a third after two more seconds. Abagail watched her just as intently as Fade watched the ceiling. Stopping just by the door, Fade stood silently until suddenly she called out, a loud sinister bark that made Miss Grouse jump a bit.

"I can see you're a stubborn one, are you not? Well know this, whoever and whatever you are, that I will not let you go near John. Whatever deviousness, however evil, you had planned will not be happening this day to him. Go away, slither away snake and hide in your hole, or else I'll come out there and take care of this myself."

The words, sounding like a threat to anyone and everyone probably but Abagail, echoed for just a second in the room. The older lady, now trapped in the body of the child she tried to steal the very lifeforce from, knew the Sky Pirate was not bluffing, boasting. Abagail knew, if need be, Fade would walk out into the hall and confront this attacker with nothing but steel and shot, just like old Blackbeard himself would do. So, remaining silent whi e sitting still in her chair, Miss Grouse watched Fade as the Sky Pirate waited by the door. After what seemed an eon, and Abagail was sure it was, Fade spoke in a whisper delivering an order.

"Keep an eye on John, don't let anything happen to him whi e I'm out here dealing with our visitor Abagail."

"I know Captain, if something happens to the shaman I am trapped like this forever."

"No," Fade whispered with a voice filled to the brim with truth, "if anything happens to John then you'll feel every ounce of my anger, understand?"

And there's the bear, Miss Grouse thought as she only nodded once while her servant whispered with concern. "Give me your gun, so I can protect the Madame.

"As if I would I ever give my gun to someone else!" The Sky Pirate Captain snapped with a look of incredulity. Then she gave one last, long glare, to Abagail before stepping out of the room. The look was to make sure she understood what would happen if John befell some nefarious fate, and Miss Grouse knew this. Just as before, there was no threat to Fade's words, nothing but a solemn promise that the Sky Pirate Captain would ensure this night would get much worse for Abagail if something happened to the shaman.

I was maybe ten minutes out of Malfeus's valley, or maybe it was ten hours, time has little significance here in the Other Worlds, when the words the Reaper had spoken upon our parting rang oddly true. Enyo would find me he said coldly, she would come looking for me, and it was her lowliest and most foul minion who found me. The trail before me led downward, into a vast canyon, high red walls rising up from the hard rock ground to seemingly touch the sky. Hues of dark and light colors mixed into the canyon rock making it look quite beautiful, if one could forget where one was. My instincts told me Enyo's familiar was approaching, something I had expected actually. The imp was small, maybe two feet high, resembling a small green dragon with wings, the kind you might find

decorating a painting of older times or as stone guarding the cathedral of a church. Thanks to the fact the imp was less than conspicuous, I could hear the thing's small claws scurry across the canyon walls as it dug for purchase while trying to remain silent at the same time, it was easy to 'detect'. I stopped and steeled myself for its company. Enyo would never let me just follow her, track her, and not keep an eye on me. She could use the imp's eyes as if they were her own; see everything it sees, like through a scrying pool. The Goddess of Lust was nothing but capable. From behind I heard a pebble fall and make the smallest of noise. A simple 'puff' in the sand as it landed, but enough of a sound that my ears told me the imp was close now.

"**Please stop embarrassing yourself Drake and come out.**" I called to the imp.

There was nothing but quiet, and the silence just frustrated me more. "**Then I'll stand here and wait for Enyo to show herself, and we both know that will not make her happy. An unhappy Enyo is worse for you then for me imp.**"

Again, there was nothing but silence, but then after what felt like a minute, the wall to my left, just a few feet away, a piece of rock shook as if the stone came to life and was breaking free from its grasp. Another power of the imp was its chameleon like shifting, which it used to a great effect on some, but with that now gone the imp looked just small and green and angry. "**Bah!**" it spat at me with its lizard face.

"**Hello Drake, no need to hide now.**"

"**How did you know it wasssssss me?**" The imp hissed at me like a snake.

"I've been in air ship wrecks that were quieter then you Drake." I answered while turning and starting off back down the trail. "I've been in fights, battles, and parades that were quieter than you imp."

"Bah!"

I walked along the trail, between the red canyon walls, keeping one ear on the imp and my eyes on the path ahead. I saw the green dragon like creature run along the wall to get ahead of me, then stop and turn back to look me in the eyes. "Why are you here Sssssshaman?"

"It was a nice day for a journey, and I haven't been to see Enyo in such a long time." I answered sarcastically walking by the imp.

"You are not welcomed here Ssssssshaman Greywolf! The mistressssss will not like you in her landssssss."

"Then the mistress can come and tell me to leave herself." I called back still continuing onward.

The imp didn't follow me this time, not from what I could hear, and this started to intrigue me, yet all my thoughts ceased when I reached the alcove just ahead. I have seen my share of sights in the Nightshades realm, from Malfeus's fields of souls to the swamps of avarice where Silas reigns, but nothing could hold a candle to Enyo and her punishments. The lustful suffer here in her lands, at her command and servants' hands, before moving on, and I am sure the fields of Malfeus or the swamps of Silas must seem like paradise after a stay with Enyo.

As I reached the opening to the alcove I heard growling, like a wild dog, and the lilting laughter of a woman, or two or three. The giggle was one of enjoyment, pleasure, and when my eyes saw what made the sound my blood pumped a little faster. When the musk of wanton sex touched my nose, my blood heated. From over my shoulder, Drake the imp laughed just a little at me and my state.

"Ssssssuccubi, lowly entitiessssss that I refusssssse to consssssssort with, but very effective."

The imp was right. There were three succubi, one with black hair and one with white hair and one with blood red locks. They were dressed in transparent gowns that hid nothing of their perfect bodies and moved on non-existent winds as if floating in water. Their hands touched each other all over and in places that would make a man's blood boil. They cooed with excitement, but not at each other. No, it was for their captive who stood chained to the canyon wall just across from them, a way to entice and toy with their soul, a man. Only he wasn't a man anymore, not in the sense I know of one. He was naked, growling and foaming at the mouth, pulling so hard on the chains that held him fast the metal tore his skin. A collar around his neck bit in the flesh making blood run down his bare chest as he yelled for his desire to come closer, begged for the trio to come and touch him just once.

"To lusssst after something to the point of losing onessss sssssself is to be nothing but an animal, eh shaman?"

"To drive someone to that point is cruel Drake." I answered.

"The Sssssuccubi did not have to lead the man here, in the Middle World he chossssse lust over everything elssssssse. Now he mussssssssst balance the ssssssscales hissssssss life of lussssssssst left."

The man growled and howled like a wild animal and the succubi giggled more. The black and the white hair reached out and acted as if they would touch him, yet just before flesh could touch, they pulled back and it provoked the chained man even more. He screamed for them, to hold them, to touch them in ways a lover should only whisper in the most intimate of settings. The poor soul was lost to everything but the lust he had carried in his heart when he walked the Middle World. Now he was a captive to it, as much as the chains that held him to the canyon wall.

"**Why do you think they come here, eh sssssshaman?**" **The imp asked, bringing me out of my thoughts. Still, I didn't answer right away and Enyo's familiar continued on without me.** "**Humanssssss, why do they do thissssss to themselvessssss?**"

Wahna's words came back to me as I shifted my attention to the imp and his question. I wondered, did it reach into my memories and use that morning to try and strike at me? Did it think my confusion about Heaven and Hell was still with me after such a long time? I smiled and shrugged my shoulders. "**Are you asking me why these souls come here, to be treated this way Drake?**"

The small dragon scurried closer and hissed, "**I know they come here screaming they do not want to be here. They come why, when they wisssssssh to be sssssssome where else?**"

I wonder, was I this sightless when I was younger. Maybe, I thought as I replied. "**Absolution is only ever earned Drake, be it with fire or air.**"

I didn't try to hide my smile as I turned from him. To see a small green dragon, look at you in complete confusion, well it is quite funny, trust me. Only, as I moved away from the imp, I locked eyes with one of the succubi, the black-haired demon. Her dark eyes twinkled as they met mine and for a brief second, I felt a longing inside my heart stir. From behind, Drake the Imp, spoke and I could almost see the smile on his face.

"Doessssss ssssssshe remind you on ssssssssomeone sssssssshaman?"

Before I could stop myself, I spoke her name in a hushed whisper. *"Fade,"*

She was perfect match for the Captain of the Crescent Moon, a twin in every aspect. The long flowing hair and matching eyes, it was like stepping back to this morning when we argued in the alley. It was like reliving the moment all over again. The succubus smiled seductively at me, a long smoldering smile meant to drag a man through a thousand thorns for a small taste. I gathered myself though, and just nodded to the entity, using the longing and feeling of love for Fade in my heart to hold the demon at bay. The succubus cooed and giggled as it went back to tormenting the one chained to the canyon wall, my blood began to cool with relief of the gaze being broken, and then with a growl that sounded like a pack of wolves, the three entities dived onto the man. They tore into his flesh with tooth and nail, and as they did he screamed, but not in pain or fear. It was pleasure, the moment we all achieve when there is no will to hold back the primal. He yelled in ecstasy as the succubi did what they were created to do, bring about the downfall of a man, to bring about his death. When there was no more noise, no more writhing from the chained man, and when the alcove fell quiet, the three entities slowly faded like smoke from a dying fire. Was it over for the man? Was his scale balanced? Maybe, but I knew better.

"When will he return?" I asked Drake.

"Sssssshortly...Hisssss ssssssscale wassssss very tilted."

I turned more than ready to leave the alcove and the black-haired succubus. The imp ran along the wall beside me quietly watching my every step. I hoped Enyo enjoyed what she had seen back there, the effect it had on me. This was a game to her, a way to pass the immortal days here in their Lower World, but to me it had come too close to home. Was that succubus put there to torture me? Was she made to look like Fade to drive a stake into my heart? was the succubus meant to say my love would end up here? I doubted it, to become one of the fallen one must wish it with all their heart and soul, and then curry favor with one of the Nightshades to complete the transformation. Fade was a free and independent soul, a Sky Pirate, sworn to live and die free from anyone's command or law, except her own. Enyo controlled her minions, ordered them at her whim, and this was not Fade by any means.

Up ahead, another alcove appeared, and I saw another man stumble out of it grabbing his stomach and throat. He was dressed in fine clothes, the kind a man of wealth would wear, and he staggered across the trail into the other canyon wall hitting it with enough force to bounce off. The imp stopped beside me as I froze to watch what was about to happen. Again, I had an idea, a glimmer of a thought, and it was enough to keep me from helping this man. I watched as he wretched once, trying to force something in his stomach out. The man wretched again, squeezing his throat hard enough to turn his knuckles white and his flesh red before, with a great spew, coins began to pour forth from him like a fountain. Gold, bright and shiny, fell from the man's mouth in waves to the dirt floor of the canyon. They clinked against each other, sparkled even, though there was no light, and drew the attention of the others.

Yes, they were others in the alcove, and as soon as the coins were falling they ran out and started to grab them up. Men and women dressed in fine clothes fighting over the money like dogs over a bone. They hit each other, bit each other, and shoved each other to get a chance to grab a single coin.

"Greed, it seems a little low for Enyo Drake."

"Lussssst isssss lussssssst, for money or flessssh, it isssss all lussssssst." The imp replied.

Then I saw the coins the men and women were fighting so hard to keep turn to sand in their very hands, turn to red dirt that flowed through even clenched fists. They screamed and wailed as the precious coins they desired more than life itself slipped away with the wind. They pleaded with the coins, as if the gold would speak, not to leave them, not to go away. Yet every single one did, every gold piece turned to dirt and became part of the canyon again. The mass began to cry and wail in anguish as one, then one among them, an elderly woman in a dress that looked handmade, suddenly started to choke and wretch like the man before her. The elderly woman stepped back, or staggered depending on how you look at it, into the alcove and all the others gave chase. I took the break to make my move and I started walking past the opening to the chamber where the mass had moved. As I walked past, I took a quick glimpse inside and noticed the alcove was large, huge, and there were more men and women in there than I could count. Greed was like the cold I thought, everyone seemed to be catching it.

The rest of the time on the trail was quiet. The imp kept to itself, which piqued my curiosity just a touch. Every entity in this realm hated me it seemed, no, loathed me would be a better description. I wasn't welcomed by any of the Nightshades, and as I have said before, they were just waiting for my time here to start, and they're minions, like the Faceless One and Drake, took extra care in reminding me of just that. Yet, here was the imp remaining quiet, and as I reached the end of the trail and the canyon walls began to open up and pull back, I stopped and turned back to Drake.

"**Where is Enyo?**" I asked.

The imp dropped down to the ground and stood up on its hind legs like a Hume. We stared at each other for a moment with no words passing our lips. The wind slowly rolled by and I thought I heard more wailing from the trail back in the canyon.

"**I know why you look for me John. I know why you are here.**"

The voice wasn't Drake's but I recognized it easily. "**Where is the girl's soul Enyo?**"

"**What if I told you I did not have it John, but I know where to go and retrieve it?**"

A deal, with Enyo? I smiled a little waiting to see where this would lead. Of all the Nightshades, she seemed to hold a special spot for me. Why though I have no clue. "**Where is she Enyo?**"

"**She will be with Silas soon.**"

"**Why Silas?**" I asked concerned a little.

The imp smiled, as best as it's maw could, and spoke. "**His intentions are his own John. I was asked to bring her to him and that is what I am doing.**"

"**Why did you steal her soul Enyo?**"

"**A debt, even among the Nightshades, must be repaid John Greywolf.**"

"**A debt?**"

The imp was quiet. I wasn't sure if Enyo was still controlling it, but then it spoke, and my question was answered. **"Are you going to follow me John?"**

"I have no choice Enyo. I came for the girl's soul and I won't leave without her."

"Then run swiftly John. I am close to Silas's land. I want to see you again."

And with the conversation done, the imp dropped in the sand. It didn't move except to breath. The possession by Enyo wore the little beast down and I was sure it wouldn't be moving anytime soon. I turned and started to jog toward Silas's land, wondering if I could catch Enyo, and then wondering what I would do if I did.

The End

###

About the Author...

*R.Kane lives in the Southern US with his family where he was born. He enjoys the occasional fishing trip for bass and throwing the ball with his Golden Retriever. He is the author of other independent titles like **'Runner'** and **'Little Wolf'**.*

Please visit his website for updates and his other works -

http://www.rkanepublications.com